EVERYTHING LEADS to YOU

Also by Nina LaCour:

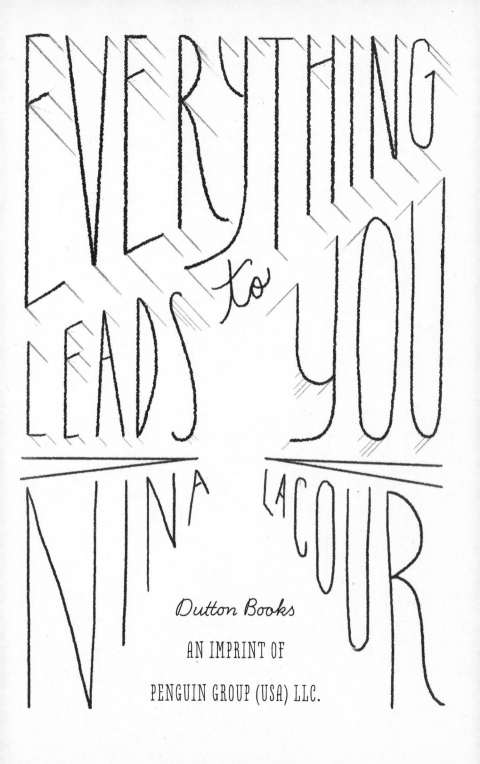

EVERYTHING to LEADS YOU

NINA LACOUR

Dutton Books

AN IMPRINT OF

PENGUIN GROUP (USA) LLC.

DUTTON BOOKS
Published by the Penguin Group
Penguin Group (USA) LLC
375 Hudson Street * New York, New York 10014

USA * Canada * UK * Ireland * Australia
New Zealand * India * South Africa * China

penguin.com

A Penguin Random House Company

CIP Data is available

ISBN 978-0-525-42588-5

Printed in the United States of America

10 9 8 7 6 5 4 3 2 1

To Kristyn and Juliet, the loves of my life

Part 1

THE VASTNESS

Chapter One

Five texts are waiting for me when I get out of my English final. One is from Charlotte saying she finished early and decided to meet up with our boss, so she'll see me at Toby's house later. One is from Toby, saying, *7 p.m.: Don't forget!* And three are from Morgan.

I don't read those yet.

I head off campus and a few blocks over to where I parked my car in an attempt to avoid the daily after-school gridlock. But of course the driver's side lock won't unlock when I turn the key, so I have to go around the passenger side and open the door and climb across the seat to pull up the other lock and shut the passenger door and go around to the driver's side again—and by the time I'm through with that twenty-second process, the cars are already backed up at the light. So I inch into the road and pull out my phone and read what Morgan wrote.

You okay?

R u coming to set later?

I miss you.

I don't write back. I am going straight to set, but not to see her. I need to measure the space between a piano and a bookshelf to see if the music stand I found on Abbot Kinney Boulevard yesterday will make things look too crowded. The music stand is beautiful. So beautiful, in fact, that if it doesn't fit I will find a new bookshelf, or rearrange the furniture entirely, because this is exactly what I would have in my practice room if I knew how to play an instrument. And if I could afford a nine-hundred-dollar music stand.

As the light turns and I roll my car through the intersection, I'm trying to ignore Morgan's texts and think only of the music stand. This music stand is a miracle. It's exactly what I didn't even know I was looking for. The part that holds the sheet music is this perfect oxidized green. When I texted my boss a picture of the stand she wrote back, *Fucking amazing!!!!* An expletive and four exclamation marks. And when I texted Morgan to tell her that this was the last time I would allow myself to get dumped by her, that breaking up and getting back together six times was already insane, and there was absolutely no way I would take her back a seventh, she replied with, *I don't know what to do!* Indecisive and only mildly emphatic. So typical.

But the music stand, the music stand.

Turning right onto La Cienega, my phone rings and it's Charlotte.

"You need to come here," she says.

"Where?"

"Ginger took me to an estate sale."

"A good one?"

"You just have to come."

"Someone famous?"

"Yes," she says.

"Sounds fun but I need to measure for that music stand."

"Emi," she says. "Trust me. You need to come here now."

So I scribble down the address, make a U-turn, and head toward the Hollywood Hills. I drive up Sunset and roll down all the windows, partly because the air-conditioning doesn't work and it's ninety degrees, but mostly because I'm driving past palm trees and hundreds of beauty parlors and taco trucks and doughnut shops and clothing stores and nightclubs, and I like to take it all in and think about how Los Angeles is the best place in the world.

I turn when my phone tells me to turn and start ascending the hills, where the roads become narrower and the houses more expensive. I keep going, higher than I've ever gone, until the houses are not only way bigger and nicer than the already big, nice houses below them, but also farther apart. And, finally, I turn into a driveway that I'm pretty sure has never before encountered a beat-up hatchback with locks that don't work.

I park under the branches of old, gorgeous trees that are full and green in spite of the arrival of summer, step out of my car, lean against the bumper, and take a look at this house. My job has taken me to a lot of ridiculously nice houses, but this one stands out. It's older and grander, but there's more to it than that. It just feels different. More significant. I'm not thinking about Morgan and thinking instead about who might have owned this house. It was probably someone old, which is good, because an estate sale means someone has died, and it's sad to dig through thirty-year-old people's stuff and think about the futures they could have had.

The double front doors swing open and Charlotte steps into the sun. Her jeans are rolled up at the ankles and her blond hair is in pigtails, and her face is part serious, part elated.

"Guess," she says.

I try to think of who has died in the last couple of weeks. My first thought is our physics teacher's grandmother, but I seriously doubt she would have lived in a house like this one. Then I think of someone else, but I don't say anything because the thought is crazy. This death is huge. Front-page huge. Every-time-I-turn-on-the-radio huge.

But then—there's this house, which is clearly an important house, and old, beautiful trees, and Charlotte's mouth, which is twitching under the tremendous effort of not smiling.

Plus it isn't swarming with people, which means this is some kind of preview that Ginger got invited to because she's a famous production designer and she always gets called to these things first.

"Holy shit," I say.

And Charlotte starts nodding.

"You're not serious."

Her hands fly to her face because she's giddy with the delirious laughter of someone who has spent the last hour in the house of a man who was arguably the most emblematic actor in American cinema.

Clyde Jones. Icon of the American Western.

She leans against the house, doubles over, slides onto the marble landing. I let her have one of her rare hysterical fits of laughter as I take it all in. I can't think of enough expletives to perfectly capture this moment. I would need a year's worth of exclamation points. So I just stare, openmouthed, thinking of the man who used to live here.

Charlotte's hysterics die down, and soon she is standing, composed again, back to her super-brilliant, future museum-studies-major self.

"Come in," she says.

I pause in the colossal doorway. Outside is bright and hot, a beautiful Los Angeles day. Inside it's darker. I can feel the air-conditioning escaping. Even though this is an amazing opportunity that will never come again, I don't know if I should go any farther. The thing is this: My brother, Toby, and I talk all the time about what movies do. They speak to our desires, which are never small. They allow us to escape and to dream and to gaze into eyes that are impossibly beautiful and huge. When you live in LA and work in the movies, you experience the collapse of some of that fantasy. You know that the eyes glow like that because of lights placed at a specific angle, and you see the actresses up close and, yes, they are beautiful, but they are human size and imperfect like the rest of us.

This, though, is different.

Because even if you know a little bit too much about how movies are made, there are always things you don't know. You can hold on to the myth surrounding the actors; you can get swept up in the story.

Clyde Jones belongs in the Old West. He belongs under the stars, smoking hand-rolled cigarettes and listening to the wind. In *A Long Time Till Tomorrow* he lived in a log cabin. In *Lowlands* he lived out of a green pickup truck, sleeping by the side of the road a couple hours at a time, searching for a woman from his past.

Clyde Jones is the savior. The good, uncomplicated man. The perfect cowboy. But as soon as I walk through this doorway he will be an actor who spent his life in a Los Angeles mansion. The ultimate collapse of the fantasy.

"Em?" Charlotte says. She steps to the left, gesturing that I should follow, and I can't help myself. A moment later I'm in Clyde Jones's foyer, the doors shut behind me, gazing at one of the most beautiful objects I've ever beheld: a low-hanging chandelier, geometric and silver and shining.

Clyde Jones was no cowboy, but his aesthetic sensibilities were amazing.

I'm still dying over Clyde's house when Ginger strides past me.

"Oh, good, Emi, you made it." Charlotte and I follow her into the living room.

"Yeah," I say, standing under the high white-beamed ceiling, next to what I can only assume is a pair of original Swan chairs positioned under a huge pastoral landscape with a clear sky as endless as the skies in his films. "It's probably better that I don't go to the studio today."

"These glasses," Ginger says, pointing, and Charlotte walks over to a shiny minibar and takes a tray of highball glasses. "Why should you avoid the studio? Oh, let me guess: Morgan."

"She broke up with me."

"Again?"

"Something about not being tied down. Life's vast possibilities."

"'Life's vast possibilities.' Such bullshit," Charlotte says, setting the glasses next to a group of other beautiful objects that Ginger must have already chosen.

I say, "Yeah," but only because that's what Charlotte needs me to say. Charlotte is the kind of friend who automatically hates everyone who has ever done me wrong. The first time

Morgan broke up with me and we got back together, Charlotte tried her best to get over it and be nice to Morgan. But somewhere around the third time, Charlotte got rude. Stopped saying hi. Stopped smiling around her. By now, Charlotte can't even hear Morgan's name without clenching her jaw.

Ginger shoots me a sympathetic look.

"It's okay," I tell her. "I'm done with movie people."

And then we all laugh, because really. What a ridiculous thing to say.

—

When Ginger is finished choosing what she wants, she lets Charlotte and me explore for a while and see if there's anything we want to buy. We find ourselves in Clyde's study, which has to be the size of my brother's entire apartment. It has high ceilings supported by thick wooden beams and an entire wall of windows with doors that slide open to the land in back. Of all the rooms, this one feels the most Western. There's an enormous rustic table that he must have used as a desk and a collection of leather chairs arranged in a semicircle facing a cavernous fireplace. Shelves line the entirety of one of the side walls, and covering the shelves are hundreds of awards including four Oscars, along with objects from his films: cowboy hats and guns and silver belt buckles.

Most people our age don't know or care very much about Clyde. His career is long over. His roles were rarely sophisticated or smart; there isn't much to recommend him to my generation. But my brother has eclectic tastes, and when he loves something, it becomes nearly impossible not to love it along with him. So over the years I became infatuated with the moment that Clyde appears on the horizon or in the saloon or riding through tall grass toward the woman he loves.

Standing in his study now feels both unexpected and inevitable. And, more than those things, it feels *meaningful*. Like all of Clyde's arrivals. Like, without knowing it, everything I've done has been building toward this moment.

"Are you all right?" Charlotte asks me.

I just nod, because how could I describe this feeling in a way that would make sense? There is no logic behind it.

I pick up one of the belt buckles. It's heavier than I thought it would be, and more beautiful up close: the smooth silhouette of a bucking horse with a rough mountain and waning moon in the background.

"I'm going to see how much they're asking for this," I say.

Charlotte cocks her head. "You're choosing a belt buckle?"

"It's for Toby," I say, and Charlotte blushes because she's been in love with my brother forever. Reminded, I check my phone and see that we're supposed to meet up with him in just under two hours.

Charlotte's flipping through records. She pulls out a Patsy Cline album.

"I can't get over this," she says. "Clyde Jones used to sit on these chairs and listen to *this* record."

We find Ginger signing a credit card slip for over twenty thousand dollars, which might explain why, when we show the estate sale man the belt buckle and Patsy Cline record, he beams at us and says, "My gift to you."

"Charlotte, will you get Harrison on the phone?"

Charlotte does, and hands the phone to the man to arrange a pickup, and then we are back in Clyde's hot driveway, out of his house forever.

—

Toby lives in a classic LA courtyard apartment, like the one in David Lynch's film *Mulholland Drive*, which chooses to focus on the darker side of the movie business, and also the one in *Melrose Place*, which was a nineties TV show set in West Hollywood that my dad lectures about in his Pop Culture of Los Angeles course at UCLA. Toby's courtyard has a tidy green lawn and a pretty fountain, and from the side of his cottage you can see a tiny strip of the ocean. We walk in, and there is his stuff, packed, waiting by the door. A set of matching suitcases that look so grown up.

He hugs us both. Me first and long, Charlotte next and quicker. Then he stands and faces us, my tan brother with his crooked smile and black hair that's always in his eyes. I feel sad, and then I push the sadness away because of what we have to tell him.

"Toby," I say. "We spent the afternoon in Clyde Jones's house."

"You're shitting me," he says, his eyes wide.

"No," Charlotte says. "Not at all."

"His house was full of the most amazing—" I start, but Toby puts his hands over his ears.

"*Dont'tellmedon'ttellmedon'ttellme*," he says.

"Okay," I say.

"The collapse of the fantasy," he says.

I know, I mouth, all exaggerated so he can read my lips.

"I love Clyde Jones," he says, dropping his hands.

I nod. "Not another word on the subject," I say. "But I do have something for you. Close your eyes."

My brother does as told and holds out his hands. I pretend I don't notice Charlotte staring at him, and place the belt buckle in his cupped palms. He opens his eyes. Doesn't say anything. I wonder whether I chose the wrong object, and then I realize that tears are starting.

"Oh, please," I say.

"Holy. Shit." He blinks rapidly to compose himself. Then he rushes to his bookshelf of DVDs and pulls one out. He's mumbling to himself as he turns on his TV and waits for the chapter selection to appear on the screen. "Saloon door . . . I'm a man of the law but that don't make me honest . . . Round these parts . . . Yes!"

He's found the scene, and we all squeeze onto my parents' old sofa, me in the middle acting as a buffer for the sexual tension between my brother and my best friend.

Toby presses play and turns up the volume. I recognize it as *The Strangers*, but I've only seen it a couple times so I've forgotten a lot of what's happening. The scene begins with a shot of a saloon door. We hear the voices of the people inside but the camera doesn't turn to them. When one person matters so much, all you can do is wait for his arrival. And then boots appear at the bottom of the door, a hat above it. The doors burst open and there stands Clyde Jones.

The screen fills with a close-up of his young, knowing

face, shaded by a cowboy hat. He scans the saloon until he sees the sheriff, drinking at a table with one of the bad guys. The camera shifts to his cowboy boots as they stomp across the worn wooden floor toward the sheriff and his buddy, who both spring up from the table and draw their guns as soon as they see Clyde.

Unfazed, Clyde deadpans, "I thought you were a man of the law."

Sheriff: "I'm a man of the law but that don't make me honest."

The bad cowboy doesn't say anything, but looks borderline maniacal as he points the gun at Clyde.

Then Clyde says, "Round these parts, lawlessness is a disease. I have a funny suspicion I know how to cure it."

The camera moves down to his holster, and Toby shouts, "Look!" and presses pause. There's the belt buckle: the horse, that hill, the moon.

Charlotte says, "That's amazing!"

I say, "Toby. I am seriously worried about you. Of all the Clyde Jones movies and all the belt buckles, *how* did you know that this buckle was in this scene of this movie?"

But Toby is doing a dance around his living room, ignoring me, reveling in the glory of his new possession.

"Thank you, thank you, thank you," he chants.

After a while Toby calms down enough that we can watch the rest of the movie, which goes by quickly. Clyde kills all the bad guys. Gets the girl. The end.

"Okay," Toby says. "I asked you both here for a reason. Come to the table."

I'm trying to hold on to the good feeling of the last hour, but the truth is I'm getting sad again. Toby is about to leave for two months to scout around Europe for this film that starts shooting soon. It's stupid of me—it's only two months, and it's a huge promotion for him—but Toby and I spend a lot of time together so it feels like a big deal. Plus he's going to miss my graduation, which I shouldn't care about because I've been over high school for a long time. But I do care just a little bit.

Toby opens the door to the patio off the kitchen and the night air floods in. He pours us some iced tea he gets from an Ethiopian place around the corner. The people there know him and sell it to him in a plastic pitcher that he takes back and gets refilled every couple days. They don't do it for anyone else, only Toby.

When we're seated at the round kitchen table, he says, "So, you know how I put up that ad to sublet my place? Well, I got all these responses. People were willing to spend *mad* cash to live here for two months."

"Sure," I say. Because it's obvious. His place is small but super adorable. It's this happy mix of Mom and Dad's old worn-in furniture and castoffs from sets I've worked on and things we picked up from Beverly Hills yard sales, where rich people sell their expensive stuff for cheap. It's just a few blocks from Abbot Kinney, and a few blocks more from the beach.

"Yeah," he says. "So it was seeming like it was gonna work. But then I had a better idea."

He takes a sip of his tea. Ice clinks. Charlotte leans forward in her chair. But me, I sit back. I know my brother, the master of good ideas, is waiting for the right moment to reveal his latest plan.

Finally, he says, "I'm letting you guys have it."

"Whaaaat?" I say. Charlotte and I turn to each other, as if to confirm that we both just heard the same thing. We shake our heads in wonder. And then I can't help it, I think of the third time Morgan broke up with me, when her reason was that I was younger (only three years!) and lived with my parents. Would it make a difference to her whether I lived here instead? Or is this time really about the vastness or whatever?

Charlotte says, "Are you serious?"

And Toby grins and says, "Completely. It's my graduation present to both of you. But there's a condition."

"Of course," I say, but he ignores me.

"I want you to do something with the place. Something epic. And I don't mean throw a party. I mean, something great has to take place here while I'm gone."

"Like what?" I ask. I'm a little worried, but excited, too. Toby's the kind of person whose greatness makes other people want to rise to any occasion. Everything he does is somehow larger than life, which is how he worked his way from a summer job as one of the parking staff to a full-time job as the location manager's assistant. And then, last month, at the age of twenty-two, he became the youngest location scout in the studio's recent history.

"That's all I'm gonna say on the subject," he says. "The rest is up to you."

We try asking more questions but when we do he just sits back and smiles. So the conversation shifts to *The Agency*, the film he's scouting for. I get to design a room for it, too, which will be my biggest job yet. It's a huge-budget movie with a young ensemble cast—Charlie Hayden and Emma Perez and

Justin Stark—all the really big young actors. It's a spy adventure, but the room I'm designing is for one of the girls when she's still supposed to be in high school, before they all become spies and start traveling around the world. It's probably going to be a stupid movie, but I'm thrilled about it anyway. A few weeks ago, Toby and I got to go to a party with the director and the whole cast and crew. I hung out with these stars whose faces are on posters all across the world. That's just one example of the kinds of things I get to do because of Toby.

Too soon, a knock comes on Toby's door—what is now for two months my door—and the film studio driver sweeps his suitcases into the trunk and then sweeps up my brother, too. Toby dangles the keys out the window, then looks out at me and says, "Epic."

The car pulls away and we wave and then it turns a corner and is gone. And Charlotte and I are left on the curb outside the apartment.

I sit down on the still-warm concrete.

"Epic," I say.

"We'll think of something," Charlotte says, sitting next to me.

We sit in silence for a while, listening to the neighbors. They talk and laugh, and soon some music starts. I'm trying to push away the heavy feeling that's descending now, that has been so often lately, but I'm having trouble. A few months ago it seemed like high school was going to last forever, like our college planning was for a distant and indistinct future. I could hang out with Charlotte without feeling a good-bye looming, take for granted every spur-of-the-moment plan with my brother, sneak out at night to drive up to Laurel Canyon with Morgan and lie under blankets in the back of her truck without worrying that it would be the last time. But now the University of Michigan is taking my best friend from me in just over two months, and my brother is off to Europe tonight and who knows where else after that. Morgan is free to kiss any girl she wants. I expected graduation to feel like freedom, but instead I'm finding myself a little bit lost.

My phone buzzes. *Why didn't you come to work?* I hide Morgan's name on the screen and ignore Charlotte's questioning look.

"Hey, we should listen to that record you got," I say, and Charlotte says, "Nice way to avoid the question," and I say, "Patsy Cline sounds like a perfect way to end the evening," which is a total lie. I don't know why Charlotte likes that kind of music.

But I fake enthusiasm as she takes the record out of its sleeve and places it on Toby's record player and lowers the needle. We lie on Toby's fluffy white rug (I got it from a pristine Beverly Hills yard sale for Toby's twenty-first birthday, along with some etched cocktail glasses) and listen to Patsy sing her heart out. Each song lasts approximately one minute so we just listen as song after song plays. Truthfully? I actually like it. I mean, the heartbreak! Patsy knew what she was singing about, that's for sure. It's like she *knows* I have a phone in my pocket with texts from a girl who I wish more than anything really loved me. Patsy is telling me that she understands how hard it is not to text Morgan back. She might even be saying *Dignity is overrated. You know what trumps dignity? Kissing.*

And I might be sending silent promises to Patsy that go something like *Next time Charlotte gets up to go to the bathroom I'll just send a quick text. Just a short one.*

"That was such a good song," Charlotte says.

"Oh," I say. "Yeah."

But I kind of missed it because Patsy and I were otherwise engaged and I swear that song only lasted *six seconds*.

"I wonder who wrote it," she says, standing and stretching and making her way to the album cover resting against a speaker.

This is probably my moment. She'll look at the song list and get her answer and then she'll head to the bathroom and I will write something really short like *Let's talk tomorrow* or *I still love you.*

"Hank Cochran and Jimmy Key," she says. "I love those lines 'If still loving you means I'm weak, then I'm weak.'"

"Wow," I say. It's like Patsy is giving me permission to give in to how I feel. "Are the lyrics printed?" I ask, sitting up.

"Yeah, here." Charlotte steps over and hands me the record sleeve, and as I take it something flutters out. I pick it up off the rug.

"An envelope." I check to see if it's sealed. It is. I turn it over and read the front. "'*In the event of my death, hand-deliver to Caroline Maddox of 726 Ruby Avenue, Apartment F. Long Beach, California.*'"

"*What?*" Charlotte says.

"Oh my God," I say. "Do you think Clyde wrote that?"

We study the handwriting for a long time. It's that old-guy handwriting, cursive and kind of shaky, but neat. Considering that 1) Clyde lived alone, and 2) this record belonged to

Clyde, and 3) Clyde was an old man who probably had old-man handwriting, we decide that the answer to my question is Definitively Yes.

The feeling I had in Clyde's study comes back. The envelope in my hand is important. This moment is important. I don't know why, but I know that it's true.

"We should go there now," I say.

"To Long Beach? We should probably let the estate sale manager know, don't you think? Should we really be the ones to do this?"

I shake my head.

"I don't want to give it to someone else," I say. "This might sound crazy but remember when you asked me if I was doing okay earlier?"

"Yeah."

"I just had this feeling that, I don't know, that there was something important about me being there, in Clyde Jones's house. Beyond the fact that it was just amazing luck."

"Like fate?" she asks.

"Maybe," I say. "I don't know. Maybe fate. It felt like it."

Charlotte studies my face.

"Let's just try," I say.

"Well, it's after ten. It would be almost eleven by the time we got there," Charlotte says. "We can't go tonight."

I know as well as Charlotte that we can't just show up on someone's doorstep at eleven with an envelope from a dead man.

"My physics final is at twelve thirty," I say. "Yours?"

"Twelve thirty," she says.

"I can't go after because I have to get that music stand and then get to set. I guess we'll have to go in the morning."

Charlotte nods, and we get out our phones to see how long it will take us to get to Long Beach. Without traffic, it would take forty minutes, but there is always traffic, especially on a weekday morning, which means it could take well over an hour, and we need to leave time for Caroline Maddox to tell us her life story, and we have to make sure we get back before our finals start, which means we have to leave . . .

"*Before* seven?" I say.

"Yeah," Charlotte says.

We are less than thrilled, but whatever. We are going to hand-deliver a letter from a late iconic actor to a mysterious woman named Caroline.

Chapter Two

We get on the road at 6:55, glasses full of Toby's iced tea because it was either that or some homemade kombucha that neither of us was brave enough to try. Toby does yoga, eats lots of raw foods. It's one of the areas in life where we diverge, which is probably good since we're alike in almost every other way: a love for the movies, a love for girls, an energy level other people sometimes find difficult to tolerate for extended periods of time.

Charlotte and I spend a while in bumper-to-bumper traffic on the 405. I allow Charlotte twenty minutes of public radio, and then when I am thoroughly newsed-out I turn on The Knife, because I am a firm believer that important moments in life are best with a sound track, and this will undoubtedly be one of those moments.

"Who do you think she is?" I ask, switching into the right lane. Charlotte's holding Clyde's envelope, studying Caroline's carefully written name.

"Maybe an ex-girlfriend?" she says. "She'll probably be old."

I try to think of other possibilities, but Clyde Jones is famous for being a bit of a recluse. He had some high-profile affairs when he was young, but that's ancient history, and it's common knowledge that he died without a single family member. With relatives out of the question, I can't think of many good answers.

We exit the freeway onto Ruby Avenue.

"I'm getting nervous," I say.

Charlotte nods.

"What if it's traumatic for her? Maybe it wasn't the best idea to do this before our finals. What if Caroline needs us or she passes out from shock or something?"

"I doubt that will happen," Charlotte says.

Neither of us has been on Ruby Avenue, so we don't know what to expect. But we do know that as we get closer to the address it becomes clear that whoever Caroline Maddox is, she doesn't live the same kind of life Clyde did. Number 726 is one of those sad apartment buildings that look like motels, two stories with the doors lined up in rows. We park on the street and look at the apartment through the rolled-up window of my car.

"Maybe she'll be someone he didn't know that well. Like a waitress from a restaurant he went to a lot. Or maybe he had a daughter no one knew about. From an affair or something."

"Yeah, maybe," Charlotte says.

We get out of the car.

After climbing the black metal stairs to the second story and knocking on the door of apartment F, I whisper, "Is it okay for us to ask what's inside? Like, to have her open it in front of us?"

Charlotte shakes her head no.

"Then how will we ever know? Will we follow up with her?"

"*Shhh,*" she says, and the door opens to a shirtless man, holding a baby on his hip.

"Hello," Charlotte says, professional but friendly. "Is Caroline home by any chance?"

The guy looks from Charlotte to me, shifts his baby to the other hip. He has longish hair, a shell necklace. A surfer who ended up miles from the beach.

"Sorry," he says. "No Caroline here."

Charlotte looks at the address on the envelope. "This *is* 726, right?"

"Yeah. Apartment F. Just three of us, though. Little June, myself, my wife, Amy."

"Do you mind my asking how long you've lived here?" Charlotte asks.

"About three years."

"Do you know if a Caroline lived here before you?"

He shakes his head. "I think a dude named Raymond did. We get his mail sometimes."

I turn to Charlotte. "Maybe she left a forwarding address with the landlord."

She turns to the surfer. "Does the manager live in the building?"

He nods. "Hold on," he says, disappears for a moment, and returns without the baby. He slides on flip-flops and joins us outside. "It's hard to describe. I'll lead you there."

We follow him down the stairs.

"Awesome weather," he says.

I say, "Well, yeah. It *is* LA."

"True," he says.

We walk along a path on the side of the building until we reach a detached cottage. He knocks on the door. We wait. Nothing.

"Hmm," he says. "Frank and Edie. They're old. Almost always home. Must be grocery day."

He pulls a phone out of his pocket.

"I can give you their number," he says, scrolling through names, and Charlotte enters it into her phone.

—

Walking back to the car, I say, "If we can't find Caroline, are we allowed to open the envelope?"

"We should really try to find her."

"I know. But if we don't."

"Maybe," she says. "Probably."

I hand Charlotte my keys and she unlocks her side, gets in, leans over and unlocks mine. I start the car and look at the time.

"We could have slept an extra hour," Charlotte says.

"Let's call the managers now," I say. "Maybe they were sleeping."

But she calls and gets their machine. "Good morning," she says. "My name is Charlotte Young. I'm trying to get in touch with a former tenant of yours. I'm hoping you might have some forwarding information. If you could call me back, I would appreciate it."

She leaves her number and hangs up.

Sometimes she sounds so professional that I can't believe the girl talking is also my best friend. At work, as long as I do my job well I don't have to talk like an adult because I'm one of the creatives. But Charlotte helps with logistics and phone calls and scheduling and making sure people show up when they are supposed to.

"I hope they call back," I say, noticing a brief ebb in the traffic and making a U-turn in the middle of the block.

"I'll follow up if they don't," Charlotte says.

"But if we can't reach them, and we can't find Caroline, then we'll open the letter," I say. "Right?"

"Maybe," she says. "But we're really going to try to find Caroline."

—

After my physics final and my Abbot Kinney stop, I drive to the studio, a little nauseous. Heartbreak is awful. Really awful. I wish I could listen to sad songs alone in my car until I felt over her. But I can't even talk about it with Charlotte, and I have to finish designing the room I'm working on now, even though I know Morgan will be on set with her sleeves pushed up and her tight jeans on and her short hair all messy and perfect. I pull into the studio entrance and the guard waves me through, and I roll past Morgan's vintage blue truck and into an open spot a few cars away, trying not to think of the first time I sat in the soft, upholstered passenger's seat and all the times that followed that one.

Morgan is off in a far corner of the set, but I see her first and then she's all I see. Filling everything. I'm carrying the music stand and I set it down in the room, but even though I'm looking at it and running my hand along its smooth wooden base, I can barely register that it's here.

Ginger says something and I say something back. She laughs and I fake-laugh and then I move a picture frame over a couple inches and immediately move it back. And then Morgan is next to me asking if I got her texts, touching me on the waist in the way that makes my stomach feel like a rag someone is squeezing.

I nod. Yes. I got them.

"I miss you," she says.

I don't say anything back because we've done this so many times before and I promised myself that I wouldn't do it again. She can't break up with me and then act like she's the one who's hurt. All I want is to flirt with her on set, to ride around in her cute truck talking all day, and dance with her at parties and lay poolside at her apartment and kiss. All the things we used to do. All the things we could be doing now if she weren't busy wondering if the world holds better things for her than me.

"Your shirt's cute," she says, but I don't say anything, just lean over to smooth down the edge of the colorful, patterned rug we're standing on. This morning I tried on seven outfits before deciding on these cute green shorts and this kind of revealing, strappy white tank top. I thought it looked summery and fun and, I'll admit, really good on me. But now I think I should have worn something I always wear so that Morgan wouldn't notice it was different and thus I wouldn't appear to be *trying* to look different.

I bend down to adjust the rug again, and it really does look good, the way the green in the music stand brings out the colors in the pattern, and I'm finding myself actually able to think of something other than her until she says, "Emi, are you not talking to me?"

And I stand up and say, "No, no, that's not it."

Because it isn't. I'm not trying to be childish or standoffish. I'm not trying to be mean. But I can't tell her that I'm not talking because I'm afraid that I'll cry if I do. The humiliation of being broken up with six times is brutal. And really, there might not be much worse than being at work with all of the people whose respect you want to earn while your first real love tells you you look pretty because she wants you to feel a little less crushed by the fact that she doesn't love you back.

I force a smile and say, "Check out this stand. Isn't it perfect?" knowing that she'll like it almost as much as I do.

"Yeah," she says. "The whole room looks really, really good."

I take a step back and look at it. Morgan's right. The room is supposed to be the basement practice space for a teenage-band geek named Kira. She doesn't have a big part in the movie, but there's an important scene that takes place in this room, and it's the first set I've designed on my own. I started with actual kid stuff. Trophies from thrift stores that I polished to make seem only a couple years old. Concert posters of a couple popular bands whose members play trumpets, which this character plays. So much sheet music that it's spilling off shelves, piled on every available surface. All of these normal things, but then a few extravagances, because this is the movies. A white bubble chandelier that lets out this beautiful soft light; a really shiny, *really* expensive trumpet; a hand-woven rug. And now, the music stand. I feel overwhelmingly proud of myself for pulling this off, and completely in love with the movie business.

"So now you're just waiting on the sofa?"

I turn to the last empty wall where the sofa will go, and nod.

"Any leads?"

I shake my head. No.

"It needs to be perfect," I say.

Early in the movie, Kira loses her virginity. She loses it to a guy who doesn't love her, but she doesn't know that in the moment. They have sex, not in her bedroom, but on a sofa in this practice room, the room that I am dressing, and I know that the scene will be disturbing because the secret is out to everyone except Kira that the guy isn't worth losing anything to. I've been trying to track down the sofa since I got the assignment. I know what I want. I know that it's going to be a vivid green, a soft material. The scene will be painful but the sofa will comfort her. It needs to be worn-in and look a little dated because it's the basement practice room; it's where the cast-off furniture goes after it's been replaced by newer and better things. But it also needs to be special enough to have been saved.

From across the studio, a guy calls to Morgan, asking her a question about plaster. Morgan is a scenic, which means that she builds the decorative elements of the sets before people like me come along and fill them. She can turn clean, white walls into the crumbling sides of a castle. She can turn an indoor space into a garden. She's an artist. It hurts to be this close to her.

"I have to go help him," she tells me. "But maybe we can grab dinner later. Talk. I'll check back in before I'm off?"

I nod.

She walks away.

Then I text Charlotte: *Intervention needed.*

Luckily, Charlotte's on the lot, working a couple buildings over. She tells me to meet her in the parking lot at exactly six o'clock.

—

After a couple hours of tinkering with my room and helping some of the set dressers, I say good-bye to Ginger (who tells me for the twentieth time how great everything looks) and find Morgan outside with her hands covered in plaster.

I tell her, "Charlotte needs my help, so I'm not going to be able to have dinner. We're in the middle of this really crazy mystery."

I wait for her to ask what it is. I get ready to say, *We're trying to fulfill Clyde Jones's dying wish*, for the awe to register on her face. But she just says, "No problem. Another time."

Another time. A period, not a question mark. As if it's such a sure thing that I will say yes.

I back my car up alongside Charlotte's so that, with our driver's side windows open, we can talk to each other without getting out.

"Thanks," I say.

"Anytime I can save you from making yet another terrible mistake with that girl please let me know," she says. Which is a little harsh, but something I probably deserve.

"Did the old people call you?" I ask.

"No. I wanted to wait for you before trying again."

I hop out of my car and cross around to hers. She puts her phone on speaker and dials. It rings. We wait. And wait. And then an old man's loud voice says hello.

"Hi," Charlotte says. "I'm sorry to bother you. I left you a message this morning. My name is—"

"*Hey, Edie!*" the man yells. "It's that girl from this morning! Calling us back!"

Charlotte and I widen our eyes in amusement.

"Now," Frank says. "I couldn't quite make out your phone number in the message. *Yes! The girl from this morning!* Let me see if I can find what I wrote down. Tell me the number again?"

Charlotte tells him.

"Oh," he says. "Two-*four*-three. I thought you said, 'Two-*oh*-three.'"

"Actually, it *is* two-oh-three."

"Two-four-three, yes."

"Actually—"

"And your name one more time, my dear?"

"Charlotte Young. I was wondering if you had any information—"

"*Yes, dear! We had the number wrong!* And her name is *Charlotte!*"

I'm trying my hardest not to laugh but I can see Charlotte becoming serious. She switches off the speakerphone and holds it to her ear.

"Frank? Sir?" she asks. "Will you be home for a little while? I have some questions that might be better to ask in person."

I wait.

"Okay. Yes. Hello, Edie. My name is Charlotte. *Charlotte.* Yes, it's nice to talk to you, too."

—

Frank and Edie are waiting for us on their porch when we arrive in Charlotte's car. It took us a little over an hour to get there and I wonder whether they've been waiting this whole time, frozen in positions of expectancy.

"Now, which one of you is Charlotte?" Frank says.

"Don't answer!" Edie says. "Don't say a word, girls. I am an excellent judge of people. Let me guess."

She peers at us. Her hair is a purple poof, like cotton candy. I can't tell if it's supposed to be brown or if she's getting wild in her old age.

"You," she says to me. "Are Charlotte."

I shake my head.

"Emi," I say, and hold out my hand.

She scoffs, says, "You look like a Charlotte," but her eyes have this fun glimmer.

Frank towers over her, surveying us through thick glasses.

"Come on in, girls," he says. "Come on in."

Inside, we sit on a plastic-covered maroon sofa with *People* magazines stacked up beside us, cookies and lemonade arranged on the coffee table. This elderly couple having us into their living room, serving us snacks with the fan blasting and the screen door flapping open and shut—it's so sweet, almost enough to take my mind off Morgan.

"I hope you like gingersnaps," Edie says. She thrusts a finger toward Frank. "He got ginger cookies. I said I wanted *plain*."

"They didn't have plain."

"How could they not have plain?"

"You were with me, dear," he says. "Lemon. Oreo. Maple. Ginger. *No plain*."

She shakes her head.

"Crap," she says. She lifts a cookie and eats it. "Crap," she says again. And then she takes another.

"Do you live in the neighborhood?" Frank asks us.

"I live in Westwood," Charlotte says.

"Santa Monica," I say.

"Santa Monica!" Edie says. "Our son, Tommy, lives in Santa Monica. You may know him. Tommy Drury?"

I shake my head. "No," I say. "He doesn't sound familiar."

"He's a lovely boy," Edie says.

"He just turned sixty!" Frank says. "He's not a boy!"

"He's *my* boy. Do you shop at the Vons on Wilshire?"

"Um," I say. "I guess. I mean, my parents do."

"It's a good Vons," Frank says.

"A nice deli section," Edie agrees. "But too crowded."

Charlotte compliments them on the lemonade ("Straight out of the box!" Edie confides) and then says, "We're looking for a former tenant of yours. Caroline Maddox."

"Who?" Frank turns to Edie, and it's only then that I notice his hearing aids.

"*Caroline Maddox,*" Edie shouts.

"Oh yes, Caroline." Frank nods.

"You remember her?" Charlotte asks.

"Yes, of course!" Edie says. "She was a very nice girl. Very nice. But she had troubles. The drugs and the men and that baby." She shakes her head. "What a shame."

Frank says, "Yes, yes. You girls must have noticed that the hedges around the path are all overgrown." He says it so apologetically. "Caroline, she used to take care of those for us. It was years ago and I worked during the days and dealt with apartment business at night. Caroline, she helped us with some of the chores."

"For reduced rent," Edie adds.

"Do you know where she is?" Charlotte asks. "Or where she moved to after she left the apartment?"

"Oh, dear," Edie says.

"Oh, dear," Frank echoes. "I hate to say it, but Caroline died."

"When?" Charlotte asks.

Frank shakes his head. "I'm terrible with dates," he says.

"I know," Edie says. "It was October of 1995. I remember because the Dodgers lost in the playoffs. Those Braves beat them Three to nothing. Three to *zip*. Terrible! I remember thinking, *What could be worse than this?* And then, just a few days later, we found Caroline in the apartment."

Frank looks off to the side, eyes glassy, and Edie picks up a cookie but doesn't eat it. We sit quietly for a little while, and then Edie begins gossiping about celebrities. I tell her about our jobs in the movies and she is impressed, especially with *The Agency*, which she's already been reading about even though shooting doesn't begin for a few months. But Charlotte stays quiet, and I can understand why. Here we were expecting to find Caroline, a living person, who would take this envelope from us and hopefully tell us about what was inside and who she was to Clyde. But instead we discover that Caroline is a dead woman. And it's unsettling, somehow, that whatever Clyde wanted to give to her was never, and never will be, received.

—

It's dark by the time we get back in the car.

Charlotte sighs. "I guess we did all we could."

"So we're going to open it?"

She nods, but doesn't reach for her bag.

I find it on the backseat and fish out the envelope. It's so thin. And I realize something that I hadn't really registered before: It's old, yellowing. I wonder how old. Old enough, I guess, for Caroline to die and someone named Raymond to move in and move out, and then for the surfer's family to follow. Maybe even older than that.

Charlotte takes the keys from her lap and very carefully rips open the envelope.

Dear Caroline,

I confess it was optimistic of me to think our lunch might transform a lifetime of estrangement into some kind of relationship. I don't think, however, that it was optimistic to think it could have been some kind of beginning, even if it was the beginning of something meager. A casual hello now and then. An acquaintanceship. But I've been trying to reach you for several months. My letters have been returned. What few phone numbers I can find for you are all outdated. I'm not disregarding the possibility of a change of heart, but, for now at least, I'm giving up.

There were things I wanted to tell you that afternoon that I couldn't bring myself to say. I told myself it was because I expected it to be Me and You, and instead it was *Me and You and Lenny*. So I found myself in the company of two strangers instead of only one. However, that might have only been an excuse. You are my only child and I was never a father to you. I don't know how a father is supposed to say heartfelt things or express regret or give a compliment.

So, here it goes, on paper, which feels far less daunting.

I was unaware of your existence when you were born. After I learned about you, I had intentions of being a good father. To put it plainly, your mother made that impossible.

She would not accept my money. She would not consider a friendship. I spent a decade trying to make amends with her but the truth is that I had very little to say. We both had our reasons for what happened that night and in the few weeks that followed. I won't presume to know hers, but in my defense, I did not make any promises or intentionally lead her on. She had what many people crave, a few minutes in the spotlight on the arm of someone famous. She did not ever know me and I did not ever know her. I would like to think that we each received something we needed in a specific period of time in our lives, but I fear that your mother's reaction to my repeated gestures spoke otherwise.

It may seem unfair of me to speak this way of a woman who is no longer in this world to defend herself. I don't wish to be cruel. Another thing I wanted to do (but didn't) was offer you my condolences. And I wanted to say that I know what it's like to be an orphan. It's possible that you feel alone in the world. I know a little bit about that, too. I suppose I thought we might bond over our specific tragedies, but instead I told you about my dogs and the weather, and you stared at your eggs and never touched them.

You are my only child. I wanted you to know a few things about me. It is true that I always wear a cowboy hat, but I am not the stoic, humorless man that I so often played. I try my best to enjoy life. I enjoy hiking through the hills behind my home. I have loved deeply, but had hopes of a different kind of love.

There is a bank account in your name at the Northern West Credit Union. Please visit them and ask for Terrence Webber. He will give you access to the account. If you do not want the money, please give it to Ava. It may seem crass to give you so much. Please don't think of it as an attempt to buy your love or forgiveness. Despite the idealistic notion that money is of little importance, money can open doors. I hope, my daughter (if you'll allow me to call you that this once), that doors will open for you all your life.

My regards,

Clyde

"So you were right," Charlotte says. "Caroline Maddox was his daughter."

"What tragedy," I say.

"So bitter," Charlotte says.

"So regretful."

Charlotte nods. "It's like he wants to tell her everything but it hardly adds up to anything."

"I know. I wear cowboy hats? I enjoy hiking?" I pick up the letter again. His handwriting is careful and shaky and everything is neat, like he wrote multiple drafts. "Who's Lenny? Who's Ava?"

Charlotte shakes her head. "I don't know."

At the end of the block, a couple men step out of a liquor store, shouting into the night. They laugh, slide into their car, pull away.

"He didn't even know that she died," I say.

We head back to the studio to pick up my car, and then we caravan to Toby's apartment, where our parents told us we could stay again tonight, and where we intend to stay for as long as Toby's away.

Driving alone, I can't but help thinking of how today is just so sad. Toby's gone, Morgan doesn't love me, Clyde Jones had a daughter named Caroline who tended Frank and Edie's garden and had problems with men and drugs and never got her father's letter or all that money that might have helped her.

And I was sure that all of this would mean something for me, too. That something had to come of wandering through Clyde's house, of our accidental discovery. But now it's just something else that has come to an end.

And it's only later, after watching *Lowlands*, with the warm breeze coming through the kitchen door and our glasses half full of Toby's Ethiopian tea, that Charlotte says, "What was it Edie said? The drugs and the men and that *baby*? Could Ava be Clyde's granddaughter?"

Chapter Three

Charlotte and I are perched on benches in the high school courtyard in our short shorts and tank tops, tapped into the school wireless connection, searching for Ava.

We start by trying to find Caroline's obituary, because we don't know Ava's last name, or even *if* Ava is really Caroline's daughter. But we search the *Los Angeles Times*'s online archive, and the *Long Beach Press-Telegram*'s, and neither of them go back as far as the nineties.

"Let's just look up Ava Maddox," I say.

It doesn't seem like Caroline was married, and from what Edie said—*all those men*—it doesn't seem like she was in a serious relationship either.

Charlotte types in the name, and a moment later we find that there are nine Ava Maddoxes listed in the country, one of whom happens to live in Los Angeles, on Waring Avenue, which is not super close but not too far either. Maybe a twenty-minute drive northeast across the city.

"Should we drive out there?" I ask.

She clicks on an icon that promises to tell us more about Ava, only to find that they want to charge us for it.

"*Forty dollars?*" I say. "No thanks. Let's just go."

"Okay," Charlotte says. We stand up and she slips her laptop back into its case and then into her bag. We agree to meet back at my car after we're finished with our respective finals—the last of the semester, the last of our high school lives.

On the way to my math class for the last time, I feel a tap on my shoulder and turn around to see Laura Presley handing me her yearbook.

"Sign it?" she asks, all flirty and cute and kind of nervous.

I force a smile and say sure.

"But how will I get it back from you?"

Her best friend, who is in my math class, says, "Should Emi just give it to me when she's done?"

"Perfect!" Laura says, as though it's a new idea and not a plan they made before coming up to me.

I take the yearbook from her and walk into class, even though I'm not going to sign it. I've never been that into high school, so I don't care much about these books made to commemorate it, and if Laura wants some kind of closure we can meet up and laugh about things one day. There was a time I wouldn't have found anything to laugh about, but it's been a long time since everything ended between us.

Laura is who made me swear off high school girls. The short version is that I've always loved kissing. I kissed more boys in elementary school and junior high than I can count. (Purely innocent, by the way. It never went past that.) And then I kissed Tara Ryland behind the science building our freshman year. When our mouths parted she stood there, blinking at me, like, *What the?* And I blinked back at her, like, *Oh my God.* But we were reacting to different things. Tara was shocked because one moment we were collecting dirt samples to measure minerality and the next she was kissing a girl. But for me it was different. I skimmed over the girl part and just thought, *Is this what it's supposed to feel like?* Because it wasn't only that she was a good kisser (which she was), it was that the kiss left me shaky, and by this time I had become almost immune to kissing. And then girls sort of started lining up to kiss me. It drove Charlotte crazy. She rolled her eyes for a year straight. In the midst of all of this, just for a couple months, I threw everyone off by dating Evan Haas. What can I say? There was just something about him.

And then Laura descended from the heights of the popular crowd. She wanted to kiss and hold hands in the hallways. She wanted to leave her group to sit with Charlotte and me at lunch, but preferably just me. She wanted to make out with me at parties in hot tubs while other kids watched. And okay, yeah, that was fun for a little while, but I was starting to fall for her and I didn't want it to be a show.

So now, in between math problems, I give my hand a break from scribbling numbers and think of those nights and days with Laura. For the last few months, everyone has been getting all sentimental about leaving high school, and I guess this is my version of that. By the end of my exam, I'm replaying the afternoon when we were supposed to drive down to the beach and just hang out, and she said, "*Or*, we could go to Alex's party. It's going to be crazy." She said it while grabbing my hip and pulling me close to her, right in view of Alex and all his friends. I pried her hand off me and stepped back.

I told her, "Let's just forget it."

Meaning our plans for that day. Meaning the rare moments when we actually seemed to be in a relationship. Meaning the utter hopelessness of high school girls who didn't know what they wanted.

This was junior year, and a few months later, when senior year started and Laura still smiled at me in this sad way every time we passed each other in the hallway, I told Charlotte, "I actually think she might have liked me."

"Of course she liked you," Charlotte said. "She just didn't know what to do with that."

By this time I had already met Morgan and was spending every waking moment trying to get her to notice me, so registering this about Laura felt like just a small thing, but something nonetheless.

Two hours and sixty-five problems later, I walk up to the front and hand my teacher my exam. He's hunched over his desk, watching silent videos on his laptop. Then, back at my desk, I surprise myself by finding a bright red pen in my backpack and opening Laura's yearbook to a front page. I'm not going to write anything sentimental, but I can give her something for nostalgia's sake. So I write in big, bright letters, *Kissing you was really fun.* I draw a heart by my name.

Then I leave school to find Ava.

—

"What are we supposed to say when we get there?" I ask Charlotte.

We're just a couple miles away now, inching through traffic, hoping not to get caught in an intersection when the light turns red.

"We'll just ask if Ava's home."

"And if she is?"

She bites her lip, a familiar sign that she's pondering. Usually something brilliant follows, so I just drive and let her think.

"We know that she was a baby in '95, so she should be

around our age. If she's older, we'll just say we got the wrong
Ava and head out. But if she *is* our age . . ."

"What if she doesn't know she's adopted?"

"I think she'll know. Her last name is the same as her
mom's. And I don't think people keep things like this a secret
anymore."

"I hope not," I say, "because that would be awkward.
Here's Waring; turn left."

We find the house, small and blue, with succulents growing in the front yard. We park and unbuckle our seat belts but
neither of us makes any move to get out of the car. I lean back.
The windshield reflects the tree above us: branches and leaves
and the road through the glass.

"If she's our age," Char says, "let's just ask if her mother's
name was Caroline. If she says yes, then she knows more of the
story than we do, and we can just tell her we have something
that belongs to her, give her the envelope, and let her know
that she can call us if she has any questions."

"Then just leave?" I ask.

She nods. "And if she says no, that Caroline was *not* her
mother's name, then we should just thank her and go."

"But what if she says no because she doesn't know about
Caroline, or because she doesn't know who we are or why
we're asking? What if we think we have the wrong Ava when
really she's the right one?"

Charlotte bites her lip again.

Finally, she says, "I don't know. We'll just have to see what
happens today and go from there."

She opens her car door and then I open mine, and I follow her up the walk to the door. Charlotte knocks and we both wait until we hear a kid's voice from the other side, asking who is it.

"Charlotte and Emi," Charlotte says. She looks at me for help, but what else are we supposed to say?

"We're looking for Ava?" I try, but it comes out a question.

The door cracks open and a little girl peers through before pushing it open wider. She has long dark hair in pigtails and a quizzical expression.

"Here I am," she says.

"You're Ava?" Charlotte asks.

"Yeah."

"How old are you?"

"Eight."

"Ten years too young," Charlotte murmurs.

"Sorry," I say. "Looks like we have the wrong Ava."

The little Ava shrugs.

"It's okay," she says. "Bye."

The door shuts.

"Okay," Charlotte says, as we turn and head down the steps, back to the car waiting in the shade. "We have to go to the library."

"The library?"

"There are things we just can't find online, no matter how much money we waste."

"But really? You think we can find answers in the library?" I'm skeptical, but Charlotte has great faith in the collection and preservation of things, and if she wants to go to the library I will go with her.

—

It turns out that 1995 is ancient history. So ancient, in fact, that we have to slide brown sheets of film displaying newspaper obituaries into a primitive machine, and then drop in quarters to make the screen light up. With the help of a cute, tattooed librarian named Joel who makes her blush as he leans over her to tinker with the machine, Charlotte starts with October 1 in the *Los Angeles Times*. Joel sets me up on a machine next to Charlotte and gives me the *Los Angeles Herald-Examiner*, which, I'm quick to point out, is obviously the inferior paper.

"It's not even a paper anymore," I say once Joel is back behind the information desk. "I'm clearly the sidekick in this mystery. I'll selflessly devote myself to the *Herald-Examiner* while you find the answer in the *Times* and get all the glory."

Charlotte smiles and changes slides.

I've only gotten through October 5 by the time my first quarter runs out and the screen goes dark.

"I thought libraries were supposed to provide information free of charge," I whisper.

Charlotte ignores me. I search and search forever. There should really be a more efficient way of doing this.

"Why do we have to search by date? We should be able to search by name."

"Newspapers don't work that way," Charlotte says, and I can tell she's getting tired of me.

An hour later, she's made it through October, and she sighs, defeated.

"My mom wants me home tonight," she says. "She's been complaining about me staying at Toby's all the time before leaving for college."

"That's understandable," I say. My parents haven't been too worried about it, but I'm staying in LA for college, living at home to save money, while Charlotte's really leaving. "I'll see if my dad can help us out."

Charlotte appears skeptical. "I feel like we're hitting a wall," she says. "I don't know if we're going to find her."

"You feel that way because you just read through hundreds of obituaries. It's depressing. But we'll find her," I say. "We just need to approach this from a new angle."

Charlotte's mom picks her up, but I keep searching, loading film and popping quarters into the machine. I make it through September and then I am finished with nothing to show for my patience and Charlotte's faith in antiquity. I still have my studio work to do, so I wander over to Joel and ask him for today's paper, which, thankfully, is in its normal paper form. I take a seat at a long, shiny table and start the weekly task of mapping out my Saturday morning garage- and estate-sale schedule.

—

My parents have gotten delivery from Garlic Flower, so I kiss my mother's cheek while she talks on the phone to a colleague, then grab a plate and a fork and heap rice and garlic chicken on my plate. My dad is watching a reality show about rich women. This is the kind of ridiculous thing you get to do for money if you are a professor of popular culture.

"Dad?" I say. "I need to vent. Mom's on the phone."

He turns the TV on mute. "Your mother has just finished reading a *New Yorker* article on emerging African American filmmakers and is now trying to coax them all into speaking to her graduate seminar," Dad says. "So try me."

My mother is also a professor, of black studies and gender studies, which basically means that while Dad observes all things pop culture with palpable glee, my mother observes and then obliterates them with whichever theory best suits the subject. Which, considering the subject I'm about to raise—perhaps the whitest, straightest, most gender-normative American icon in all of cinema—makes my dad the far-better sounding board anyway.

"Okay," I say. "It starts with Clyde Jones."

"I'm intrigued."

I tell him the story from the beginning: Charlotte's phone call, which came at the perfect time because it meant I didn't go to see Morgan; all the cool stuff in his house, Toby's belt buckle and Patsy Cline; and then, finally, the letter; and Frank and Edie; and the library and all of those obituaries from all of the papers.

"Do you know how many newspapers there are in Los Angeles?" I say.

"I know of quite a few," he says. Then, "So Clyde Jones had a daughter named Caroline who died in an apartment on Ruby Avenue. And you need to learn more about her in order to find someone named Ava who may or may not be her daughter."

"Exactly," I say. "And, really, why is it so difficult? Why can't I just search 'Caroline Maddox' and have an obituary pop up?"

My dad strokes his beard in a way that's so cinematically thoughtful that I have to try not to laugh.

"Why do you want to find her daughter?"

"There might still be money in that account that belongs to her."

He raises an eyebrow, so I try again.

"It seemed to really matter to Clyde."

Still, he is unconvinced.

"Okay," I say. "Look. It's just important to me. I just feel like it's important."

He seems satisfied by this answer.

"And how do you know that Caroline died in September or October of '95?" he asks.

"Edie said something about the Dodgers losing in the playoffs."

"That's right," he says. "Three—nothing."

"You should hear this woman talk," I say. "She's really great. 'I said I wanted *plain*,'" I imitate. He laughs, so I keep going. "'Do you shop at the Vons on Wilshire? Nice deli section. Too crowded, though.'" He laughs harder. "'Those Braves beat them three to nothing. Three to *zip*. Terrible!'"

"Wait," he says. "The Braves?"

I take a bite of my dinner and nod while chewing.

"They lost to the Braves in the playoffs in '96. Not '95."

I swallow. "Are you sure?"

"Yes. The Dodgers lost three—nothing in the playoffs in '95 to the Reds, and then again, three—nothing, to the Braves in '96. Sounds like Edie got her years mixed up."

I stop chewing. Stare at him.

"Are you sure?"

"Emi," he says, tapping his head. "There is a world of Los Angeles history in here. I am absolutely sure."

But I still run to the computer to make sure. And moments later, I find it on the Major League Baseball site. The Dodgers and the Braves. 3–0. 1996.

I groan, head in hands. "Why didn't we check this *before* we spent all day in the library?"

"Hey, at least you have a new direction," Dad says.

"Easy for you to say. You like this research stuff."

"True," he says.

I take out my phone and text Charlotte.

Braves beat Dodgers in 96. Back 2 library. 2 p.m.?

Chapter Four

After seven weeks, fifty-two garage sales, and sixteen estates, the impossible happens: I find the sofa.

It's upstairs in a Pasadena house, my fourth and farthest stop of the morning, in a dressing room adjoining the master bedroom.

I push through the hoards of people to get to the woman who is clearly in charge and tell her I'll take it.

"The one in the dressing room?"

"Yes," I say.

"Hm," she scrunches up her face. "That one's on hold."

I laugh because the universe must be playing a trick on me. But she doesn't crack a smile, so I get serious.

"Nothing said it was on hold," I say.

"I know but one of my clients expressed interest at the preview."

"Expressed interest? That's hardly putting something on hold. Did she pay a deposit?"

"No."

"Then I should be able to buy it. I can pay you right now."

"Why don't you check back this afternoon?"

"I'll pay you double," I say.

"Fine," she says. "But I need it out of here immediately. I don't want it here when she comes later. This way I can blame it on someone else. You have a truck?"

I scoff like that's a ridiculous question. It's a scoff that says *Of course*.

While her assistants lug the sofa downstairs, I madly call

all the buyers whose numbers are programmed into my phone. But all I get is voice mail after voice mail and I start to panic. The assistants ask me where the truck is and I tell them someone's pulling it around. "You can just set it down here," I say, and they set it on the dried-up grass of the front yard, bordering the sidewalk.

I sit on the cushions and try the next number. This way, if the woman comes, I'll just refuse to get up. I'll be ready to channel Clyde Jones. *If you want the sofa, you'll have to get past me first.*

But soon I am out of numbers. I guess no one wants to work on a Saturday, but besides the studio buyers, I only know one person with a truck. I can hear Charlotte telling me that she would rather rent a truck than have me call Morgan for help, and she would be right to say it, but I can't take any chances with this sofa. It's everything I hoped it would be, only better: vivid green and soft, with these gold embroidered leaves, so delicate I didn't notice them when I first saw it from across the room. In the first music-room scene, when the daughter is practicing, it will seem pretty but plain. Later, though, once she's lying on it under the boy's weight, and there are close-ups of their hands or feet or faces, people will see the thread and the leaves. I can picture the girl's hair spilling over the side, blending with the gold, like she's tangled up in a forest. There's something fairy-tale-like about it, which is perfect, because fairy tales are all about innocence and ill will and the inevitability of terrible things. They're all about the moment when the girl is no longer who she once was, and with this in mind, I surrender all doubts and shreds of dignity and call Morgan.

She answers on the third ring.

"I found a sofa," I tell her. "It's perfect. Please tell me you can help me get it to set."

"Where are you?"

"Pasadena," I say.

"*Pasadena?*"

"Yeah," I say. "I'm sorry. But the couch is amazing. The couch is one of a kind, the best couch in history, the—"

"Okay, I'm at brunch with some people. I'm paying the bill. Text me the address."

I hang up and text her, and then I lie down on the sofa and look up at the clear sky. Time passes and people pass, carrying the remnants of a dead woman's life. I allow myself to imagine Morgan telling me she wants me back. I try to limit this particular daydream to two or three times per day, or else it becomes difficult to pay attention to the people and things around me. I've been lucky to have sofa hunting and Caroline Maddox as distractions, but now I have the sofa and I'm starting to agree with Charlotte that Ava might be a lost cause, and where will that leave me? The answer is simple: It will leave me in too many moments exactly like this, lying down somewhere, my mind occupied by the sound of Morgan saying *I want you back* (which is not a difficult sentence to imagine because it's already happened five times in real life), placing her hands around my waist and pulling me toward her, kissing me in that passionate way that says *I never thought I'd be able to kiss you again and now that I have you I'll never let you go.*

I'm absorbed by these thoughts when Morgan's face appears above me. Next to hers is a woman's I don't recognize.

I sit up. "Isn't it even more amazing than you could imagine?"

"It's really cool," Morgan says. "It'll look great in close-ups."

Even though she's saying the right things, I almost wish she wasn't. Another person might see this sitting in the sun on a Saturday morning in Los Angeles and think it's just a sofa, a castoff from an estate sale, no more or less special than any other sofa. Morgan understands, though, that it is, in fact, more special.

"This is my friend Rebecca."

"Hi, Rebecca." I channel Charlotte, stand, extend my hand like a professional, trying not to wonder if Rebecca is in some way affiliated with vastness.

"Morgan's been telling me about you," Rebecca says.

"Oh."

"Good things," she says.

"Great."

I'm too confused to say anything else. Is Morgan telling her about me because she's her new girlfriend? Is she telling her how great I am out of pity?

"I'm sure you guys have things to do," I say, grabbing one of the sofa's gorgeous arms. I feel really young and really foolish and desperate. I wish I had a limitless supply of friends with trucks. I wish I didn't need her. I wish I had called Charlotte instead so she could have facilitated a truck rental. That is Charlotte's job, after all: facilitation. Why didn't I let her do her job?

The three of us carry the sofa to the bed of Morgan's blue truck and lift with all our strength. It slides in.

"I'll follow you guys," I say, and turn and get into my car before they can say anything else to me.

—

All the way to the lot, I try to think about life's vast possibilities. Not as a means of self-torture, because I'm not that type of girl. But as a means of trying to get over Morgan. Life *is* vast. Many things *are* possible. Morgan was right about that. So even if she is dating Rebecca now, maybe the world isn't necessarily over for me. There are still Ava Maddoxes to find and sets to create and girls to kiss and colleges to attend. It's possible that someday I will hear a Patsy Cline song and the heartbreak will barely register. It will be some distant, buried feeling. I won't remember how much it once hurt.

By the time we get to the lot I am resolving to make it on and off set without crying. I park closer to the entrance than I usually get to because hardly anyone is here, and I ignore Morgan's and Rebecca's residual laughter as they climb out of the truck. I take down the tailgate and start pulling out the sofa, which is unbelievably smooth and plush. And when we set it down in the music room, this room I've created, it becomes official: This is the perfect room, the perfect sofa, the perfect set for heartbreak.

Morgan stands back and looks, but Rebecca walks all around it, paying attention to the sheet music and picture frames and the posters and trophies and rugs.

"You did this yourself?" She touches the top of the music stand.

I nod.

"The sofa really does suit the room. It feels authentic. How did you find it?"

"I looked for a long time," I say. "I went to fifty-two garage sales and sixteen estates."

"I'm sure you saw a lot of nice sofas, then."

"Yeah," I say. "But I knew what I wanted."

Rebecca turns to Morgan and smiles a smile that says something. It isn't a language I'm privy to, but it doesn't seem like pity, so I don't let it get to me.

"I'm going to call Theo," she tells Morgan. "Really nice to meet you," she says to me. She looks me in the eye. She shakes my hand again. I notice that she's older than Morgan by at least a few years, but that doesn't necessarily mean anything.

She goes outside and I ask, "Who's Theo?"

"Her boyfriend," Morgan says. "Why?"

"No reason," I say, looking into her face for the first time today. She looks back at me. I can tell that she likes what she's seeing.

"Want to see what I've been working on?" she asks, gesturing to the far side of the set, where she's been building the little brother's room.

I pull out my phone; it's one thirty.

"Wish I could," I say, "but I have to meet Charlotte at the library."

She laughs like she knows I'm playing hard to get, and I have to admit that it feels good to turn her down.

—

At 4:46, with Charlotte at the machine next to me scouring the *Los Angeles Times*, I find Caroline Maddox's obituary in the *Long Beach Press-Telegram*.

Her name appears next to a small, grainy photograph.

"Char," I say, and there must be something in the way I say it that tells her I've found it, because she sighs and says, "Finally."

She scoots her chair closer to me. We read together.

> Caroline Rose Maddox passed away on October 7, 1996. Born in Beverly Hills in 1974, she had a lifelong dream of being an actress. She had small parts in dozens of films, including *The Restlessness*, directed by Scott Bennings, in which she played a waitress in the climactic scene. In addition to acting, Caroline was a gifted gardener and a compassionate, loyal friend. She is survived by her four-month-old daughter, her best friend, Tracey Wilder, and the hundreds of people whose lives she made brighter by her presence in them.

"This is really sad," I say.

"The acting stuff?"

"All of it. That she died, I guess. And the acting."

"We all die," Charlotte says.

"Well, yeah."

"Sorry. It's just that the acting part seems the worst. I mean, she was an extra. Her character didn't even have a name but it was her greatest accomplishment."

"Hopefully, she was proud of it," I say. "We should find the movie. *The Restlessness*? I haven't even heard of it."

Charlotte gets out her laptop and transcribes the obituary, word for word.

"Ava's name isn't even in it," I say. I read it again. "Who do you think wrote it?"

Charlotte bites her lip. "I'd assume Tracey Wilder," she says. "She's the only person mentioned by name."

"Hey," I say. "We should search for Ava Wilder. It would make sense, wouldn't it? If I had a kid and I died, you'd adopt her, right?"

"I think your parents or Toby would probably—"

"But if I didn't have parents or a brother. If Clyde Jones was my dad but you didn't even know it. If, for all you knew, I had no one but you. You'd adopt her, right?"

"Of course," she says, starting a search for Ava Wilder.

Three in the entire US. One in Leona Valley, a town that borders the desert.

We stare at the screen.

"Search for Tracey," I say.

Charlotte's hands fly across the keyboard.

Twenty-one Tracey Wilders in the US. Charlotte starts to scroll down the list and I see it before she does.

"Oh my God," I say, and Charlotte gasps when she sees it: Tracey Wilder, Leona Valley, California. Next to her name is a phone number.

"Let's call her."

"Tracey or Ava?" Charlotte asks.

"Ava," I say. "Definitely. Clyde wanted the letter to go to Caroline, but he said she could give the money to Ava. Tracey has nothing to do with it."

We gather all of our stuff and Charlotte returns the microfilm to Joel-the-cute-librarian and we walk fast toward the exit.

"You call," I tell her.

"Okay," she says, "but let's get in the car so it'll be quiet."

Down in the garage we can't get service, so I have to drive up to the street; and even though Charlotte's ability to have a successful phone conversation in no way requires my full attention, I pull into a loading zone because I'm too nervous to drive.

She dials the number and I lean in close enough to hear a boy's voice say hello.

"Hi," she says. "My name is Charlotte. Is Ava home, by any chance?"

There is a pause, and then the kid says, "No, she isn't."

"Would you mind taking a message?"

"Ava's, um. . . I mean, I can? But I don't know when she'd get it."

"Oh," Charlotte says.

"She doesn't live here anymore."

"Is there another way to reach her? Another number?"

"I don't really know where she is," he says.

Charlotte bites her lip.

He says, "I can take your number, and if I talk to her I'll give it to her, but I don't know when she'll get it."

"Okay," Charlotte says, and she leaves him her number.

"I'll give it to her. If she calls, I mean."

"Okay," Charlotte says again. I can tell she doesn't want to hang up and I don't want her to either.

"Bye," the kid says.

She doesn't say anything, but soon there's a click.

And now it's just Charlotte and me, illegally parked in downtown Los Angeles, all of the answers lost in the vastness.

Chapter Five

On Monday, I go straight to the room Morgan's been working on. I can play hard to get only for so long. Really, I am easy to get. And I keep thinking of how she drove all the way to Pasadena to pick up the sofa, and how she's been saying nice things to Rebecca-who-has-a-boyfriend about me, and how she wants to show me this space she's been working on, because she cares about her work and knows that I also care because we are aligned in this way among many others.

Her back is to me when I walk into the room. She's putting up wallpaper, sponging the corners of a panel to smooth it out.

"This is gorgeous," I say, because it is. The paper is the pattern of a night sky, panel after panel, with glowing stars forming constellations. It's perfect for the little boy, who has an interest in science and whose room is shot primarily in night scenes.

She steps away and smiles at me. I allow myself to notice how good her arms look in her tank top, tan and strong but still unmistakably *girl* arms. And because the music room is finished and I knew that I wouldn't be doing anything too hands-on today, I wore a skirt and a skimpy shirt to show off my girlishness, too.

"I'm mostly running errands today," I tell her. "But I wanted to check it out. Since I couldn't, you know, on Saturday."

"That's right," she says. "You and Charlotte had a library party to attend."

"We were actually doing something pretty interesting," I say.

"I can imagine." She turns back to her work and I watch her hands as they smooth down swirls and stars.

To the right is a bunk bed built out of light-colored wood.

"You built this?" I ask her, and she nods.

I climb the little ladder and sit on the top bunk. It would be so easy to forget that all around us people are working, moving planter boxes of trees to go on the opposite sides of windows, painting sets and assembling furniture, supervising and surveying and engaging in conversations. So easy, because here is a bunk bed and rumpled sheets, here is a model of a hot-air balloon floating from the ceiling, here is a white wall steadily becoming less white as Morgan applies panel after panel of deep blue wallpaper. It's all a fantasy, so it's easy, for a few minutes, to get lost in it.

"I've always wondered what it would be like to be on the top bunk," I say, even though the idea has never occurred to me.

"And?"

"It's great," I say. "So cozy. You haven't been up here?"

"Not since I finished building it."

"Why don't you join me?"

She smiles and shakes her head.

"Hey, what are you doing later?" I ask, trying to ignore Charlotte's inevitable disapproval. I already had to explain myself about Saturday morning's encounter.

"I have plans," Morgan says.

"What kind of plans?"

"Mmm," she says. "I don't know if you want to hear about them."

"Oh," I say, and the glorious world of little boy's bunk beds and hands smoothing stars and beautiful arms and short skirts disintegrates. I skip the ladder and hop down instead.

"Well, have fun."

"Em," she says. "I'm sorry if this is hard."

"Yeah, okay."

"No, really." She sets down her sponge and leans against the bed, looking at me. "I really like you; I just can't be tied down right now."

"That's such a cliché thing to say," I tell her. "If I saw that in a script I would laugh."

She shrugs. "It's how I feel right now. When you're ready to hang out as friends I would love that."

My phone buzzes and I check the screen. It's Charlotte texting, *I thought your sofa was green?*

"Charlotte's here," I say. "I have to go."

"Okay," Morgan says. "Thanks for coming by. And my friend Rebecca might want to talk to you. I gave her your number. It's about good things."

"Sure," I mutter, and head to the music room.

I see Charlotte as soon as I round the corner.

"Of course it's green," I say. "I'd call it, like, a cross between forest green and kelly green. What would you call it?"

"Um," she says, "light gray?" And then she turns to look into the room and I turn with her.

My sofa is gone.

I spin away from her and out of the building until I'm in the bright sunshine of the lot with Charlotte behind me saying, "Emi, let's just talk about this for a second. Let's just take a moment to calm down."

But all I can say is "Clyde fucking Jones," because it's *his* sofa in the place of my perfect one.

I storm through groups of smiling people and stern people and people talking on cell phones and carrying Starbucks cups and into Ginger's building and past her secretary and into her office. She's on the phone and holds up a finger for me to wait. So I stand there, in her perfectly decorated room, adorned with posters from all the famous movies she's worked on, until she hangs up and says, "This must be about the music room."

"What happened to my sofa? Did you see it? Wasn't it perfect?"

She says, "It was a nice sofa. But we got so many amazing things that day, *together*, remember? You and me and Charlotte."

"Of course I remember that day," I say. "What does it have to do with my music room?"

She sighs as if she's just so busy and I am so unreasonable.

"Emi, first, it isn't *your* music room. You've done a really lovely job, but you are an intern and I am the production designer."

"Yes," I say. "I'm aware of our respective positions."

"*Okay*," Charlotte says, sweeping into the office, having apparently been hovering right outside the door. "I think it would be a good idea for Emi and me to take the afternoon off if that would be all right with you, Ginger. She's been working really hard and didn't get much sleep last night and, you know, things with Morgan are still a little rocky, so—"

"Fine," Ginger says. "Go. Emi, tomorrow you'll see that the couch complements your efforts beautifully." But she says it coldly, with more edge than I've ever heard in her voice, and I start to worry about everything, because she'll be my boss on *The Agency*, too, and I know that I'm just an intern. I'm easily replaceable. Maybe there are hundreds of geniuses of teenage decor. Maybe my niche isn't even that special.

I follow Charlotte out of the office and the building and toward her car. She opens the passenger side for me and I tumble in.

"I just have to wrap up a couple things," she says. "And then I'll come back. Don't go *anywhere*, okay?"

"Okay."

"I can't believe you talked to her that way."

"I know. Me neither."

She nods, satisfied, and shuts my door.

I get out my phone and try Toby.

A moment later, his voice rises above many other voices and music in the background.

"Hey, little sister."

"Hey. Where are you?"

His face appears on my screen but the image is dark and grainy and I can barely see the curves of his face.

"Café," he says. "London."

"London. That's far away."

"Yeah," he says. He leans closer to the camera; his face gets bigger and I can see him better. "They talk funny here." He grins, leans back.

"Come back," I say. "Come closer."

He does.

"Hey, is something wrong?"

I nod and I feel my eyes well up and I wish so much that they wouldn't. But it's Toby and I know that if anyone will understand it will be him.

"My sofa," I start, and shake my head because I need to pull myself together.

He waits. If I could see his face better I know that I would see concern, and I hate that he is so far away, and I hate that Morgan is going on a date tonight, and I hate that Los Angeles is full of so many miles and so many bars and so many people for her to be with instead of me.

"Oh, man," he says before I've had to explain. "They went with something else?"

"It's terrible," I say. "It's modern. And *gray*."

"But, Em, you love modern."

"Not for this. It isn't right."

"Gray," he says. "Okay. Could be worse. What about throwing some pillows on it?"

"No," I say. "I don't want to *throw pillows on it*. I understand this scene. I understand why it's important and what it should feel like, and I know what should be in the shot to make it feel the way it's supposed to. And I found it. I looked so hard. I found it."

"You still have the rest of the room, right? That Neutral Milk Hotel poster? You still have that, right? And the trophies. Those are classic."

"I don't want you to try to make me feel better," I tell him. "I just want you to listen."

I can see people getting up from a table behind him, people everywhere, moving around in the dark.

"Toby," I say. "I don't know if I want to do *The Agency* anymore."

"What? No, wait a second. You're really bummed right now. I totally get that. But just let yourself feel like that for a while and then let it go. Do you know how many times I've found locations I've known were perfect only to have the location manager say he wants something different? It sucks. I know it does. But it's the way it works."

"It's Ginger," I say. "She tells me she trusts me and that I can do whatever I want, and then when I'm not even there, without even talking to me about it, she just makes this change and ruins everything."

"Not *everything*."

"I don't want to keep working with her. I want to work for myself."

Toby clears his throat. He leans back in his chair.

Finally, he says, "This is how it works. You bust your ass. Not everything goes your way, and then, after a while, you get to that point. You get to make your own decisions and people look to you for approval on *their* work."

"Yeah," I say. "I know."

"You will move up in the studio," he says. "I know you can do it. You just have to bite that tongue of yours and not let her see you so upset."

"She already has."

"Well, show her you're over it."

I nod.

"See this project through. See *The Agency* through. Then see where you are."

"Okay," I say, but my heart isn't in it. There is this distance between us, and I can't tell him everything I'm thinking, which is that I don't know that I *want* to move up in the studio if working for the studio is going to be like this. If I can search for months and months in so many places, and then have all that work undone in a moment.

Charlotte appears by the driver's side window.

"Charlotte's escorting me off the lot," I say.

"That bad?"

"Yeah," Charlotte says, buckling her seat belt. "She told Ginger that she was 'aware of their respective positions.'"

"Damn," Toby says with a half smile, half grimace. "Go cheer her up, okay?"

"I'll do my best," Charlotte says.

—

As Charlotte drives us off the lot, she says, "I'm taking you to the canals."

"That's a good idea," I tell her. "I love the canals."

The canals are why Venice is called Venice, but not that many people know about them. Most people who don't live here just head to Abbot Kinney for food and shopping, or the beach for the beach. But the canals are beautiful. They were designed by Abbot Kinney himself, and they are lined with houses, so when you walk along the canals, you're basically walking through people's front yards.

We park and cross over a footbridge and begin our maze-like stroll.

To our left is water; to our right are the illuminated living rooms and kitchens of the insanely wealthy and stylish.

"I couldn't live here," Charlotte says. "These people are so unselfconscious."

That's where Charlotte and I diverge, because I could totally live here. What's the point of decorating your home if nobody gets to see it? But on a night like tonight I understand where Charlotte's coming from, because I wish more than anything I could find someplace dark and quiet and away from civilization.

"Clyde fucking Jones," I say.

"Yeah," she says. "I'm so sorry I didn't get to see the room the way you planned it."

"I didn't even get pictures!" I moan. "It looks so stupid with that couch."

"It doesn't look stupid—it's a really nice couch—but it also doesn't look like a cast-off piece of furniture."

"No," I say, "it doesn't. It looks like a four-thousand-dollar Adrian Pearsall sofa, because that's what it is. I thought this movie was supposed to be about a normal middle-class family."

"At least Kira gets to lose her virginity on a really nice piece of furniture."

"It doesn't even matter," I say. "It changes the whole mood of everything. Ginger can have her mid-century-modern teen sex scene. I was going to give her a fairy tale."

We cross another bridge and I have to pause to stare into the house in front of us because it's just so amazing. The entire side is glass. A spiral staircase rises from the living room to a lofted bedroom. In the gleaming, silver kitchen, just a few feet from us, a man is cooking dinner.

"I'm really hungry," I say.

"Me, too," Charlotte says.

We wander farther.

"Morgan's going on a date tonight."

Charlotte sighs. "And *how* do you know this?"

"I kind of ran into her today. I think my life might be falling apart."

"A little."

"She keeps flirting with me."

"She's a terrible person."

"I don't think so."

"That's the problem."

"So what are you going to do about my brother?"

I swear, she stumbles a little when I say it.

"What do you mean?"

"You should just tell him how you feel."

"Em," she says. "That was a long time ago."

"Nice try," I tell her.

She's referring to this time in sixth grade when she wrote me a note during third period telling me she had a crush on an older boy. She was trying to be subtle but I already knew. Everything Charlotte feels is obvious to everyone. I wrote her a note back that said, *Does he happen to be in 10th grade? Does he happen to share my DNA?* which I thought was clever, considering we were in science class at the time.

She blushed and never wrote me back.

"I've been thinking a lot lately," I say. "Life is short. People die. I mean, think of all those obituaries we read. Think of Clyde and Caroline. You should talk to Toby. He hasn't had a girlfriend in a while. He's probably just waiting for you to graduate and now you've graduated."

"I'm really hungry."

"Just think about it," I say.

"I'm out of money or else I would want tacos."

"I wouldn't mind, you know," I say. "It wouldn't make things weird between us. I've had, like, six *years* to get used to the idea."

"Okay," she says.

"Good. I'm broke, too, but there's some stuff we can cook at the apartment."

—

Back at Toby's, we cook dinner. Either the emotional strain from the day has caught up to us, or we've allowed ourselves to become so hungry that all we can think of is food, because our conversational skills are reduced to this:

"Should I add garlic to this?"

"Did you wash the lettuce?"

"How old do you think this cheese is?"

"Is there too much garlic in this?"

Finally, Charlotte lifts the plates and I follow her outside to the patio, to the warm night air and the *ranchera* music from next door.

Toby's neighbors are having a loud conversation in Spanish, shouting and laughing, and I wish I could follow but I took French in high school.

"What are they talking about?" I finally ask.

"Hairstyles," Charlotte says.

"What about them?"

"Whether someone's hairstyle is out of fashion or not."

"Is it?"

"The loud guy thinks so. The woman with the softer voice thinks it's timeless."

The loud guy says something especially loudly and they all laugh.

I smile. They sound so happy.

"What did he say?"

"I didn't understand it."

"Oh."

"Why aren't you eating?"

A moment ago I was ravenous but now I can't imagine taking a bite. The heartache comes in waves and this particular one is the enveloping kind.

"I'll save it for later," I say.

"The girl or the couch?" Charlotte asks.

"Honestly?" I say. "The girl."

Charlotte shakes her head and eats her pasta while I move mine around on my plate. She doesn't say anything but it's fine with me because I wouldn't be able to even fake interest in anything Charlotte might want to talk about. I keep wondering who Morgan is going on a date with, and what this girl has that I don't. Her own apartment? The legal right to drink?

"That girl is so—"

"Just stop," I say. "It's not what I need right now. I don't care how terrible she is. I don't care that you hate her."

"Okay," Char says, her voice soft. "We'll leave how I feel

about Morgan out of it."

"Thank you."

"But I do have something to say."

I force a bite into my mouth. Force myself to chew.

"It's over," Charlotte says.

I stare at her. I swallow.

"Um," I say.

"It's time for you to accept it. She was your first love. That's a huge deal. And I know how much she's meant to you, and that it isn't easy to accept that it's over. But it is. It's over."

Tears rush in without warning.

"Okay, I take it back," I say. "I'd rather just hear about how much you hate her."

"Em," she says. "You did a really good job of loving her. You put up with all her bullshit. You were a really good girl-friend. And now it's time for you to find someone who will love you back."

She scoots closer to me and grabs my hand. She waits for me to look at her.

"I'm sorry I made you cry," she says. "But you really need to hear this."

I nod.

"It's over," she says, once more. "Okay?"

"Okay," I whisper, but I don't really know what I'm agreeing to.

Charlotte stacks my plate on top of hers and moves them out of the way, but neither of us gets up. I could sit here in silence all night, which I'll admit is rare for me. I don't want to think about the fact that Morgan never loved me, even though

I know that Charlotte is right. And I don't want to think about the decisions I'll inevitably have to make tomorrow. I'm caught between self-preservation and self-righteousness, between apologizing to Ginger and quitting. Neither option feels good. So I just want to listen to the sounds of the neighbors' conversations and their lively music, all of these words I don't understand.

—

Charlotte's phone rings so she goes inside to answer it, and an especially good song comes on. I wish I knew what it was so I could find it again.

I hear Charlotte say hello.

And then I hear her say "Ava."

I turn around and she's wide-eyed, pointing to the phone pressed to her ear.

"Thanks for calling," she says. "I know you don't know me—"

She looks confused. "La Cienega Bakery?" she asks. "No, I don't know anything about that."

"Speakerphone!" I mouth to her and she nods and switches over.

A raspy voice says, "Oh, okay. I applied for a job there a while ago, so I thought . . . It doesn't matter. So *who* are you?"

"I'm Charlotte. My friend Emi is here, too."

"Hi," I say.

"This might sound strange, but we have something that was meant to belong to Caroline Maddox."

Ava is quiet on the other end, and I look down at the

phone and see that it's trembling in Charlotte's hand.

"Caroline?" Ava finally repeats, her voice breaking on the question.

I say, "We got this letter for her, so we tried to find her but then found out that she died, so we've been just kind of connecting some dots, and eventually we found you—"

"You have a *letter* for *Caroline*?" Ava asks.

Charlotte says, "It's kind of a long story. It would be better to talk in person, if that works for you."

"What are you doing now?"

"Now?" Charlotte asks. "We're just hanging out at our apartment."

"In Venice," I add.

"I can be there in twenty minutes."

"Oh," Charlotte says. "Okay."

I give her the address, and then we hang up.

I stare at Charlotte. She stares at me.

I scan the living room. Clyde Jones stuff is everywhere. Toby's desktop computer screen is full of search windows for Caroline and Tracey and Ava, as is Charlotte's laptop, resting open on the coffee table.

"Shit," I say, and we begin closing screens and putting away Clyde Jones DVDs because neither of us wants to look like we've been collecting all the information there is to have about the girl who is about to walk through our door and possibly hang out for a while.

And somewhere in the frenzy of sweeping evidence and cleaning up our dinner dishes, the gravity of the moment captures me. I feel a camera panning across the room as if I'm watching us from a distance. A counter covered in garlic peels and cutting boards and bread crumbs. The door to the patio ajar. Two girls in a colorful, lived-in living room. They don't know what's coming, but one of them—the one with the far-away expression and the dark hair, the one whose eyes betray that she hasn't been sleeping well—she has felt on the verge of something.

And when they hear a knock at the door, it's this girl who crosses the room to answer it. She turns the knob, and here it is—like Clyde appearing on the horizon or emerging from the tall grass—a redhead in the doorway of a Venice courtyard apartment. A curious gaze, a tentative step inside. The curve of her mouth when she smiles, the raspy timbre of her voice when she says hello.

Chapter Six

As soon as I open the door I wish we'd had just a few more minutes, because Ava is standing in the doorway looking movie-star pretty, looking *Clyde Jones* pretty, and I am facing her in a shirt with a red tomato-sauce smear on the chest, my hair in a messy ponytail, realizing that in spite of all our planning I have no idea how to deliver the news we summoned her to hear.

"Hey. Come in," I say, but I'm fighting the urge to tell her never mind.

Charlotte and I have involved ourselves in other people's lives in a way that suddenly makes me uncomfortable. Like there was a NO TRESPASSING sign in front of a family's driveway, and not only have we trespassed, but we've gone through their garage, opened all of their private boxes, rifled through their photo albums and diaries to discover dozens of secrets that were never meant to be revealed.

Ava is here, though, in the middle of Toby's cozy living room, thanks to luck and fate and our will to find her. Charlotte is offering her the last of our Ethiopian iced tea and she is saying yes. She's slipping a worn brown leather purse from over her shoulder and apologizing.

"What for?" Charlotte asks.

"I must have been difficult to get ahold of," she says. "You must have tried hard."

"It took us a while," I say, pouring the tea into a little blue glass.

"Yeah," she says. "Well, it's been a strange year."

She tries to say it casually, like her year has been just averagely strange, which doesn't really fit with the kid on the phone who had no idea where she was or if she would ever be calling home again.

I hand her the glass. Her fingertips graze mine in the transfer.

She takes a sip of tea and looks at us, expectant. She wants answers, obviously, the reasons that we tracked her down, the information that we have. But all I can do is take her in because it's uncanny, her resemblance to Clyde. Even more than the red hair and the green eyes, her features are like his: the slant of her cheekbones and her delicate nose, the slight crookedness of her smile as she looks quizzically at us. These are the features that, in spite of Clyde's bravado, made him always a little bit vulnerable, made us always worry for him and hope that he would survive the shootouts and get the girl.

Ava pushes a strand of hair behind her ear and I notice that she's even dressed a little bit like Clyde. Everything she has on looks vintage: brown leather boots and high-waisted denim shorts, a leather belt with a dulled brass buckle.

"This is really good," Ava finally says, breaking our silence. "I've never had tea that tastes like this."

"I'm glad you like it," Charlotte replies, and I wonder if she's been thinking the same things that I have. Between her gift for social interactions and my tendency to over-share, we don't usually suffer through awkward silences like this. I try to pull myself together.

I say, "It's Ethiopian, from this restaurant around the corner." And then I launch into an explanation of Toby's charm and this apartment and the request he's made of us, and as I do, I can feel myself getting farther and farther from the reason we have her here with us right now. "He said we have to do something epic," I say. "So if you have any ideas feel free to share them."

I know that I'm going on about nothing of any importance to her but I can't stop talking. Clyde Jones's granddaughter is sitting in our kitchen and trying to downplay some kind of distress, something that's kept her away from home for a long time.

I can still feel where her fingers brushed mine.

And we have a letter that is going to change her life.

"How did you connect Caroline to me?" she asks once I've stopped rambling.

"The library," Charlotte says.

"The library?"

"I know, right? It was Charlotte's idea."

Charlotte says, "We found Caroline's obituary in the newspaper, and it had Tracey Wilder's name in it. Emi guessed that Tracey Wilder might be your mom? Your adoptive mom? That's what we've been thinking."

"Caroline and Tracey were best friends. Tracey adopted me when Caroline died. I was just a baby, though."

Ava lifts her hands to her mouth and bites a short, unpolished nail. I notice the small freckles that dot her cheeks and the bridge of her nose. She catches me staring at her and my eyes dart away. So stupid. I should have just smiled.

"So what is it that you have?" she asks. "For Caroline?"

I glance at Charlotte, hoping she'll know how to take it from here. I'm not good at this at all. I'm so much better with imaginary people and their imaginary lives.

Charlotte says, "I really don't know the best way to tell you this, so I'll just show you what we found."

She walks into the living room and takes the letter off the coffee table. I can't even look at Ava, I'm so nervous. Charlotte gives her the envelope and Ava takes out the letter. I go sit on the sofa to wait. I would leave the apartment and walk around the block a few times if I could.

Ava is quiet for a long time, standing in the kitchen. I hear the pages rustling. She must read it several times. Charlotte comes to sit next to me but we don't say anything.

Finally, I hear Ava walking over to us. She sits on Toby's orange chair.

"Am I reading this right?"

Charlotte and I nod.

"Is this Clyde . . . ?"

"Jones," I say. "Yes."

"Clyde Jones was my grandfather?"

We nod again.

"I know that's what it looks like but I just keep reading it over and over. There could be another explanation."

"Yes," Charlotte says. "There could be."

"But everything leads to you," I say. "All the names and the dates of everything."

"Who's Lenny?"

"We don't know."

Ava studies the letter again. "So Caroline's mom died a long time ago, but her dad was alive all this time. I guess I always assumed that both of them had died, or else my mom would have told me about them."

"Maybe Tracey never knew about Clyde," I say.

"It's possible," she says. "How did you find this letter?"

We tell her all about ourselves and our jobs in the movies.

"Wait," she says. "You design sets for real movies? How *old* are you?"

"We're eighteen," I say.

"I don't design sets," Charlotte says. "I make phone calls and run errands. Emi is the genius."

I roll my eyes even though I really love compliments.

"But even if you're a genius," Ava says, "isn't that a really big job? People go to school for that, right?"

"I don't technically design them," I say. "My name probably won't even be in the credits. My brother got me this unpaid internship a couple years ago and I've just sort of worked my way up from there. I'm still an intern and I barely make minimum wage, but my boss let me submit a proposal for this sixteen-year-old's room and she really loved it, and now they're just sort of into me for some reason, so I have a next job lined up, too."

I decide to leave out the unfortunate events of this afternoon. Even I know this night should be about Ava and not about me, and I'm hesitant to mention that her grandfather (admittedly without his knowledge) took part in the destruction of my room and, indirectly, may lead to the early demise of my career, too, if Ginger decides to blacklist me for talking to her the way that I did.

"That is such a cool job," she says. "I used to take drama in high school, freshman and sophomore year. I loved to stay after rehearsals and watch people paint the sets. I mean, I know it's not the same thing. These were just high school plays. The sets weren't even that good, but it was just fun to watch everything come together. Sometimes the backdrops would be double sided. One side would look like a living room or something, and then they would turn it around and it would be a sidewalk scene?" She blushes. "I'm sure it doesn't compare at all to what you guys do, but it just made me think of it . . ."

She trails off and I realize that she's embarrassed, and Charlotte must notice it, too, because she rushes in and asks, "Did you act?"

Ava nods. "I started to get really into it, but Tracey made me quit."

"Why?" I ask.

"She claimed that rehearsals kept me out too late and that my grades were slipping." She shrugs. "I never tried that hard in school. Drama was the only thing I ever liked."

"I guess it runs in your family," I say.

Ava looks down at the letter, as though she's forgotten about all of it for a moment.

"Do you realize how huge this is?" I say. "Clyde Jones's life was pretty much a mystery. All people knew was that he was kind of a ladies' man when he was younger, and that he then became a recluse, and that he never had a wife or children. And now, here you are, and it turns out that even the little we thought we knew about him wasn't true. *You*," I say, pausing for effect, making sure that she's really understanding this, "are the secret granddaughter of the most iconic actor in American film history."

Ava shakes her head in wonder. Then she looks down and smiles. It makes me relieved and happy, like we aren't invading anything with this information, aren't trespassing at all. Like what we've done is more like picked a bunch of wildflowers and left them on a stranger's doorstep, something wild and beautiful, ready to be discovered.

"I've never even seen a Clyde Jones movie," she says.

"Are you joking?"

"I can picture him in his cowboy hats and everything, but no."

I shake my head. "Insanity."

"It's not that insane, Emi," Charlotte says. "Not everyone grows up in a household like yours."

"Well, you came to the right place," I say to Ava. "We have the complete collection. Do you have plans?"

The sunburst clock above Toby's TV shows that it's almost eleven. I see her glance at it.

"I have time," she says. "I just have to make a quick phone call first."

"Great! Char and I will choose one."

She wanders back into the kitchen to find her phone.

"*I'm glad she didn't freak out,*" I whisper as Charlotte and I position ourselves in front of Toby's extensive DVD collection.

"Yeah, she seems really calm about it," Charlotte says.

We choose *A Long Time Till Tomorrow* because it's quintessential Clyde. *Lowlands* is my favorite but Ava can get to that one later, after she has at least a basic knowledge of his career so she can appreciate the ways in which it departs from his usual role. I can hear bits of her conversation. Toby's place is small, and she isn't trying to be secretive.

"I'll drive us," she's saying. "Yes, really. Okay, see you in the kitchen at one fifteen."

She's obviously talking to someone she knows well, but she isn't saying anything about what she just discovered. If it were me, I would be calling everyone. I would be ecstatic, but all she seems to be is curious.

She walks back in and sits down.

"Sorry," she says. "I had to call my friend Jamal. I'm driving us to work later."

"Where do you work?" I ask.

"Home Depot," she says.

"Really?"

"Is that weird?" she asks.

"I just can't picture you in one of those uniforms, or, like, helping people cut the right-size pieces of Masonite."

"We work the early-morning stock shift. We don't help customers. It's an okay job and Jamal's my best friend, so that helps."

I nod, and Charlotte asks, "Have you known each other for a long time?"

"Almost a year. But we were best friends after barely a week of knowing each other. Things like that happen fast when you don't have anybody else."

I'm struck by the simple truth in that statement, but agreeing with her would be dishonest. I can't even pretend to know what being so alone would feel like. And she doesn't look like she's waiting for a response anyway. She's made herself comfortable in the chair, watching the screen, waiting for the film to begin.

"All right," I say, back to business. "We're starting with *A Long Time Till Tomorrow*. This is Clyde in his first lead role. 1953. Lee Dodson is the director. This is the movie that made Clyde Jones, Clyde Jones, if you know what I mean."

She nods.

"Ready?" I say.

"Ready."

I press play and the twangy music starts. Charlotte sits on the white rug, Ava on the orange chair, me on the sofa. The first couple scenes play. Charlotte laughs at the stilted dialogue and I examine the sets, which are spare and rustic.

And then, twelve minutes into the movie, Ava starts sobbing.

—

She cries for a while, knees pulled up to her chest, these sobs that sound like she will never stop.

Charlotte and I keep offering her blankets and mugs of mint tea but she keeps telling us she'll be okay.

"Should we call your mom?" I ask Charlotte, because her mother is a therapist and speaks in a soft and coaxing voice that I will never be able to successfully imitate.

"If she doesn't stop, yeah," she says.

But, eventually, Ava does stop.

"This is so embarrassing," she says, forcing a laugh. "How stupid."

"No," I say. "Not at all."

"Do you want to talk about it?" Charlotte asks her.

"I don't even know where I would start," she says, and I can tell Charlotte's ready to let it go but I'm not. It's not just that I'm nosy—which, admittedly, I am—it's that I believe in this kind of thing. If you find a letter in a famous man's house, and that letter ends up belonging to his daughter who died before she got a chance to get it, and you spend days chasing false leads in search of the granddaughter, and when you do find her, she isn't where she's supposed to be so you resign yourself to an answerless future, but then (suddenly, amazingly) the answer appears in your living room, sobbing on a bright orange chair, you don't just let it go.

So I tell Ava, "We have time. Start anywhere," and she finally accepts the mug of mint tea and begins.

"I ran away about a year ago," she says.

"Why?" I ask.

"A few reasons. But my mom—Tracey—was the main one. She made it impossible for me to stay." She shakes her head. She doesn't want to tell us about it.

"You can go ahead," Charlotte says. "So you're away from home."

She nods. "At first I was living in my car, but then eventually I found a shelter downtown."

Charlotte asks, "Is that where you live now?"

Ava nods.

"Oh my God," I say.

"No, it's fine. The counselors are okay. It's just this big house with a lot of teenagers living there, and we have chores and they help us find jobs. It's where I met Jamal.

It's fine. It's just that I've been spending all this time trying to adjust to living without a family, and now you guys show me this letter, and suddenly I'm watching my grandfather in a movie. And I never really thought about my grandparents at all—I just knew they were dead—and I don't know anything at all about who Caroline was or what her life was like."

She takes a sip of tea, stares down into her mug.

"I know so little about where I come from," she says.

"Tracey hasn't told you?" I ask.

"I used to ask her a lot of questions but I gave up. She's really into self-improvement. Like reinventing herself? That sort of thing. She says there isn't any use dwelling on the past, so it's as if all of it—Caroline, my life as a little kid—disappeared."

"That's intense," I say.

She still looks on the verge of tears but she laughs anyway.

"Intense is a good word to describe my mother. Everything I know about Caroline I had to figure out by myself, but I couldn't ever find much." She forces a smile. "I guess I should have gone to the library."

"I typed up Caroline's obituary," Charlotte says. "Do you want to read it?"

Ava says yes, so Charlotte gets up to find the computer. I study the TV screen, where Clyde is frozen in profile against a bleak landscape, and say, "You look like him."

"I kept thinking that when we were watching. My mom and my brother, they look so much alike. I've never looked like anyone."

"Your brother?" I ask. "Is that who answered the phone when we called?"

She nods. "He's Tracey's son. She was married for a few years to this guy from her church. It didn't last."

Charlotte places her laptop on the coffee table, and Ava slips down onto the rug to read about Caroline.

"She was in movies?" she says when she's finished.

"It sounds like she was mostly an extra," I say. "But yes."

"I had no idea." Her eyes well up again but I can see her blinking, fighting it. After a little while she says, "Maybe that's why Tracey never wanted me to act."

"Yeah, maybe so," I say.

Together, Charlotte and I tell Ava everything we've learned about Clyde and Caroline. Every question we've asked, every answer we've gotten. She loves hearing about little Ava, and laughs over my impressions of Frank and Edie, but her face gets serious when we get to what they said about "the drugs and the men and that baby," and it all feels different now, that "that baby" is the girl sitting here with us, learning all of these secrets from her past for the first time.

And then, in the middle of everything, when it seems that soon we'll resume our movie and continue the night, Ava says, "The clock."

She points at Toby's sunburst.

"Is that time right?"

"Yes," I say.

"Then I have to go."

I look at Charlotte, hoping she'll have a plan for what we'll do next, why we'll need to see one another again, but Ava is already halfway across the living room.

Her eyes are still pink, her face soft from crying, but when she pauses in the doorway to say good-bye, she looks like Clyde Jones—the cocky, crooked smile, the charming glimmer in her eye.

"Thanks," she says, "for finding me. Not everyone would have done all that." And then she disappears into the night.

Chapter Seven

The next morning, I knock on the ajar door of Ginger's office.

She looks up from her desk, not terribly thrilled to see me.

"I've come to apologize," I tell her, and she nods and waves me in.

I have a speech prepared—Charlotte and I rehearsed over coffee this morning—and I recite it. It involves a little bit of groveling, a little bit of flattery, some self-deprecation, and a fair amount of regret. It ends with a concession: "Though it isn't what I had envisioned for the room, it is a beautiful piece of furniture for such an important scene, and I'm sure that it will have mass appeal without sacrificing style."

"I'm glad you feel that way."

"I do," I say. "I also have a couple of changes I would like to make to the rest of the set in order to make this new direction cohesive."

"I'm listening," she says.

"First of all, I don't think the poster works anymore. Now that it's a more polished room, I think we should go for more professional-looking wall art. I was thinking of this framed Miles Davis poster." I show her an image on my phone.

"Yes, I approve. What else?"

"The music stand," I say, trying not to sound bitter. "I know we both love it, but—"

"The music stand stays. Emi, I know you feel like I changed your entire concept for the room but I didn't. We can strike a balance between stylized and naturalistic here. You can pull that off. Take the afternoon to make the changes you want, and I'll go down to look at the end of the day."

So I take the afternoon.

As I'm going back through the room, thinning out the stacks of sheet music, rearranging the decorative objects, I keep thinking of Ava's exit. She disappeared as quickly as my sofa did, and with barely more warning. I thought that we would at least have her phone number, but Charlotte told me it was blocked, which means that it's up to her to get in touch with us if she ever wants to see us again. And why would she? We're just two random girls who happened to discover something that belonged to her. Now she has the letter and if she chooses to learn more she can. She doesn't need us. I try to talk myself into feeling glad that we got to play a small part in something so interesting. Something that was part of real life.

But, self-delusion aside, I can't handle the thought of this being over.

So when my phone buzzes in my pocket, even though she never had my number and it would be almost impossible, I am overwhelmed by an irrational, electric hope that it's her.

"Hello?" I say.

"Emi?" a woman says. I don't know who she is, but her voice doesn't have the raspiness of Ava's, and I feel stupid for even hoping. "This is Rebecca. We met the other day. I'm Morgan's friend."

"Yeah, of course," I say. "Hi."

"I'm calling to offer you a job."

"Oh yeah?"

"I'd love to tell you about it if you have time."

"Sure," I say. "That sounds great. When did you have in mind?"

"Five o'clock today, if possible."

I take a step back and look over the room. It looks pretty good, and I think it's what Ginger wants it to be.

"Yeah," I say. "I actually just finished work for the day, so I'm free."

—

I meet Rebecca and her boyfriend, Theo, at a café in Silver Lake. They're sitting outside against these brilliant blue tiles I love, drinking matching cappuccinos.

"Thank you for coming on such short notice," Theo says, speaking with a prominent accent that I'm fairly certain is South African. "Rebecca has been raving about you."

"Really?"

"Yes, really." She nods and smiles at me, these cute tiny lines forming by her eyes.

"You should hear her go on and on about the sofa," Theo says.

"They didn't end up using it."

"What?" Rebecca gasps. "Oh no."

"I know, right?" I say. "That trip out to Pasadena was all for nothing."

"Well, I don't know about that," she says. "But what did you do?"

"Honestly? I had a meltdown. And then I spent the afternoon today figuring out how to make the room work with what my boss chose."

"But it looked better before, I imagine," Theo says. "The way you had envisioned it."

"Definitely," I say. "But it isn't my movie, you know? I don't get to make the calls. I understand how it works and I can appreciate my boss's point of view."

I'm switching into interview mode now, because I don't know what they are going to offer me, but I do know that Morgan and her friends do really cool projects, and Rebecca and Theo just have that thing some people have that makes you want to be in their company, no matter what they're doing. I have a portfolio to build and experience to gain, and if Rebecca saw what I did and liked it, then maybe she'll let me do more of what I'm good at.

"Yes, but what if you had a situation where you knew that the choice you made was the right one. Let's say, then, that someone tells you to change it to something hideous. And let's say that the person making the call wasn't even in the art department. Totally didn't know what he was talking about. What would you do then?"

I don't know what the right answer to this question is. Maybe it's a trick because he hates it when the people who work for him are defiant, or maybe he wants someone who can stand her ground. So I just answer honestly.

"I guess I would take a little while to think about it. I'd really consider his point of view. And then, if I was still certain I was right, I'd tell him no," I say. "I'd explain why."

"And if he said, 'Do it anyway'?"

"I'd try to explain again."

"What if he said, 'I'm the boss, listen to me.'"

"You're saying he's not in the art department?"

"Yes."

I hesitate. I think about what Ginger would do, if the film director or a producer tried to change one of her concepts after she had worked so hard on conceptualizing and planning. After it all had been approved. She wouldn't let anyone get away with that, no matter how powerful or intimidating he might be.

"Then I'd tell him that he hired me for a reason, and that was because I know what I'm doing and I'm good at it," I say. "I'd insist, I guess. I'd insist that it stay that way as long as other people whose artistic visions I respected also agreed that it was good."

Theo leans back and smiles.

"I like you," he says.

"See?" Rebecca pokes his shoulder. "He was afraid you were too young."

I shrug. "Yeah, I get that."

"But Morgan said you were strong willed. She's very confident about you. We tried to hire her. She was in a seminar I taught when I was in grad school, and I've always loved her work. But she's double-booked as it is. So I asked her for a recommendation and she told me about you."

"I'm grilling you because I need someone who won't be afraid of me," Theo says.

"Are you the director?"

"Yes, I am. Rebecca is producing."

"And you need a . . . ?"

I don't want to make a fool out of myself if what they're looking for is an intern and what I say is something much more prestigious. I'm hoping they'll say it's a set dresser job.

It would take me years to get that position in a studio, but it might be possible that a small film would take a chance on someone like me.

"Production designer," Rebecca says.

"*What?*" I say.

"Well," Theo says, "basically, your job would be art department."

"You could hire one person to help you," Rebecca adds. "But I know that isn't much. It's a huge job. A huge job. And the pay is disgraceful, and we begin shooting in four weeks."

"Four weeks?"

"Afraid so. But we would give you so much creative freedom."

"Here," Rebecca says. "Take the screenplay. Just give it a read and see if it speaks to you."

I don't even say anything. I just take the screenplay out of her hands and open to the title page. *Yes & Yes*, by Rebecca Golden and Theo Fitzgerald. And seeing their names there floods me with gratitude. I am touched. This is their film, their money, their effort of love, and they are willing to trust me with so much if I say yes.

"I'll read it," I say. "I'll read it tonight."

"I hope you enjoy it," Rebecca says.

"Of course she'll enjoy it," Theo says. "Can't you see? She's our kind of people. She has the love."

—

For some reason, I don't tell Charlotte. As soon as I walk into the apartment I slip my bag, with the screenplay inside, in the corner of Toby's living room and then I join her on the patio where she's staring at her computer screen.

"What are you working on?"

"I'm enrolling for classes," she tells me.

"What are you taking?"

"A bunch of GE stuff. But also Intro to Museum Studies."

"So fun," I say. But I really thought Charlotte would switch over to film studies once I got her the job at the studio. I thought "the love," as Theo put it, would be contagious, especially since Char is so good at everything she does and has the perfect mind for the production side of filmmaking. But I guess her attention to detail and impeccable social graces will serve her well in the museum world.

"You're already registering?"

"I leave in a month and a half."

"Don't remind me."

"Don't you need to pick your classes soon?"

"Probably." I shrug.

"You should know when your registration date is."

"Yeah, I'll look it up." Everything seems less urgent for me since I'm staying in LA for school, and now, with the fantasy of a production design job hovering within reach, school almost feels unnecessary. But I know it's not. I know it's going to open the world up in a new way. Soon I'll be able to sit with my parents and watch TV, well schooled in all of their critical theories. It will be nice to keep up with them. And I'll learn so much more about the history of film and production design. I'm not naive enough to imagine that I know all there is to know about how films are made.

Still, I don't want the summer to end so soon.

"Have you thought about what we should do with the apartment?" I ask.

"Yes," she says. "But I can't come up with anything epic enough."

"I know," I say. "It sucks. Let's go get tacos and sit on the beach."

So, after Charlotte finishes her college stuff, we walk to our favorite food truck, and then head to the ocean, dodging roller bladers and skaters and bicyclists, kicking off our sandals at the edge of the sand and making our way to an open, welcoming spot to eat and watch the sun set over the ocean.

"What's even in Michigan anyway," I say to her. "Lakes? So what."

"I'll miss you, too," she says.

We hear a buzzing and both of us reach for our phones. Morgan hasn't texted me in three days. My screen is blank.

"Look," Char says, and holds hers out to me.

This is Ava. Are you and Emi free tomorrow? I have something to show you!

"Tell her yes," I say.

"Should we have her come to Venice again?"

"Sure," I say. And then I change my mind. "No, actually. Let's meet at the Marmont!"

Charlotte laughs and shakes her head.

"The Marmont. Okay. Something tells me that's not the kind of place Ava usually goes."

I snatch Charlotte's phone away and type, *Meet us at the Chateau Marmont. Sunset and Havenhurst. Hollywood.*

Charlotte peers over my shoulder.

"You know the cross street by heart?"

"Of course." I say, handing her phone back. "Is it weird that I feel relieved right now? It was kind of awful to think it was over."

"I don't think it's over," Charlotte says. "There's so much we don't know yet. I kind of feel like it's only over if she doesn't ask us for anything, but it's possible she'll need help figuring more out, and if that's the case we should help her."

"I hope she asks us," I say. "There's no way Clyde Jones's granddaughter should be living in a shelter and working the overnight shift at Home Depot. It's, like, against the laws of the universe."

Charlotte laughs.

"I really liked her."

"Yeah, I bet," Charlotte says.

"No, really," I say. "Not only because she's, like, heart-breakingly beautiful. She told us things about her life. She wanted to stay and hang out. She doesn't even know us. Not everyone would do that."

"Yeah, I liked her, too," Charlotte admits. "We'll see what happens tomorrow."

The sun hovers low over the water, the clouds around it all pink and violet.

"I've been wondering," I say. "You know what I said the night we found the letter? How I felt like there was something significant about it?"

"Yeah, I remember. It's the only time you've ever said anything like that."

"I've just been thinking that maybe Ava is someone I'm supposed to know."

"Know?"

"It isn't just because she's so pretty. Or because of Clyde. I know it sounds crazy but I swear there's this thing about her. I feel like I was meant to know her."

Charlotte traces circles in the sand.

"You don't think she'd be interested in me," I say.

"I'm not saying that."

"Yeah but you aren't saying anything. That says a lot."

"You should give yourself some time to get over Morgan. Start slowly."

"Why do you have to be so practical?"

"One of us has to be. We could end up being Ava's friends."

"I'll need more of those once you're gone."

"I'm not going to be 'gone.' I'm going to be away for college."

"But then who knows. You'll go be an amazing museum director somewhere. You could end up in New York. You could end up in Chicago. This might be it for us, right now, on the beach. After this everything will be different. You'll forget your love of palm trees and fear of snow. You'll spend all your time in a fancy office bossing people around and discovering stolen seventeenth-century sculptures."

I have a lot more to say, but Charlotte is pushing me over into the sand.

I try to continue in spite of her assault: "You'll be recruited by the Louvre. You'll live in Paris and marry a handsome Parisian who is, like, half French, half Moroccan, and looks exactly like my brother and when the time comes to renew your American citizenship you'll say, Who needs *les États-Unis* anyway? Sand in my eye!" I gasp.

She stops pushing me and stands up.

"Let's go," she says. "You're ridiculous and I have work to do."

I stand up and follow her.

"You'll start saying that American movies are stupid, all spectacle and no substance, completely overlooking the hundreds of beautiful, quiet films that come out of the US every year, let alone the fact that spectacles are, in themselves, incredible."

Charlotte stops walking and turns to face me. She puts her hands on my shoulders.

"I'm going to Michigan because it's the best school for what I want to do. I don't know where I'll go when it's over. But you will always be my best friend, and I will never be the kind of snob who says that all American movies are stupid. If I ever make a gross generalization like that, please point at me and laugh until I feel sufficiently humiliated."

"Okay," I say, and a tightness forms in my throat. She smiles at me, a smile of sympathy and her own sadness, too.

I didn't even mean for this to be a heartfelt moment, but I guess I need it. It sucks to lose your best friend, even if only to distance. Even when it isn't really losing her at all.

—

I start reading at eleven thirty, when Charlotte is asleep. I'm lying on the couch with a small brass lamp (snagged from my grandpa's garage) turned on so the light doesn't wake her up. The average screenplay is between 90 and 120 pages, one page per minute of screen time. This one is 111, which means that I will be able to get through it tonight, or at least get a good-enough sense of it to know whether I want to take this insane opportunity.

By page three, I'm infatuated.

Yes & Yes has two main characters, Juniper and George, both of whom work in a small Los Angeles market. George is in his mid-forties, and as the screenplay unfolds we learn that he's been living in Oregon but has moved back to Los Angeles, into his childhood home, to care for his ailing father who ends up dying and leaving George the market. Now George is in a slump. He's still living in the house he grew up in even though his parents have died, and he's working in the store, something he never intended to do.

Juniper, who turns twenty in the film, wants to be a botanist. She's taking community college classes while working in the market, and she's been having a rough time since her elderly boss got sick and died. He had treated her like a daughter and she needed that because she's a lonely and kind of fragile person.

Here is the moment everything begins: A woman, Miranda, walks into the market, picks up a basket, begins to roam the aisles. She takes a grapefruit, a box of oatmeal, a bar of chocolate. Juniper is shelving baby food only inches away when, without warning, Miranda drops to the floor and has a seizure. Juniper drops a jar of baby food and it breaks. George sprints over from his post at the register. A customer calls the paramedics, and as they wait for the sirens to come Juniper and George sit by her, both of them captivated and afraid.

Juniper and George don't fall in love. Instead, they become friends. They bond over this experience and as they're sitting around wondering who Miranda really is with a fervor that borders obsession, they're really talking about what they imagined their lives would be and how their real lives aren't measuring up. They learn about themselves and each other.

Finally, at the end, Miranda comes back into the store. She doesn't even acknowledge them, which makes sense because even though it was a significant moment to Juniper and George, Miranda was having a seizure. She doesn't remember them. She buys her fruit and then she leaves, and they're stunned and feel slighted but we know by then that it was never really about Miranda. It was about the two of them all along.

"Charlotte," I whisper at two in the morning. "Wake up. I need to tell you something."

She opens her eyes.

"What's wrong?"

"Nothing," I say. "I have something amazing to tell you. Something incredible happened to me this afternoon."

She sits up and rubs her face.

"I was with you earlier," she says.

"Yeah, it was before that. I got offered a job as a production designer."

"Turn on the light."

I flip it on and she squints.

"Are you talking in your sleep?" she asks me.

"No," I say, plopping down next to her. "I got offered a job by someone Morgan knows from film school—Rebecca, remember, who was with her when they picked up the couch?"

"Okay."

"It's for a film she wrote with her boyfriend. I just finished reading the screenplay."

"Okay."

"I'm going to take the job. It's the most beautiful story. There's no way you could ever call it stupid. Will you read it?"

"Right now?"

"Yeah," I say. "Please. I know it's two in the morning."

"Why didn't you tell me about this earlier?"

"I was afraid that it was going to be a bad movie. I mean, *me*? A production designer? I thought it would be a joke. I didn't want to act excited about something that was probably going to be terrible."

She swings herself out of bed. "Make me coffee."

"Seriously? You'll read it now?"

"My best friend has just been offered a *really* important job for a project she thinks is beautiful. Of course I'm going to read it now."

So she takes a seat in the orange chair and I make coffee for us both and she reads. She drinks her coffee, she turns the pages. At one point, she gets up to use the bathroom but then she comes straight back. I force myself not to look over her shoulder or ask her what she thinks. Instead, I start gathering my ideas for the sets. We'll need to have George's house and Juniper's apartment; the market; a park. It's a lot to get together in four weeks, but I'll only have to work on decorating one location at a time.

A lot of the scenes are in the market, so I make a list of all the markets I can think of, from small produce stores to larger groceries that still have a small-town feel. Most of the work for this part will simply be to find a place that will say yes to letting us film there. George's and Juniper's places will be more complex because they need to reflect who they are.

This is what I love about production design. The writers imagine the story, tell us where people are and what they do and say. The actors embody the characters, give them faces and voices. The directors and producers transform an idea into something real. But the art department, we do the rest. When you see their rooms and you discover that they love a certain band, or that they collect seashells or hang their clothes with equal space between each perfectly ironed shirt or have stacks of papers on their desks or a week's worth of dirty dishes in the sink and bras strewn over brass doorknobs—all of that is *us*.

The art department creates the world. When you walk into someone's house and you see all of their things—the neatness or the clutter, the objects they have on display—that's when you begin to really know someone. Maybe there's a guy you think is your friend but then you go to his house and discover his walls are covered in taxidermy animals and trophies and you never even knew that he hunted. Maybe it's creepy, maybe the mounted heads look deranged, not preserved exactly right. Or maybe they're perfect and you can tell he's proud, that he's really good at something. Either way, it makes him more interesting. All of that is important and a lot of the time it isn't in the script; it's something the art department gets to imagine.

Rebecca and Theo have described Juniper's apartment as small and humble and containing many plants, and it will be my job to decide everything else. Is she neat or messy? Are the plants perfectly lined up on windowsills or are they cluttering every surface with dirt everywhere? Does she have art on her walls? The answer is yes. She has art on her walls, maybe something scientific.

I see her apartment in blues and greens, mostly; she's a little melancholy.

George is melancholy, too, but while Juniper's apartment needs to reflect who she is, he's living in a house he didn't decorate, a place that's been preserved for a long time. He's heartbroken over the death of his parents. In one scene he cooks an egg and eats it and washes the dishes right after, which seems like a ritual. Like the way he was taught to do things by his mother. He'll keep everything neat, exactly as it was before they died. I'll need to create a set that looks dated but cared for. He needs to seem like a guest there.

Coral. The color scheme will be corals and pinks and maybe some yellows, like the house is trying to comfort him.

When he eats his sad, single egg, he'll eat it off a dainty plate with scalloped edges and a floral pattern.

I make long, curving lists. I sketch out a couple of the vignettes for both of the houses. I work on the scenes I remember because Charlotte has my copy of the screenplay and I don't want to take her out of the story. Then I grab my laptop and browse for images to show Rebecca and Theo so they can get a feel for what I want to create. I find a few pieces of furniture on design blogs that I want to track down for the set, so I look them up and take note of where they came from, and I find the most gorgeous coral-y wallpaper to go in the kitchen of George's house, and the address of a nursery in West Hollywood that carries all kinds of exotic plants.

And then I hear a sigh and I look up and it's Charlotte. She's closing the screenplay. She doesn't say anything at first, and I can feel myself stop breathing as I wait, and then she says, "You're right. It's so moving. I love the characters. The pacing is perfect."

"Will you do it with me?" I ask her. "They said I can hire one assistant. I need someone to help me stay sane."

We're basically finished with our current project at the studio, and since Charlotte's leaving for school soon, it's also her last project there. Still, there's a good chance she'd like to spend her last few weeks at home laying low, getting ready for school and spending time with her family. So I am prepared to beg.

But she doesn't make me.

"Sure," she says. "You'd make me do tons of work anyway. I might as well get paid for it."

"So I should go for it," I say. "Right?"

I just want to hear her say yes.

"Yes."

Chapter Eight

The next day at noon, I meet Theo and Rebecca at their house just a couple blocks from the café where we had our first meeting. Their backyard is like a tiny jungle. A white iron table set with sparkling water, lemonade, and three glasses sits flanked by tropical plants.

Before sitting down, I take a look at the details. Vines curl up the fence and in one spot Theo and Rebecca have hung objects from the branches: several hand-carved masks, a few small mosaics assembled from bright pieces of pottery.

"These must be from where you're from," I say to Theo, and he nods. "South Africa?"

"Yes. Cape Town."

"You must have spent a lot of time outdoors. And you still do, obviously."

He cocks his head. "How is it obvious? I mean, you're right, but . . ."

"Most people don't decorate their outdoor spaces this way," I say. "They have outdoor furniture and a few decorative things, sure, but they don't, for example, have pillows that look like they were sewn by hand on the chairs, or framed photographs of their family members hanging on the exterior walls of their houses."

Theo and Rebecca have both of these things. They also have a collection of enamel pots and mugs that contain carefully tended succulents.

I pick up one of the mugs to show them.

"Some of these would be great for Juniper's place," I say, and Rebecca pauses on her way to the table, a cutting board heaped with fruit and cheese in her hands, and says, "So you read it?"

"I read it."

"And?" Theo asks.

"I loved it," I say. "It's beautiful. And I would be honored to be the production designer. And I don't care how little it pays."

This morning, I thought about playing it cool but then I changed my mind; it isn't my strength.

They beam at me and we take our seats at the table.

"I have a lot of ideas," I say, taking out my laptop, opening the screen and showing them the images I've collected. I reference all the places in the script that lead me to the decisions I've made about the characters, and Theo and Rebecca are asking questions, and saying *Yes, blues and greens!* And Theo's saying *Coral? Like orang-y pink? That's brilliant!* And Rebecca's saying to him *Didn't I tell you?* And to me, *Your aesthetic is exactly what we want. These ideas are perfect.* And somewhere along the way, this thing happens between us.

It becomes our film instead of only theirs.

We go over the budget and it's almost nonexistent. There's enough money to pay a small amount for the locations, but barely anything left over.

"We can save money for decor if we can use locations for free," I say. "I have somewhere in mind for Juniper's apartment."

"Yeah?"

"My brother's place. He's out of town now so it wouldn't be a problem. It has great light and it's small and a lot of what's in there already would work for Juniper. It would give us a good foundation, at least."

"Excellent," Theo says, and I tell him I will send pictures later today, and they say that pictures would be great at some point, but that they trust my vision so there is no rush.

"Where are we with casting?" I ask them in between bites of sliced peaches.

"We got Benjamin James," Theo says.

"For *George?*"

He nods.

"I can't believe you guys didn't tell me about that yesterday!"

Rebecca smiles. "We thought we could use it today if you were a tough negotiator."

"Right," I say. "Well, it would have worked. Who else?"

"Lindsey Miller," Rebecca says. "She's playing the woman who has the seizure."

"*Lindsey Miller?* That's huge."

Theo says, "Yes, we've been tremendously fortunate."

"She's a friend of ours," Rebecca explains. "Her agent is a real hard-ass but she was able to talk him into letting her do it as long as we can shoot all her scenes in two days."

"Are those dates set?"

They nod, so I get out my phone and start calendaring. The days are late in the production schedule, which means that our grocery store scenes will be the last ones we film, which is probably for the best considering that the store might be the most difficult location to secure. We brainstorm some markets to approach.

"So who is playing Juniper?" I ask.

Theo sighs and Rebecca rubs her forehead.

"Don't worry," she tells me. "We're going to find someone."

But it's clear that *she's* worried, and with only four weeks until production begins, I can understand why.

"We *had* Sarah Williams," Theo says. "She's the reason we pushed the entire shooting schedule up. But after the Oscar nod she was in such high demand. She had to back out."

"That sucks," I say. "But it makes sense."

And it does. Sarah Williams is the new "it" girl—too new to the scene to be hated by anyone, just established enough to grace the covers of all the high-end magazines. But even though having her as our female lead would have been incredible, a different idea is coming to me.

"Have you been auditioning other people?"

Rebecca laughs and Theo holds up a hand.

"In my defense—" he begins.

"Over *one hundred* other people," Rebecca says.

"Please. In my defense. This is the most important role of the entire film. If we don't have a strong Juniper, our film will be worthless."

"She's based on his sister," Rebecca explains. "No one is good enough."

"Sarah Williams was good enough," Theo mutters. "Anyway, we're getting a new group of girls next week. Our casting agent friend has been recording auditions for us."

"What scene are you having them read from?"

"Forty-two," Rebecca says. "When she—"

"Talks about the florist. Tells George that story. I love that part."

They stare at me.

"I don't have it *all* memorized or anything," I say. "But I made a lot of notes on that scene. It's the first time we're in the break room, and there are a bunch of things that I want to get in the shot. Like wine crates for them to sit on, hooks for the aprons to hang from, a board that shows the shift schedule for the week . . . That sort of thing."

"We originally wrote it to play out as a flashback," Rebecca says. "So you would see the flower stand and everything happening as Juniper tells the story. It's one of the things we had to cut considering the budget. But as long as we have great performances, we think the actors will be able to carry the scene."

They want to hear about more of my ideas, but I steer them back to Juniper as soon as I can.

"We have an A-list cast," I say. "Does that mean you need a star for her part?"

"We've talked a lot about that," Rebecca says. "At first we thought yes, but we changed our minds."

"It was out of desperation, really," Theo adds. "No star who wanted to do it was right for the part. But we have enough name recognition with Benjamin and Lindsey."

"So you'd consider an unknown?"

"As long as she was the right unknown," Theo says. "Then yes."

—

Even after I've left, I don't want to stop planning. I've never felt so awake.

As soon as I get back to the apartment I set myself up on Toby's patio with my sunglasses and my laptop and scour the Internet for art to go on Juniper's walls. I want lush, lived-in sets for this film. Nothing too spare or too modern.

A couple hours later I find what I'm looking for on the site of a vintage store in Minneapolis. Eight botanical prints from a book published in 1901. The prints are yellowed in a way that makes them look valuable and rare, and the plant drawings are so pretty—all delicate blossoms and leaves and root structures. They are so clearly right for Juniper that I only hesitate for a moment when I see the price. Yes, they are a third of the budget we have allocated for Juniper's entire apartment, but I am sure that I'll be able to beg and borrow for almost everything else, so I get out my credit card.

—

Ava appears in the doorway of the Marmont bar, scanning the room for us, clearly relieved when she sees me wave.

"I'm sorry I'm late," she says as she steps down into the bright, sunken seating area where we've claimed a table. "I had no idea what door to go through! And I kept thinking I was somewhere I wasn't supposed to be and that someone was going to know and throw me out. What *is* this place?"

She drops her purse on the red worn carpet and pulls out a velvet upholstered, high-back chair. Her hair is up today, bobby-pinned and messy, and she's dressed in the same shorts and belt as last time, today with a white shirt loosely buttoned and rolled up at the sleeves.

"It's a hotel," I say.

"A ridiculously overpriced hotel," Charlotte adds. "For celebrities and people desperate to see celebrities." She catches sight of something in the courtyard. "And for women who make me terrified of growing old."

We follow her gaze to where two elderly ladies are rising from their table, wobbly on their matchstick legs and high heels, their breasts huge and fake, the skin on their overly made-up faces pulled tight by many surgeries. Their lips are so swollen they must hurt. I look away.

"The Marmont is more than that," I say. "It has a lot of history. Clyde Jones used to hang out here, so I thought it would be the perfect place to meet up with his granddaughter."

"He did?"

"All the stars at that time did. And sure, lots of people come here just to be seen, but people do serious work here, too. Like Annie Leibovitz? She's taken some of her most famous portraits here. People have written novels here. Sofia Coppola filmed an entire movie here. And there have been a lot of tragedies, too."

Charlotte says, "Emi loves tragedy."

"That's because all the best stories are tragic."

"Tragedies like what?" Ava asks.

"So many of them. Have you heard of John Belushi?"

She shakes her head no.

"He was a comedian, part of the original cast of *Saturday Night Live.* He died here in 1982. He was only thirty-three,

and that night he was partying with all these other celebrities—Robin Williams and Robert De Niro and lots of other
people—and then he OD'd. They found him in his room. Bungalow Three."

"That's terrible."

"Yeah, so sad," I say. "Are you hungry?"

She nods and I hand her a menu. Almost immediately, her
brow furrows, and I know that it must be because everything
costs way more than it should. You can't even get a cup of soup
for a decent price. So when the waiter comes I jump in and
order a bunch of things.

"Does this sound okay?" I ask them. "I thought I'd order
stuff to share."

Ava nods but she looks worried.

"Our treat," Charlotte adds.

When the waiter leaves, Ava says, "I'll at least get the tip."

Char and I try to shrug it off.

"No. I insist," she says.

"So you had something you wanted to show us?" Charlotte asks.

I hadn't even remembered that part of why we were here,
but now, as Ava nods and reaches into her purse, I'm dying to
know what it is.

"It's just a photograph," she says. "I realized after I texted
that I should have told you that. You might have thought it was
something really big, but . . ."

I reach out my hand and she places the photo in my palm.
Charlotte leans closer to me to look.

"It's my mother," Ava says.

"Caroline," I say.

Looking at the photograph, Caroline becomes real in a way she wasn't when she was just a name on a letter found in a dead man's mansion. She's wearing her hair similarly to the way Ava is now, one wisp of it falling over her face. Her style is perfect, effortless nineties grunge: ripped-up jeans and a flannel shirt unbuttoned over a camisole, its sleeves rolled up to the elbows. Her arm is a blur of motion, as if she's about to push the strands of hair out of her face. She's outside in the sun on what looks like a street in Long Beach. She is fair and red haired and green eyed, caught in an everyday moment, casual and happy.

"She's gorgeous," Charlotte says, and it's true.

"It's amazing how much you guys resemble one another," I say. "You and Caroline and Clyde. Those are some strong genes."

I stop there. I don't ask the thing I want to, which is how it feels to see such a strong biological connection when none of them really knew one another. I wonder what Ava feels when she looks at this photograph, whether there is any recognition, anything nestled in a faraway memory that registers this woman as more than someone who shares Ava's features. If the declaration *It's my mother* is only factual, or if, somehow, she can still feel it.

"I've been wondering," Ava says. "When you met the old people at the apartment . . ." She reaches out for the photograph and I hand it back to her. She studies it and then takes a breath. "Did they happen to tell you how she died?"

"No," I say. "They didn't."

Charlotte adds, "Just that they found her in the apartment."

Ava nods. She puts the photograph back into an envelope, places the envelope inside a book, and then zips the book up into her purse.

"I went through this phase when I was five," she says. "That's when I remember Tracey really changing, pulling away from me. I felt like my life was suddenly all wrong. I spent a lot of time thinking about how Caroline might have died."

The waiter arrives with another guy behind him, placing fries and deviled eggs and bruschetta onto the table. He asks if we need anything else and we say no and I hope that Ava will continue when he leaves.

Charlotte and I don't say anything, and Ava resumes her story.

"For some reason, I always pictured her in a lavender dress, even though I've only seen this one photo of her. Sometimes I imagined pill bottles near her. Sometimes a bullet wound. Sometimes there was no kind of evidence, and it was like she just curled up on the carpet and went to sleep."

She takes her napkin and spreads it out onto her lap. She looks out the window.

"I always imagined it with carpet," she says. "I guess I wanted it to be softer for her."

"I still think it's strange that Tracey wouldn't tell you things," I say. "It seems so wrong to make you guess."

"We got in so many fights over it. For a while I thought it might be because she felt like *she* was my mother, and maybe I was hurting her feelings by bringing up Caroline."

"Maybe that's true," Charlotte says.

"No. I mean, maybe it was when I was really little. She used to say this thing all the time: 'Don't do this to us.' She'd say it to motel clerks or landlords when they tried to kick us out, or to her bosses when they told her she couldn't bring me with her to work anymore."

Charlotte frowns. "What a terrible thing to have to say."

"Yeah, but it didn't feel terrible. I guess I just focused on the 'us' part. It was never scary when I was little, even when we had to spend the night in the car or something, because we were always together. Even when she had boyfriends, she took me on all their dates. If the guys weren't nice to me we just left."

She reaches out and takes a french fry between her slender fingers. Before putting it in her mouth, she says, "One of them gave me one of those small trampolines. The kind where only one person jumps at a time? We kept it in the living room. Tracey could touch the ceiling when she jumped."

She smiles, remembering this, and I can almost see it: A girl in her mid-twenties in a sparsely furnished apartment at night. The glow of a Goodwill lamp, of streetlights through a curtainless window. A four-year-old redhead, lying on the carpet, watching as the girl jumps again and again, amazed at the contact of hands against ceiling, filled with the wonder of someday growing big, the promise of someday growing up.

But the story takes a turn, of course. Ava tells us that it was around the time she started kindergarten. She could see the way Tracey looked at the other parents. They were a little older; they were so confident; they gathered in bright clusters on the playground at the end of the school day, their wedding rings glinting in the sun. They offered one another advice and commiserated and laughed with their heads thrown back and their mouths open, hoisting babies onto their hips, praising and consoling and disciplining one another's kids as though they were their own.

"Suddenly Tracey started acting differently. She left me at home alone. She complained about dropping me off and picking me up from school and making dinner. I didn't understand it at all then, but I think she was just realizing that this wasn't a life that she had chosen for herself, you know? It's not like she really wanted a kid when she was twenty. She never told me how it all happened, but my guess is that it was impulsive, that Caroline died—her *best friend*—and there I was, all that was left of her, and I'm sure that Tracey loved me and couldn't imagine losing me, too. But that doesn't mean that she really wanted to be a parent. Or that she was ready to be one."

I find myself leaning forward across the table, too eager for this story, so I make myself sit back and drink my iced tea and swallow all my follow-up questions. I let Ava eat in peace for a minute as a minor celebrity walks past us to the patio and people try not to notice, as a hush falls and then, gradually, conversations resume around us.

The truth is I don't know anyone who has led Ava's kind of life. I divide my time between a world of relatively well-adjusted families and private school and the world of filmmaking, where the stories are often filled with all of this—young, troubled women, rejection and death and love—but they are so clearly constructed and controlled, the fate of everyone already determined.

"Charlotte isn't totally right about me," I say. "I love tragedy, but what I love the most is redemption."

"I'm sorry. Did I miss something?" Charlotte asks with a smirk.

Ava cocks her head and studies me. I find myself not knowing what to say next, because what I'm thinking about is how movies are written in scenes, and how those scenes are shot out of order. You don't start filming at the beginning and end at the end. It all has to do with locations and schedules. Sometimes, the last scenes are shot first, so you know that the couple reconciles, or the hero kills the aliens, or the addict gets clean. You already know that everything will turn out okay, so when it's time for the earlier, harrowing scenes, you can get swept up in them safely. You can let them wreck you and allow the wrecking to feel good.

I want a happy ending for Ava. I want to have that sense of peace so all the sad details of her life become just parts of a journey that ends well. Sitting here in the Marmont is a good start, even if she doesn't know that she belongs here yet. But it can't just be about who her grandfather was and the money she is hopefully going to get. Fame by association is the emptiest kind.

I reach into my bag and take out *Yes & Yes*.

"I just got a new job working on this film. It has a beautiful ending," I say. "And this is a *huge* long shot, but I think you should audition for one of the parts."

Ava's eyebrows shoot up in surprise but she doesn't say no. Instead, she reaches out and takes it.

"I know that acting in high school plays isn't at all the same as acting in a movie, but you said that you really liked it, and I figured it would be worth a try. Something about the character makes me think of you."

I don't go on, because if I had to identify what it is about Juniper that reminds me of Ava, my answer would be that they both seem lonely, both seem a little bit lost in the world.

I can feel Charlotte watching me as I show Ava the scene she would need to read from for the audition, and I can't tell if she approves or not. She checks her watch, tells us she'll be right back. While she's gone, Ava reads the scene to herself and I scoot my chair closer to read it with her, and I am struck again by how much I love this script, how proud I am of the project.

She smiles when she's finished, green eyes bright.

She asks, "When would we do this?"

"We have to submit the audition tape soon. Like, the day after tomorrow, probably. We can film it at my brother's apartment."

She nods. "I have to work tonight but I have tomorrow off so I can practice during the day."

Charlotte appears at the table.

"Are we forming a plan?" she asks, which is a relief because I know that if she disapproved she wouldn't say anything encouraging.

"Audition two nights from now," Ava says. "I have lots of work to do."

"We'd better let you get started then."

"What about the check?"

"Oh, I took care of it while I was up there. The service here is terrible. They would have kept us waiting forever and Emi and I have a meeting to get to."

Ava pulls out her wallet. "At least let me give you a few dollars."

"When you get your money from Clyde you can take us out to celebrate," Charlotte tells her.

Ava hesitates. "You're assuming the money is still waiting for me. There might not be anything left."

"I think it'll be there," I say. Because how could it not be? Who else would have retrieved it?

"Can I borrow this?" Ava asks, still holding the screenplay. "I want to read the whole thing. It would help me understand Juniper better."

I grin at her because it's exactly what she should be doing. And I have to temper the lilt in my step, try not to smile quite so wide as we're leaving.

Ava is in my life for at least a few more days.

Chapter Nine

An hour later, Charlotte and I are sitting on the floor of Rebecca and Theo's living room with the rest of the crew, all of us together for the first time. There's Charlie, the director of photography, quiet, in thick-rimmed glasses; the sound guy, Michael, with his little brother/assistant who doesn't seem too much older than me; the stylists, Grant and Vicki, who are both decked out in feathers and fringe. All of us are doing what entire teams would do on a studio production, like Grant and Vicki, who usually only do wardrobe, will also be in charge of hair and makeup. As Rebecca hands us copies of the production schedule and I see how quickly this needs to come together, I start to realize the enormity of the job I have just accepted. Everyone is overextended on this project, but even with Charlotte's help, I'll be doing the jobs of at least seven people. I'm the production designer and the set decorator, the buyer and the leadman, the set dresser and the swing gang, the prop master and the PA. Charlotte's my art director, but apart from her I'm on my own.

I'm trying to listen to what Rebecca's telling us but the list of tasks are swirling through my brain and soon I'm feeling sick. I guess it shows because Charlotte leans over to me and whispers, "You can freak out later, but not until we're in the car."

I nod and swallow and Vicki hands me a platter covered in cheese and fruit and little slices of bread, but I pass it to Charlotte without taking anything. All I keep thinking is seven weeks, fifty-two garage sales, and sixteen estates; that's what it took to find *one* sofa. And now I have fewer than four weeks before our first day of shooting, when Juniper's apartment needs to be entirely finished and George's house needs to be well underway.

And I'm wondering what I'm doing sitting here when I should be in West Hollywood begging to borrow plants, or searching for artwork to hang on Toby's walls, or ordering wallpaper for George's kitchen. They're talking about renting lights, what kinds they'll need, what day they should get them. They're talking about the camera and the lenses and the style of cinematography. None of this has to do with me, and all I can think of is how I will barely have enough money to buy the wallpaper, which means I'll need to put it up myself, and that if I mess up I won't be able to afford more panels.

Then the door swings open, and like an answer to all of my worries, Morgan strides in.

"Hey, you made it," Rebecca says, and I feel Charlotte stiffen next to me, and for once I'm not wondering if Morgan wants me back and am instead wondering how much I will be able to get her to do for me.

Morgan perches on the edge of the sofa.

"One liner?" she asks, and Rebecca hands her the schedule. She glances at it and nods.

"Morgan's going to help us out when she can," Rebecca says. "Mostly she'll be helping you, Emi."

I nod and blush because around the others I can act like I know what I'm doing, but Morgan knows how inexperienced I actually am. I don't know why she recommended me for this.

When the formal part of the meeting is over, Charlotte leaves to ask Rebecca about details—how we'll transport furniture, whether we can thank people who donate set elements in the credits, that sort of thing.

I ask Morgan if we can talk outside and she says sure and follows me out to the jungle patio.

"What did I get myself into?" I ask her.

"Is that how you say thank you?" Morgan says.

"Thank you," I say, "but this is crazy."

"It's an excellent script. This group is insanely talented. Charlie shot a film that went to Toronto last year. Grant and Vicki have worked on really important films. Do well on this and you'll get some serious recognition."

"Okay," I say. "I just need to know how to do well."

"You already know that. You just have to move faster. I have so much preproduction work to do for *The Agency* that I can't commit to Theo and Rebecca, but I'll help you out with as much as I can, so tell me what you need."

"I'm going to need some wallpaper."

"Easy."

"I'm going to need to have pots hung from a ceiling in a way that won't cause permanent damage."

"I can rig that up."

"I might need some things upholstered."

She smiles. "It's a lot quicker that way."

"Fifty-two garage sales quicker. I should have figured that out."

She shakes her head. "You'll learn these things. Show me what you have in mind."

So I show her what I've gathered and she looks serious as she listens, and when I'm finished she says, "This is why I recommended you."

That sentence? It sounds as good as *I want you back.*

"The film is going to be a big deal. You know about the casting already, I'm sure. Benjamin James, Lindsey Miller . . ."

Hearing her name these stars makes everything feel simultaneously more real and more dreamlike.

"I know," I say. "I can't believe this."

"People are willing to work their asses off for practically nothing when the material is good enough," Morgan says.

"Why are you being so nice to me?" I ask her. "Is this out of pity?"

"No," she scoffs. "You've earned this. If I couldn't take the job, I wanted you to have it. And this way I get to stay involved."

She glances at her phone.

"Look, I have to run," she says. "But call me for anything. I mean it. And just let me know when you start getting materials and I'll figure out when I can help you get them up."

Back inside, Charlotte is typing on her laptop as Theo talks to her.

"This girl knows what she's doing," he says when I join them. "I might have to borrow her from you once in a while."

An hour ago, I might have cried at this prospect, but Morgan has made me confident so I say, "It would be selfish of me not to share her."

"I have to follow up with Rebecca about something," Charlotte says. "Then I'm ready when you are."

I take out my phone to check the time, and on the screen is a text message from Ava: *Halfway through the screenplay!*

I write back, *Do you love it?*

She says, *Yes.*

Then I join Rebecca and Charlotte and listen as they go over the budget. Basically, we're going to talk our way into procuring most of the things we'll need, but we're saving a little money by using Toby's place for Juniper's apartment.

"Theo," I call, and he comes back over to us. "Do you have any leads for George's house and the grocery store, or should I start those searches?"

"I have a few places in mind for George's," he says. "I'll make us some appointments. But in the meantime if you find some possibilities go ahead and schedule some of your own. We'll go look at them all together."

Charlotte and I arrive home to a package leaning against Toby's front door, and even before we've stepped inside I'm already ripping it open. Each sheet has its own line drawing of a plant, hand tinted in subtle greens and whites and browns, with its Latin name printed in small letters at the bottom.

Juniper's botanicals, even more perfect in person.

—

Later that night I get a call from Morgan.

"Guess where I am," she says.

"Um?"

"Screening Room Five. You know Harvey? The projection-ist? He's getting today's footage ready for the execs tomorrow."

"Sounds like Harvey's a good friend to have."

The executives and department heads get invitations each day to view the footage from the day before. Gathering in small screening rooms to watch multiple takes of the same scenes from various angles and points of view might sound tedious to some people, but I've been dying for an invitation to the dailies since I started interning. Space is limited and I've never gotten to go.

"There's more," Morgan says. "Today they shot scenes eight and twenty-two."

I'm so immersed in *Yes & Yes* that it takes a moment to remember what these scenes were. But only a moment.

"Holy shit," I say. "How does it look?"

"It's your room," Morgan says. "I wouldn't start without you."

So twenty-five minutes later I'm walking into a projection room that is empty besides Morgan and her new buddy Harvey, a guy probably in his sixties with thick glasses and a comb-over. When I thank him for letting us sit in, he tells me he's just doing his job, but it's clear that he's loving having us as an audience. I doubt he usually takes his time the way he is now.

"I've set up the dailies almost every night for forty years," he says. And then he proceeds to tell me forty years' worth of stories. All the famous films of which he's seen every take, all the stars who needed a dozen takes to get something right.

"Did you ever show dailies from a Clyde Jones movie?" I ask.

"Sure did. *Silver Stirrups*. Not his finest film, but certainly his last one. He should have quit while he was ahead. Before that one was *Midnight River*. Now *that* would have been going out with a bang. But even in *Silver Stirrups* he only needed a couple takes for each scene. He was a real professional."

At that, Harvey ascends the stairs to the projection room, leaving Morgan and me alone.

"Clyde Jones?" she asks. "Are you suddenly into Westerns?"

I just shrug. I'm not even tempted to say something evasive like, *I'm asking for a girl,* or *He reminds me of someone.* Even though saying those things would be true, there is something about how I'm feeling right now that makes me want to keep quiet about it. Something about Ava I want to protect. Every time I'm reminded of her it feels like I'm keeping a secret. Not only about her famous grandfather but about her crooked smile and her raspy voice. About her hesitations and her confessions and her focused, private thoughts.

Morgan is heading toward seats in the center and I follow her, sink into the plush red velvet. Some of the most influential people in the business have sat in this screening room, probably in this exact seat. I check out the console between us and see that with a press of a button I could call up to Harvey and ask him to play something over or speed through something else.

A scene begins but it isn't of the music room yet.

Harvey's voice comes out of the speakers: "I have to go through scene sixty-eight before I get to the ones you're here to see. It's a quick one, though, so hold on to your hats."

Morgan laughs.

"This guy is amazing," she says.

I turn to see her face, lit by the screen.

"I like him," I say.

"Yeah." She smiles at me. "I do, too."

"I couldn't tell if you were being sarcastic."

"You should hear his other stories. Katy and I ended up at a bar with him a couple weeks ago. He shut the place down."

On the screen, the father is entering the living room of the house in a hurry. The first shots follow his face closely. But then the next shots show the room. I recognize Clyde's highball glasses resting on a gleaming bar cart. The sofa and rugs and chairs are all in muted tones and around the room are pops of color: red roses in a vase, full-color family portraits on a wall, a mostly turquoise globe.

It's easy to see what Ginger was doing when she planned this room. Every detail that we notice is important. The flowers a reminder of the couple's anniversary. The globe an indication of the distance about to come between them. The portraits depicting the happy family so we can see how much they stand to lose by the misfortune about to strike them.

Even before the scene changes to the music room, I realize why Ginger replaced my green-and-gold sofa with Clyde's gray one. Then the clapper flashes onscreen, *Scene 8, Take 1*, and there is my room, larger than life, and my entire body is flooded with my own wrongness.

Ginger has used the same strategy in this room. Almost everything is muted except for the important parts: the music stand to show us the daughter's talent, the trophies to show her youth and innocence. My sofa would have commanded too much attention for Ginger's concept, and while her choices are not the ones I would have made, I can see that they make sense. They work well for this film. *Really* well for this film, in fact.

My sofa would have looked great if this room were in isolation, but it's part of a film where every scene will be cohesive. When Ginger told me that she was the production designer she probably wasn't just on a power trip. She was probably trying to tell me that she was the one with the vision for film, that she knew every aspect of the sets and the locations. As an intern I knew only a sliver.

I thought the music room was mine but it was always hers.

"How does it feel?" Morgan asks.

I'm embarrassed to know that I was wrong, to remember the things I said and how ridiculously young I must have seemed to Ginger. And I'm sad to see what this room could have been if I'd had complete control over it. How close it is to my version of perfect. But somehow, I'm also proud of it. I may have just been an intern, fulfilling someone else's vision, but I did it in a way that was my own. It's possible that no one else would have chosen that particular music stand or that poster. The sheet music is still scattered and I love the messiness of it, how it feels lived in and more authentic than the living room.

And then there is the simple, pure thrill of seeing my first work on a big screen in a private screening room on the lot of a major studio.

I take a breath, overwhelmed by all of it. What I feel is too complicated to explain to Morgan, so I just smile and let her interpret that however she wants to.

—

Forty minutes later we are in the parking lot, standing in between our respective vehicles, trying to brush off the awkwardness of having watched countless takes of a girl losing her virginity. Morgan leans against the side of her truck, and since I'm standing on the passenger side of my car, I figure it's never too soon to begin the unlocking process.

When I emerge from the passenger's seat, she reaches for my hand. Against my better judgment, I let her take it. I feel the familiar tightening somewhere below my stomach when I think of all the times she's touched me. Maybe I'm supposed to step into her now, like so many other times when she took my hand. Maybe we're supposed to be kissing, bodies pressed against the truck. But instead I just stare at my hand in hers until I find my voice.

"What are you doing?"

"Are you going to make me ask you?"

"Ask me what, exactly?"

She shakes her bangs out of her eyes and really looks at me.

"If you'll come back. I want you back."

I close my eyes and when I open them again I make sure that I'm looking at something other than her.

This conversation isn't that different from the five others we had before getting back together. But it feels different, because wanting someone is not the same as loving her, and now I understand that Morgan does not love me. When you love someone, you are sure. You don't need time to decide. You don't say *stop* and *start* over and over, like you're playing some kind of sport. You know the immensity of what you have and you protect it. So I look into Morgan's eyes, and I say, "I can't do this anymore."

"Oh," she says, letting go of my hand. "I thought you wanted to."

I've never been on the lot this late. Most of the buildings are completely dark, only a few lights shining from offices. I met Morgan only a few buildings over, by a set built for a TV show, and it was bright and hot and I was a newer and more confident version of myself. I was the girl people wanted to kiss. I didn't know what it felt like to be unwanted.

"To you I was just a girlfriend in a long string of girlfriends," I say. "But it was something else for me."

"You had girlfriends before me."

"That's not what I'm saying."

I can almost hear Charlotte telling me that Morgan was my first love, telling me that it's over. And if Morgan needs me to, I'll repeat both of these things to her so that everything is clear and final. But soon she says okay and she doesn't ask me anything more. I guess she knows already.

My one-sided love was probably obvious to everyone all along.

She sighs and then smiles. And even though the smile is just further proof that I don't matter that much to her, I find myself relieved. I don't feel any trace of the satisfaction I once imagined would come with turning her down. I just feel tired and a little bit sad.

"So what happens with you now?" she asks. "Is there someone else?"

"I don't know," I say. "There might be."

"That sounds like a yes."

"No," I say. "Really. Nothing has happened. I'll be shocked if anything ever happens."

"That'll make one of us."

And then she's stepped forward, she's put her arms around me. It's a good-bye, so I hug her back, breathing in the tangerine shampoo that I will associate with her forever, remembering how we used to shower together in her tiny blue-tiled bathroom after days spent by the pool, and how in the beginning, when things still felt easy and right, holding her close like this—underwater, in the sunlight, in the quietest nighttime hours—was the best feeling in my life.

When she starts her truck I start my car, too. But after she's pulled out and disappeared, I turn off the engine again. In the parking lot, I sit for a long time, nothing but stillness and darkness through the windows.

Then I dial Charlotte.

"Okay," I say when she answers.

"Okay?" she asks.

"Yeah," I say. "Okay."

This time, I know exactly what I mean.

"Oh," she says, after a few seconds of silence. "Good."

Part 2

———

THE LOVE

Chapter Ten

"I read it twice," Ava says, dropping her purse on Toby's couch and perching on the armrest. "I've never read a screenplay before and it took me a while to get used to it. But once I did the story just took off. All of the characters feel so real."

"They do, right?" I say.

"I like how it's so focused on all these tiny details. Like the baby food jar that cut Miranda's ear."

"We were thinking you could sit in the orange chair," Charlotte says, attaching the camera she borrowed from her mom on its tripod.

Ava takes a seat as I tell her that I agree.

"It's like this intimate peek at life through all these details, and that's part of why the sets are so important, even more important than they are in other films, because so much of how the characters see the world is through these small objects and observations that other people wouldn't make."

"This looks good," Charlotte says, and when I join her behind the camera I discover that "good" is an understatement. Maybe she is talking about the lighting and the framing of Ava's face, but as Ava goes over her lines I find myself captivated. Some people who are great looking in real life just don't look right on-screen. The attractiveness doesn't translate. But Ava looks even more beautiful through the camera. Even without makeup, even though she isn't aware of us at the moment as she turns the pages of the screenplay, she is luminous.

But the question hovers over the room: Can she act?

"Should we run through it?" I ask her.

"We can record it a few times, right?"

"Sure," Charlotte says.

"Then let's just start. I practiced a lot today and I just want to dive in. If that's okay."

"Yeah, that's fine," I tell her. "I'll read George's lines from over here. And when you look up, look toward me instead of directly into the camera."

She takes a deep breath. She sets the screenplay in her lap. "I'm ready."

Charlotte presses a button and the red light of the camera begins to flash. She nods at Ava.

"My name is Ava Garden Wilder and I am reading for the part of Juniper."

She shifts in Toby's orange chair and sits a little straighter. She glances at the screenplay. Closes her eyes. Opens them again.

She begins.

JUNIPER

Listen. I don't think it's stupid. I
think that sometimes people want something so much that they manifest it. Or
at least they try to.

GEORGE

That's kind of you.

JUNIPER

No. It's not kind of me. It's just what
I think.

(Pause)

Okay. I'm going to tell you about this
thing that happened to me once. I've
never told anybody.

GEORGE

All right.

JUNIPER

This was, like, two years ago. I was
taking Botany 101 and we were studying
Ranunculaceae and I was obsessed with
them. Like, they were all I ever wanted
to look at. And I was walking home, up
Divisidero to my shitty little rented
room, and I passed a flower stand, and
there was a bouquet of them. Really gorgeous ones. They weren't cheap and I was
almost broke. It was a choice between
dinner and flowers and I chose flowers
because it was a dark time in my life
and my room was hideous and my heart was
broken and I needed something beautiful.
The florist was an immigrant, probably
in her thirties, and her English wasn't
great. I told her I wanted the flowers
and she nodded and said something to me

that I didn't understand. And then she
said, "I love you, okay?"

GEORGE

Really?

JUNIPER

Yes. And she repeated it. "I love you,
okay?" she said. And this thing happened. I suddenly got the sense that
everything was going to be okay, that I
was going to be okay. It might have felt
to me like the world was crumbling. I
may have been totally alone and broke
and doomed in all my relationships, but
this could happen. This florist could
see something in me that would make her
profess this. I didn't have to understand where it was coming from; I could
just accept it. So I said, "Thank you."
And I smiled at her. And she looked
confused for half a second but the confusion passed and she took the flowers
and wrapped them up and I gave her the
money. She said good-bye, and I thought,
How amazing. To tell me she loved me and
then just go on with her job.

GEORGE

That's a great story. Nothing embarrassing about it.

JUNIPER

I'm not finished. I started walking home.
It was raining by then and I kept thinking about the florist. I wondered what
country she was from, how long her journey to California had been, who she left
behind and who she took with her. For
once, the rain wasn't cold and the pan-
handlers weren't begging. I stopped and
looked at myself in the reflection of a
café. I remember thinking that I looked
like the kind of person I would want to
know if I just happened to meet myself.
That might not sound like a big deal to
you, but...

GEORGE

No. I understand how that could be a big
deal.

JUNIPER

Suddenly, everything was so pretty. The
rain, the shiny sidewalks, the downtown
skyline. And especially my ranunculus. I
lifted them up to see them.

(Pause)

They were wrapped in this terrible tissue paper with tacky pink cursive that
said "I love you" all over it.

GEORGE
(Softly)
Oh.

JUNIPER
Yeah. She hadn't been asking my permission to love me. She had just assumed
that the ranunculus were a gift for
someone I loved. And who, presumably,
loved me, too.

GEORGE
So what did you do?

JUNIPER
(Pause)
I threw them away.

—

We are all silent. Charlotte turns off the camera. Ava sets the
screenplay, still open to the scene, next to her on the chair. I
look toward the patio, in the direction of the ocean, and try to
identify the feeling that has taken me over.

It's an ache. A heavy sadness. The kind that is brought on by heartbreak and then perpetuated by everything that reminds you of the way it's broken. The kind that feels impossible to shrug off or tuck away. But there is another feeling, too, surfacing, and soon I discover that it's the kind that makes the heartbreak almost something to savor because it is so simple and true. Like the Patsy Cline song on the night this all began. Like the most gorgeously written screenplays. Like the most graceful performances.

And then I feel myself break into a smile, and when I turn to her, I see that Charlotte is also beaming.

The answer is yes. Ava can act.

"Let's try it again," Ava says. "I want to pause longer before I say 'I threw them away.'"

"Fine with me," Charlotte says. "But you did a really great job."

"Yeah," I say. "It seemed perfect to me."

And her performance isn't the only thing perfect about this situation. Everything we've been planning is coming together. Here she is: Clyde Jones's legacy. And as I watch Ava go through the scene three more times, each time capturing the emotion in a way that I imagine is even better than what Theo and Rebecca are dreaming of, I become more and more sure that we are witnessing something important.

Not only will *Yes & Yes* be a great film, but it has the potential to introduce the world to Ava Garden Wilder, and Ava Garden Wilder to the world.

When Ava feels satisfied and we have finished recording, we sit and watch the different takes and choose the best.

"When will you give it to Theo?" Ava asks.

"I'll send it tonight," Charlotte says. "But I'm not sure when he'll watch it. It could be a couple of days."

"The question is," I say, "should we tell him who you are right away, or should we save it for after he's seen it and is narrowing people down."

Ava cocks her head.

"Who I am?" she asks.

"Clyde Jones's granddaughter," I say.

Ava tugs at the frayed hem of her cutoffs.

"I don't know," she finally says. "It's just . . ."

"What is it?" Charlotte asks when she doesn't continue.

"I wasn't good enough?" she asks.

"What do you mean?" I ask. "You were great."

"It's just that I don't think I want them to know," Ava says. "If I'm going to get cast in this movie I want it to be because they think I'm right for the part. If I get it, I want to get it because I'm good."

Even though this isn't what I expected, I tell her I understand because I know how she feels.

"I always wonder whether I get to work on the cool projects because of Toby," I say. "Most of the interns never even get to give their opinions about the sets, let alone design a room. Usually I don't worry about it, but every once in a while I start to doubt myself."

"But now you have this film," Ava says. "So you must have really proven yourself."

I shrug. "It's pretty much the same thing. I got this job because of Morgan."

"Morgan?"

"Her ex," Charlotte says with disdain.

"My ex who happens to be a brilliant set designer with way more experience than I have."

Charlotte rolls her eyes.

"What are you disputing?" I ask her. "The level of experience is a concrete fact."

"The brilliance is debatable."

"Not really. You need to learn to separate the artist from the person."

Ava laughs an uncomfortable laugh.

"Maybe I should change the subject," she says.

"Thank you!" I say.

"I was thinking. Would it be okay if I tagged along with you sometime while you worked? I'd love to see what it's like behind the scenes. Whether or not I get the part."

"It might be boring. It's just a lot of looking through books and magazines and shopping and trying to talk people into giving me stuff for free."

"There's even Dumpster diving sometimes," Charlotte adds. "Which can be gross."

"And going to garage sales and estate sales at their closing time to see if we can get great deals on things."

Ava smiles. "That doesn't sound boring to me."

But it's hard to believe that Clyde Jones's granddaughter, who now turns out to be an amazing actor herself, wants to tag along with me while I bust my ass on this project. Still, she seems genuine, so I tell her that the day after tomorrow might be a fun day. I'll be location scouting for an exterior to use for Juniper's apartment because the outside of Toby's apartment is too nice for a single twenty-year-old who goes to school and works part-time in a grocery store.

"That sounds great!" she says. And then, I swear, I see her blush.

She gathers her purse and hands me back my script and slips out of the apartment. I wander onto the patio and listen to her car door shut, the engine start, the sound of her driving away, and then I go back inside where Charlotte is working on her laptop and probably will be for hours more, and even though our dishes are scattered across the counter and I have merchants to beg and plans to review, I change into my pajamas. Ignore Char's surprise. Wash my face and brush my teeth and climb into bed, thinking the entire time of Ava's voice speaking those lines, of her hair falling over her shoulders and her eyes wide and hopeful. The way her entrance into our lives was as breathtaking as any great film's heroine's. The way she looks at me sometimes, which I think is different from the way she looks at other people.

I am almost sure that it is different.

"Good night," I call to Charlotte, and ignore her when she calls back, "*Seriously?*" I rest my face on a pillow. Close my eyes. Because all I want is eight hours to dream about Ava Garden Wilder.

—

Then, the next afternoon, standing in a garment-district textiles store, as I'm deciding between blue and green fabric for the curtains in Juniper's apartment, my phone rings and it's her.

"I know we're scheduled to hang out tomorrow," she says. "But I'm wondering if you'll do me a favor today."

"Sure," I say. "When?"

"Well, now, actually. It'll take a few hours. Are you busy?"

"I'm just finishing up," I lie. I am nowhere close to finished, but I'm the kind of busy that feels eternal, the kind where you can't say *I'll be done in a few hours* because the truth is you will never, ever, be done.

"Should I meet you somewhere?" I ask.

"I can pick you up in Venice."

"Okay. I can be there in twenty minutes."

"Thank you so much. I'll explain everything on our way."

"On our way?"

"To Leona Valley," she says. Then, as though she's afraid I'll change my mind if she stays on the phone, she says good-bye and hangs up.

I choose blue. An underwater, electric blue.

"Nice choice," the manager says, and I thank her again for giving me a hefty discount in exchange for a thank-you in the credits.

"*Yes & Yes*," she says, "right?"

I nod. "You'll hear about it. It's going to be a beautiful movie."

Back outside, I consider what to do about Charlotte. I know she's busy with a family thing today, but it would be a major omission not to mention that I'm heading into the desert with Ava. So I take out my phone, and I let her know. *Hmmmm,* she writes back. Followed by *!!!* And, finally, *Remember: slow.*

Chapter Eleven

When I pull into Toby's driveway, I find Ava perched on the hood of her car, reading a thick paperback. She hops off when she sees me and says, through my open window, "It might be a better idea to take your car if that's okay."

She's smiling but I can tell she's nervous. Worry darts behind her eyes.

I don't even turn the car off. I just say sure and she lets herself in. She looks a little different today, a thin line of shimmering gold eyeliner making her eyes even greener. Pink faintly smudged on her lips. She catches me looking.

"I have a tendency to put on makeup when I feel nervous," she tells me. "And then I don't like the way it looks so I end up taking most of it off."

"Why are you nervous?" I ask her, thinking of the blush on her face when she left us last night. It returns now, and she twists a strand of red hair around a finger before answering me.

"A few reasons, I guess," she says. "Going back to Leona is one of them. Taking you there with me is one of them. Jamal ended up working a double shift so he couldn't come with me."

"I'm happy to help."

"Do you know how to get there?"

"I assume the 405 to start," I say.

I've hunted for furniture in almost every city in Southern California, so I know the urban sprawl well. The sad cities that call themselves part of LA even though they feel so distant from it; the rough, flat, gritty neighborhoods; the sterile suburbs with perfectly mown lawns; the wealthy, mysterious, unattainable hills. I never got as far as the desert, but when you need to get out of LA, the 405 is what takes you away.

She nods yes. I pull out of the driveway and onto the road.

I assume that she'll explain why we're going, what we're going to do once we get there. I'm trying to be patient and let her get to it eventually, but instead she tells me about Marilyn Monroe.

"This book was in the donation box at the shelter, and I immediately thought of you. I mean, does it get any more tragic?"

She flips through the paperback, which I now see is the kind of biography that would make my dad cringe—the kind packed with conspiracy theories and so-called explosive revelations.

"There's this part where it talks about her imagining that Clark Gable was her father because her mom showed her a picture of a man who looked like him and told her he was her dad, even though her dad was supposed to be another guy."

"So depressing," I say.

"Yeah," she says.

We're on the freeway now, and it's one of the rare afternoons when traffic is light and we can actually go the speed limit, so I'm barreling toward the desert, about to perform some unknown favor.

"So," I say. "Leona Valley."

She nods. "You want to know what we're doing," she says.

"I mean, I'm a little curious . . ." I shrug like it's no big deal.

"I need to get my birth certificate."

"From your house?"

"Thursday afternoons are a good time. Tracey has a knitting circle, and Jonah goes to guitar lessons. Not that it would be that bad if Jonah came home. I want to see him, but, I don't know . . ."

"I get it," I say. "Like, you miss him, but maybe you're not ready to see him yet."

She nods.

"So where do I come in?"

She grins at me. "Lookout girl," she says. "Getaway driver."

"Wow. When you said favor I thought you'd want me to, like, run lines with you or help you paint your bedroom or something."

She laughs, but I feel immediately insensitive for joking about paint when she doesn't even *have* her own bedroom. And though she doesn't seem to mind, it only gets worse when she tells me why she needs it.

"So, you know how Clyde mentioned the guy at the bank in his letter?"

"Right," I say. "The money."

Even though the money has always been part of all of this, it hasn't ever quite been real to me. Not in the way the feeling that took over me in Clyde's study was real. That was something I could believe in, but the money seemed more abstract. I guess it's easy to ignore the promise of fortune if the money isn't intended for you, and if you have no use for it because you live in a nice house on a safe, tree-lined street in the best city in the world, and your parents have a college fund all tucked away and probably other money, too, for weddings and things you haven't even thought about yet because you've never had to worry about anything financial.

"I called the bank and he was still there," she said. "Everyone else is dead, but not Terrence."

"Did he tell you anything?"

She nods. "I went there yesterday afternoon and met with him in a private office. I showed him the letter and my driver's license, and he told me that there was an account with Caroline and me on it, but since my name is different now from what it was when Clyde knew about me, I have to show him my birth certificate."

"How much is in there?" I ask, and then rush to say, "I don't mean dollar amount. Just a ballpark. Like enough for a vacation somewhere, or enough to change your life?"

"He can't tell me yet," she says. "But I asked him if it would be enough for me to afford to rent my own apartment for a few months until I get a job that pays well and his face got all twisted, like he was trying not to smile, and he said yes."

"A definitive yes," I say.

She nods.

"So that's great. That's awesome."

"I need to get out of the shelter," she says. "I really like Venice, actually. I think I might find a place there. Here's our exit."

I turn off the freeway, already imagining Ava and me in her new Venice apartment, decorating all the rooms, spending all this time with each other.

We drive past a couple of restaurants, some dirt lots and tractors, and Ava has me turn left onto a residential street. We pass a nineties-era house, brown and beige.

"Okay, make a U-turn," she says.

"Did we go the wrong way?"

"I just wanted to make sure no one was home. It's that one we just passed."

I pull up in front of her house. The shutters in the front windows are closed; junk mail sticks out of the box by the door. A few small pots of pink flowers line the path to the door, surrounded by a bright green lawn.

I turn off the car.

"Okay," Ava says. "Tracey drives a white station wagon. She has long hair that she will probably be wearing in a braid. If you see her coming, call me."

"Got it."

"I can go out the back door when she goes inside and then come back around to you."

"That sounds good."

"But she shouldn't come home for another two hours. She has her knitting circle until eight and she usually stays longer, talking."

"Okay."

"But I don't know for sure. Things change all the time, I guess, and I've been gone for a while."

She's staring at the front door, not moving.

"It's good we have a plan, then," I say. "We probably won't need it, but if she comes, I'll call you the second she rounds the corner."

She bites at a nail.

"I'm ready," she says.

"Okay," I say. "Good luck."

A silent minute passes, and then she gets out of the car.

I watch her try to unlock the front door but she's having trouble. She keeps looking at her keys and trying again. Then she leaves the front door, grabs the nearest pot of pink flowers, and walks to the side of the house. I can't see her anymore, but I hear a crash and a shattering, and that's when I get nervous. Because being a getaway driver for a girl who just wants to avoid her mother is one thing; it takes on another meaning when actual breaking and entering is involved.

I wonder if I should start the car, just in case we have to move fast. I pull Ava's name up on my phone so I can call her immediately, trying not to look away from the street as I do it.

I don't know from which direction Tracey would come.

It's difficult to keep watch in two opposite directions at one time, but I do my best.

A slam comes from the house.

It's Ava, walking out the front door. She cuts across the lawn, empty-handed.

"I need help," she says at the window. "I can't find anything."

And I thought my heart rate was already dangerously high.

"What kind of help?"

"I need you to look with me. There's so much shit everywhere. I can't go through it all."

"What about watching for Tracey?"

"She won't come. I was being paranoid. She's had the knitting circle every Thursday for years. For half my life. Come on!" She starts back toward the door and I swear, this girl must be magical because this is not the sort of thing I do.

And yet, moments later, I am standing inside Tracey's house.

"Let's look here first," Ava says, and crosses the carpet to the area of the living room with a dining room table and an armoire. I follow her more slowly because I'm standing in the house where Ava lived until a year ago and it would be impossible for me not to at least glance at what's inside. Not much light filters in through the slats of the shutters, but even after Ava flips on the chandelier that hangs low over the table, the room is hardly lit. Wood-paneled walls surround us, adorned with careful paintings of landscapes and animals. I step closer and Ava verifies my hunch.

"Paint by numbers. Tracey loves the kind of art that comes with instructions."

The table is covered with an impeccably ironed yellow tablecloth. A ceramic vase sits in the middle, full of paper flowers.

"These are actually really pretty," I say, touching a red paper petal.

"Thanks," she says, looking down at them. "I made those. They were supposed to be a peace offering, I guess, but she never put them out when I lived here."

"Maybe she put them out because she misses you."

She turns away.

"I don't think so."

She kneels on the carpet at the base of a giant armoire and gets to business, pulling the drawers until they all jut out, overflowing with papers that flutter and envelopes that crash to the floor.

"Look at all of this," she says. "Junk mail. Like, five *years'* worth of junk mail. *Shit.*" She buries her face in her hands.

"What happened at the door?" I ask. "Did you bring the wrong keys?"

"No," Ava says. "I guess she changed the locks."

"Okay." I imagine Charlotte standing with us, taking over. "We need to be strategic about this," I say.

Ava looks up at me and nods.

"Where are all of the places we should look? Show me."

"Well, this is the first one."

I say, "Let's forget about this. We can come back later if we don't find it, but I don't think it would be in with the junk mail."

"There's more than junk—"

"Did you have this before you moved here?"

"No, she got it a few years ago."

"So your birth certificate is older. She would have brought it with her when you guys moved here. It wouldn't make sense to find a new place for it so many years later."

Ava stands up.

"Her room," she says, and leads me down the hallway into a room covered in rose wallpaper with a matching country-style bedroom set. If I had more time I would take pictures of it and use it as inspiration for part of George's house. We head straight to the closet, though, where Tracey's clothing dangles from wire hangers above a sea of boxes and below a shelf stacked high with even more boxes.

"Looks like Tracey hates throwing stuff away," I say.

Ava nods.

"I wish these were labeled," I say.

"That would be nice." She laughs, and even though it's a tense laugh, it feels good to hear it. It makes me hopeful.

We grab boxes and start going through them. I'm trying to be neat about it: removing the things one by one until nothing is left, putting the pile back in, closing the box back up. Ava, however, is dumping the contents on the floor and scattering them all over, leaving everything everywhere, reaching for another box. She's moving faster than I am, but I don't think speed is the point.

She wants to cause damage. She wants her mother to come back from her knitting group to a smashed-in window and a house torn apart.

I don't know enough about the history of Ava and Tracey to decide exactly how I feel about this, but the way I feel doesn't seem important at the moment. Nor does keeping a few boxes in order when the rest of them are getting smashed under Ava's boots as she stands to pull more down.

So I stop trying to be careful.

"I'll hand them to you," I say, and she nods. I take down box after box and she pours everything out: old mittens and scarves and novels and CDs and videotapes. So many papers and photographs and envelopes. It could take weeks to go through everything.

When all the boxes are out of the closet, we sit on our knees on the rose-colored carpet, surrounded by rose-patterned wallpaper, and sift through all of Tracey's private possessions. We toss the clothes and books and trinkets onto Tracey's impeccably made bed until all that remains are papers and folders full of more papers and letters with different addresses.

Ava grabs a couple boxes and says, "Just put it all in here. You're right, it has to be with this old stuff."

I say, "Everything?"

"We don't have time to go through it all."

"The letters, too?"

"Yes," she says.

She's picking up handfuls of papers and dropping them in her box. I watch her tear through a few stacks, discarding some papers and dropping others in the boxes, until she opens a green folder and freezes. She doesn't look at me, but I can tell: She's found it.

I can't see the paper, but she isn't trying to hide it from me either. She takes two sheets from the folder and sets them on the bed: Tracey's and Jonah's birth certificates. Then she crosses the room and puts the folder into her purse.

I expect the discovery to end our business here, but Ava comes back and continues to fill boxes with Tracey's photographs and letters.

I stare at the piles on the carpet. When I finally look up at Ava, she's crying silently, still working fast. She can feel me watching her, I guess, because after a couple of minutes she says, "I don't know anything about my own life."

Pushing away how wrong this feels, I help her pack everything she wants to take.

After we're finished we run our first boxes outside and drop them by the car, then return for our final two boxes.

On our way out of the house, I say, "Don't you want to get any of your old stuff? Like, from your room?"

I know that if I left home in a hurry, there would be dozens of things I would miss. I want to see where she lived and slept and did her homework. I still can't place her in this house.

"I can't go in there."

"Why not?"

She doesn't answer me. She just shakes her head.

Even though it's dangerously close to eight o'clock, we go out the front door. I'm behind her and I move to close it but she says, "Leave it open," so I do.

A few people are out on the street. A man two doors down is watering his lawn but we don't look at him and he doesn't seem to notice us.

I do the unlocking as fast as I can and we throw the boxes into the backseat. I feel like Thelma and Louise without the husband and the boyfriend. Like Bonnie and Clyde without the guns and the murder. It's a hot night and it's still bright outside and as I turn on the car Ava rolls down her window and we pull away as if we've done nothing unusual.

—

"Charlotte is going to freak out when I tell her about this," I say.

Now that it's over, I'm shaking. Ava sees my hands.

"Are you okay?"

"Yeah," I say. "I'm fine. I'm fine. That was just crazy. I can't believe we did that."

I'm stopped at a stop sign a few blocks away from Tracey's house and since no one else is on the road around us, I allow myself to just sit for a few breaths, until they come easily again. And, soon, they do.

The heat lingers but the light is fading fast. And even though I've just trashed a woman's house, allowed her front door to be left wide open, aided in the theft of her possessions, I feel like I've fulfilled a responsibility. I chose to pursue Clyde's letter. I could have listened to Charlotte and handed it off to the estate sale manager, but I didn't. Maybe I knew from the beginning that it was going to complicate my life somehow.

And here Ava is, right next to me, thanking me with every glance she shoots in my direction.

It's simple: She makes the uncertainty worth it.

I take my foot off the brake and head in the direction of the hills.

"Turn right here," Ava tells me, softly. "There's one more place I want to go."

I let her direct me, wind up a hill, park under a tree near a cherry orchard. When we get out of the car, Ava hops over the fence. I stand on the other side, facing her.

"It's cherry season," she says. "Have you ever eaten cherries right off the tree?"

I shake my head. "The Santa Monica farmers market is the closest I get to nature."

I feel myself grinning, and soon we are plucking cherries from branches until they fill our hands, walking to a stretch of grass as night begins to fall.

We eat in silence, looking up at the sky, lying close together but not quite touching.

"I want to explain," she says.

"You don't have to," I tell her.

"But I want you to know that I'm not usually like that."

"Oh, really? You don't usually throw flower pots through windows?"

She smiles.

"No," she says. "I don't typically throw flower pots through windows. I don't steal things or wreck people's houses. And, I guess while I'm at it, I'll say that I don't usually cry in front of people either, especially on the night that I meet them."

"That night was uncharted territory for all of us. We don't usually track down mysterious girls and shock them with the secrets of their ancestry."

"It had been a hard day."

"Why?"

She sighs.

"I thought I ran away, but I didn't."

"What do you mean?"

"Tracey told me all the time that she wished I would leave but I didn't believe that she meant it. So when I finally did leave, I didn't turn on my phone for almost a month, because I thought that if I did someone could track it. I moved my car all the time because I was afraid the police would be looking for me, but I wouldn't drive it long distances. Jamal and I took the bus to Home Depot every night. It took us an hour to get there and back."

"Two hours on the bus every day?"

She nods. "It's okay, though. That's how we became such close friends. At first I thought we wouldn't really hang out even though we worked together. He had this kind of hardness to him at first, and I didn't think he'd be interested in getting to know me, this boring white girl from the desert. But we had a lot of time to get to know each other on those bus rides."

I'm about to tell her that she is anything but boring, but she doesn't give me the chance.

"Anyway, even after I moved into the shelter I was so afraid that Tracey would track me down and make me go home. I missed Jonah but I waited to call him until my eighteenth birthday, because then I'd be free."

"Is that when he gave you our number?"

"Yeah. I called you guys right after."

"It was your birthday?"

She nods. "When Jonah answered, he yelled at me. He was, like, 'Why haven't you called me? Why has your phone been off?' I told him I had to keep it off because I was afraid they'd trace it. I asked him about the car, if Tracey filed anything, a missing person's report, if they were looking for me. He was quiet for a long time. Then he told me no. He said she hadn't done anything like that. So then I knew that I hadn't run away, not really. She wanted me gone. She was through with me."

"Ava, that's terrible," I say.

Then Ava sits up and points.

"The first person I ever loved lives in that house," she says.

"Really?"

She bites a cherry off its stem and nods.

I sit up.

Below us, a ranch house stretches out in a long L, its windows bright in the dusk.

And before she says it, I feel it coming. Through the energy that is passing from her to me. From the tremor in her voice and the way I can still feel the place on my palm that her fingers touched when she handed me cherries. The way she's been blushing and the way she looks right now, her brow furrowed, her eyes bright.

The person she loved is a girl.

"Her name is Lisa," Ava says. "All summer we hung out at the aqueduct. Got drunk. Talked about running away."

"What happened?"

"She was afraid people would find out about us," she says, after a long pause. "So she confessed to her parents."

"Confessed? This isn't the fifties."

"Yeah, well, it isn't Los Angeles, either. The reverend of her church blames gay people for everything. Like every storm and national tragedy is a manifestation of God's wrath. That kind of thing."

"That's insane."

"Tracey's a congregant there, too."

With that sentence, Ava's life with Tracey snaps into focus. It's like the final touches to a set, when random pieces of furniture and arranged objects suddenly become a room in a home where people could live.

"And Tracey found out about you guys, too?"

Ava nods.

"There was a lot of yelling. Things were broken." She pauses. "*I* broke some things," she says. "I packed some clothes and a few books and then I waited for the house to get quiet, and when it did I climbed out of the window and drove away."

"And you didn't go back?"

"Not until today," she says. She turns to face me. "Not until with you."

If this were a different moment, I would go with this feeling and kiss her. Sitting shoulder to shoulder, her mouth is so impossibly perfect and so impossibly close. But even I know enough not to kiss a girl while she's telling me these things. It's not that kind of intimacy she's after, no matter how warm and close and inviting Ava is right now, no matter how much she makes me wonder how I could ever have been a mess over someone else.

So instead I ask her to tell me more about Lisa.

"The short version is this," she says, "I fell in love with one of my best friends. I'm almost sure she fell in love with me. There were a few weeks that felt like magic, but I think I knew all along that it would end."

She stares hard at the house.

"I used to spend the night over there a lot. With her."

"Her parents didn't know?"

"They thought I was sleeping on the air mattress."

"Oh."

"It lasted for about a month. I've never been so sleep deprived."

I smile, but feel a tightness in my stomach, over what I'm not sure. Probably over a lot. Like the way I could say the same sentence and mean it about the few nights I was able to spend with Morgan by telling my parents I was somewhere else.

But also, maybe, the tightness is a little bit hopeful, a little bit over Ava and the possibility that the two of us could be sleep deprived together one day. It's a thought that I push away, though, because I am beginning to understand Charlotte's hesitation. She doesn't want me to get hurt again, and let's face it: I am just a small part of Ava's potential rise to stardom. I've been around enough young actresses to know that an amateur production designer, an intern, really, would never hold her attention for long.

So I try to pull myself from fantasies of someday, back to this still-warm ground and cool night air and clear sky and bright stars and company of a girl who is telling me part of the story of her life.

"It was the strangest thing. One morning I woke up in Lisa's bed and I had that feeling that came on all the time: that our time together was going to be over. Soon we would have to pull our clothes back on and go, one by one, into the bathroom. We wouldn't sit too close at the breakfast table. We wouldn't look at each other for too long at any moment, even when we were the only two people in the room, because at any time, without warning, someone could walk in and see that look and find us out. The light was coming through the curtains and it was too soon. I wasn't ready to get out of bed with her yet. So I lifted the sheet to cover our heads and I said that I thought we should tell people. 'Tell people what?' Lisa asked. I should have known that was a bad sign. *Tell people what*. But I didn't. I just said, 'About us. We shouldn't have to hide it.' The sun was coming up fast; not even the blinds and the sheet could keep it out, and I could see Lisa's eyelashes and the curve of her ear. I could see her lying awake and not answering me. Finally she moved away from me and reached for her pajama pants and the sheet fell away and we were there, in the sunny room, and everything was bright. She told her parents that night, but not in the way that I'd hoped. She told them that I had been coming on to her, that I had tricked her into all of it."

"And they believed that?"

Ava sighs. "I made it easy for people to believe bad things about me," she says. "It's something the counselors at the shelter have helped me understand. I gave Tracey all these reasons to reject me so that I could stop feeling so powerless."

I wait, but she doesn't tell me anything more.

"Well, Lisa's going to regret it," I say. "When she hears about you. She'll probably want you back."

"I doubt it."

"No," I say. "You don't understand. Your life can change as soon as you want it to. All you have to do is tell people who you are, and soon Lisa will be in line at the grocery store and she'll see you on the cover of *Vanity Fair*. She'll buy it and read the interview and find out along with the rest of the world. The interview will be all about Clyde and Caroline, and your upcoming movies and your lunch dates with famous people on the Chateau Marmont patio. Your portraits will be shot by Annie Leibovitz and you'll be wearing Yves Saint Laurent or whatever. You'll be so far removed from this place that Lisa will wonder if you even remember her."

Ava doesn't respond at first, but she's really thinking about it. Her face is so serious in the moonlight, her eyes fixed on me, taking in every word.

"Maybe," she says, but I can't tell if she means it.

So I keep trying.

"Even if we leave Clyde and the movies out of it," I say. "There's still this thing that happens after you break up with someone. It barely takes any time to work. All you have to do is continue with your life, and then when you find yourself in a room with her again it's as if you're a different person. Maybe your posture is a little more confident. Maybe your laughter is louder. You're wearing perfume she's never smelled before and you have a new way of pinning back your hair. You don't even have to say anything because your presence alone is enough to say *Look at who I am without you.*"

She smiles.

"That scenario sounds a lot more realistic," she says.

We leave a pile of cherry pits on the grass, hop the fence again, get back into my car. The space between us feels electric, each breath is something we're sharing. Once we're on the road, ahead of us is only the dark hills and the sky, and we drive in silence and I don't even turn on the music until we're back in Los Angeles, hundreds of taillights stretching endlessly before us, the clutter of roads and freeways that could take us anywhere.

Chapter Twelve

I guess the realization that Ginger was right about my sofa has shaken my confidence, because this morning I find myself in Theo's backyard having requested a meeting to go over my progress. Recognizing Ginger's concept made my vision for this film clearer. I don't want stylized, I want naturalistic. Instead of drawing the audience's attention to a few meaningful objects, I want everything to be meaningful.

"I want the places to really look lived in," I say to Theo now.

"Yes."

"I want, like, dishes in the sink and a sweater draped over a chair."

"Love it."

"And I'm trying to think of how to make it cohesive. Juniper's apartment will look a lot different from George's house but I need to make them feel like they are from the same world. Like, emotionally."

Theo nods and I notice some suppressed amusement and realize that I'm seeming young again. Of course the different sets should be cohesive in some way. That's probably something people learn in their first production design class, but I haven't taken any classes and even though it's probably something I knew on some instinctual level, I didn't totally understand it until Morgan and I watched the dailies.

So I stop talking about things I should already know and instead show Theo what I've planned so far. I've refined some of the vignettes and now that we're sure we're using Toby's place for Juniper's apartment, I've been able to figure out what should go where to make the most impact. And I stop feeling young and start feeling brilliant again because everything I show him gets him more and more excited. The shade of blue I chose for the curtains makes him clasp his hand over his heart.

"Isn't it amazing," he says, "what a certain shade of blue can do? How it can make a person feel?"

"And I also found these gorgeous botanical prints."

I've been saving this for the meeting's finale because I am certain he will love them. But even before he looks at my laptop screen where I've pulled up a photograph, his tone changes.

"Mmmm." He squints and shakes his head.

"What?"

"Not botanicals."

I push the screen closer to him. He must just have a different idea of what botanical prints would look like.

But he looks at the image and says, "These are lovely. Perfectly lovely. But they aren't going to work."

I stare at him. I don't understand. They are so perfect for her. They cost so much money.

"Why not?"

"Juniper loves plants, yes. But you've covered that with the actual plants in her apartment. She's more than just a botany student. We need to see a different side of her."

"Okay," I say. "So what do you have in mind?"

He smiles and points at me.

"That's your job. I don't know what should go on her walls, but I do know it isn't botanicals. Now, I know you were planning to scout Juniper exteriors today but I was in and out of sleep all night with nightmares that we didn't find a store. We were all gathered and ready with the costumes and equipment and then we realized we had nowhere to go."

"So grocery stores today," I say, trying to recover from the shock of the botanical rejection. "I'm on it."

—

Theo is right. So clearly, painfully right.

I drive away feeling, once again, like such an amateur. Botanicals are the obvious choice, the first impulse meant to be replaced by a better one. I have to tell a better story with Juniper's set, but I don't yet know what that story should be.

Charlotte texts that she'll join me on the grocery search after she gets out of a producer's meeting with Rebecca, so I drive down to the Silver Lake café and wander outside, under telephone wires, past grand houses with bars on the windows, waiting for her to be finished.

"Emi," Rebecca says, appearing behind me on the sidewalk with Charlotte at her side. "I'm so glad I caught you. Please tell me that you don't have five a.m. plans for Sunday yet."

"Um, does sleeping count as a plan?"

"I'm getting us VIP access to the Rose Bowl flea. Can I bribe you with cappuccinos?"

"VIP access to the Rose Bowl is enough of a bribe in itself. Should I meet you at your place?"

"Perfect. I'll see you then."

On the drive to the first grocery store on the list Theo gave me, I fill Charlotte in on what Ava told me about Lisa and running away, about our trip to Leona Valley. She is less shocked than I thought she'd be.

"Aren't you at least a little bit impressed?" I ask. "Ava threw a flower pot through the window. We trashed the house and *stole* things."

"Tracey deserves it," Charlotte says. She seems distracted so I ask her what she's thinking.

"I just feel like we're missing something important. Maybe Ava will get some answers reading through Tracey's stuff."

"Probably. She took a lot."

"But I wish there was someone we could talk to who knew them all."

"Yeah. Me, too."

"Was there a dad listed on the birth certificate?"

"It said 'Unknown.'"

"That doesn't give us much to work with."

"I know," I say. "And we still don't know who Lenny is."

It takes us five grocery stores to find one that I would consider using. We don't want it to look like a chain or a liquor store, and because Charlie, the DP, shoots using almost all natural light, we need a relatively small space with a lot of windows. The Great Foods Market is exactly what we're looking for. Rows of bright produce take up most of the store, with just a few racks of dry goods. It's light and airy, but small enough to read immediately as independently owned.

Charlotte and I approach the cash register together, and I think of the way Toby can hand business owners his card, flash the name of the studio, and be immediately legitimate. We have more explaining to do about who we are, what this film will be. At least we have the stars to name. A girl around our age slips into the back to get the owner, and soon emerges a sixty-ish, pudgy white guy with slicked-over hair. At first he looks unsure, but when I name Benjamin James and Lindsey Miller, his entire demeanor changes.

"Yeah," he says. "I might be able to do this."

I beam at him.

"Your store will shoot so well. It's a really nice space. I'm so glad we discovered it."

"I'm glad you like it, honey. My guess is you'd like to have a few full days to shoot. I mean with no customers, besides what you'll be shooting at night."

"That would be amazing," I say. "Would that work?"

"Yeah, it's possible, it's possible." He beckons us over to the dry goods and we follow. "You'd probably want to move some things around, right? See, all the shelves here, they look like they're attached to the floor but they can be pushed. It's not impossible."

I shake my head in happy disbelief. This is going so much better than I thought it would. I glance at Charlotte but she doesn't share my enthusiasm. She's staring at the owner with skepticism.

"How much do you want for this?" she asks.

He pauses, stands a little straighter.

"Ten grand a day," he says.

Charlotte laughs.

I feel like I've been punched. How could I not have realized that this guy was only after our money? I'm sure there are legends out there about how much shop owners have been paid to have their stores turned into movie sets.

Sadly, I tell him, "This isn't that kind of movie."

"I could accept five," he says.

Charlotte shakes her head. She pulls the list from my pocket where a corner is peeking out and unfolds the paper. She reaches across the counter and helps herself to a pen, then scratches out the name and address of the Great Foods Market.

"Next stop Figueroa Street," she says.

—

We return with nothing.

"It's quite all right, Emi," Theo says. "We'll keep on the search."

Charlotte disappears to another room with Rebecca so I go outside and sit on the front stairs of the house. Soon she will be finished and we will head home.

For now, though, I call Ava. I can't help myself.

"I found it," she says when she answers, her voice rushed and urgent. "*The Restlessness.*"

"We need to watch it," I say, glad for the distraction.

"I know."

"Want to come over?"

"Yes."

"We're in Echo Park, but we can be back soon. Give us an hour?"

"Can I bring Jamal with me?"

"Yeah, of course," I say.

Charlotte meets me outside and I drive us out of Echo Park, past the Silver Lake bars and cafés and boutiques, into downtown with its towering buildings, and onto the freeway.

"This must mean something, right?" I ask, after filling her in.

"What?"

"That she wants to watch it with us? She must really like us. We have a connection."

"We should probably prepare ourselves for another emotional night," Charlotte says.

"I think we're really good for her. I think she likes being around us. We're exactly what she needs right now."

Charlotte turns to me from the passenger seat. I can feel her disapproval even though I'm merging onto the freeway and not looking at her.

"What?" I ask.

"She's been kicked out of her house, she's been living on her own for a year, practically homeless, and she's about to see her mother, basically for the first time other than a photo, in a tiny role in an obscure movie. I do think we're good for her, and I *hope* that's all you're focused on."

"Don't you think she's so great, though?"

"Yes, I think she's great."

"Don't you think the way she bites her nails is so charming?"

"Yes."

"I really love red hair. I never really thought about red hair before, but it's so pretty."

"Emi."

"*Okay*. It's not like I'm going to do anything about it, I just think she's—"

"Really great," Charlotte says. "I know. She's really great."

It turns out that what Ava tracked down is a VHS tape. I open the door and there she is, standing next to Jamal, holding the video in her hands like the rare and precious object it is.

"Uh-oh," I say, and her face loses all its excitement.

"Thought so," Jamal says to her, and then he sticks his hand out for me to shake.

"Jamal," he says.

"Emi," I say, and he smiles and nods, *What's up?* and I like him immediately.

Ava says, "I thought you'd have one. You have all those records, all this old stuff . . ."

"Yeah," I say. "Record players are romantic. VCRs? Not so much. It's fine, though. It just means we have to go to my parents' house."

"Which actually might be a good thing," Charlotte says, appearing from somewhere behind me. "Because they will feed us."

Charlotte is out of gas so we take my car and Jamal has a laughing fit over the lock situation.

"Hey, at least I have a car," I tell him.

"What makes you think I don't have a car?" He shoots a mock-offended look at me. His face transforms from friendly to hostile, and it's so sudden and calculated that even though he's joking I get a glimpse of what his life might have been like before the shelter.

But I shrug off the thought and say, "I heard all about those long bus rides to Home Depot."

"So you're giving away all my secrets now?" Jamal asks Ava.

"What secrets?" Ava says. To us she adds, "I tell him every-thing about my life and he tells me very little."

"What can I say? I'm a good listener."

Ava rolls her eyes, and we begin the short drive from Ven-ice to Westwood, up Venice Boulevard past Venice High and a costume rental shop and several beauty parlors. Charlotte calls my parents to give them a heads-up that we're coming over, and when she hangs up she turns around to see Ava.

"We told them about Clyde and you and everything," she says. "So don't be surprised if they're excited to meet you."

But excited is an understatement.

We walk through the door and my mother breezes past Charlotte and me and basically swoops down on Jamal and Ava like a mother eagle saving her lost children from the wild.

"Ava," she says, placing her hands on Ava's shoulders. "The girls have told me all about you. You are a strong and beautiful young woman. Don't let anyone tell you otherwise. And what is your name, young man? Jamal: handsome, grace. Welcome, both of you, to our home. Would you like water? Tea? Perrier?"

I am mortified, but I try to tune her out and join Dad in the kitchen to peruse the take-out menus while Charlotte sticks with our new friends, hopefully ready to snatch them from the eagle's claws if her grip gets too tight. Dad and I look through seven menus only to decide on Garlic Flower like we always do, and he pretends to consult the menu before he orders all the dishes we always get.

When he hangs up, he comes in the living room but kind of hovers on the periphery. He's a pretty outgoing guy. It's weird that he isn't introducing himself, especially since my mom is talking to Jamal about the rich and tumultuous history of his hometown and Ava is perched on the edge of the sofa, looking uncomfortable even though Charlotte's sitting with her.

"Dad," I say. "Come meet Ava."

Dad takes two strides toward her and sticks out his hand.

"P-pleasure to meet you, Ava," he stammers.

And then I realize what's held him back. My father is star struck.

"Hi," Ava says, standing to shake his hand.

"I'm a huge fan of your grandfather's work," Dad says. "I wrote my senior thesis about his pivotal role in creating the mythology of the American West."

"*Okay*, Dad," I laugh.

Ava looks nervous.

"I never actually met him," she says. "But Emi and Charlotte showed me one of his movies. Well, part of one."

"You have his nose," Dad says. "And his freckles."

"I didn't know he had freckles," I say.

"Most people don't know," he says. "The studios thought the freckles made him look too boyish, so he wore heavy makeup to cover them. In 1966, when he was presented the Oscar for best actor in *The Stranger*, the public first got a glimpse of them. It was in all the gossip columns."

Ava cocks her head and her hair falls over one shoulder.

"Really?" she says. "It was gossip-column worthy?"

"Yes. In fact," Dad says, "I have a collection of Dorothy Manners columns in my office. I have the one where she talks about his 'boyish appearance at the Oscars last Monday.' Want to take a look?"

Ava nods and stands and follows Dad down the hallway, and then Charlotte and I are together on the couch while Mom is saying, "Really? You didn't learn about the Watts riots in school? *In* Watts? What on earth were they teaching you if not that? You have to know the history of where you come from. Okay, so it started like this . . ."

I say, "I felt kind of bad about us all descending on their mellow evening just because we wanted them to buy us dinner, but I think we just made their night."

Charlotte nods. "This is a dream come true for the Miller-Price household."

Finally, our buddy the delivery guy rings the bell.

He waves at me from the other side of our glass door as I open it.

"Hey, Eric," I say.

"Hey, Emi," he says. "Big order this time."

"We have guests," I explain and, when Mom joins us with an article she clipped from the Sunday *Times* for him, I mouth, *Good-bye*, and take the food to the kitchen.

Charlotte and Jamal and I pull out plates and silverware.

"Hey," Jamal says. "I think your mom likes me."

"Yeah, probably," I say. "Why?"

"She called me handsome and graceful."

"She was telling you what your name means," Charlotte says.

"My name means 'handsome and graceful'?"

"Apparently, yes," I tell him.

He laughs.

"I didn't even know you were black," he says.

"Yeah," I say. "My grandpa's black, so I'm a quarter."

He leans back to get a better look at me.

"Yeah, I can see that," he says. He drifts to the refrigerator and studies the photographs hanging there. "Who's this?" he asks, pointing to a photo of Toby and me. We're dressed up for the premiere of a documentary Dad was featured in, and I see it as Jamal must be seeing it now: Toby several shades darker than me, his hair thicker and curlier, his eyes dark brown to my amber.

"My brother," I say.

"Same dad?"

I nod. I could tell him about all the teachers who had Toby first and who tried to mask their surprise when they discovered that I was his little sister. Or the times when I was a kid when strangers mistook my mom for my babysitter.

But I decide to keep it simple for now.

"The mysteries of genetics." I shrug.

"For real," he says. And then, a moment later: "You have a cool family."

I don't know what to say in response. I don't know anything about Jamal's life, but the fact that he lives in the shelter with Ava obviously means that his home life wasn't exactly ideal. I suddenly feel very shallow for being embarrassed when they first came in. There are far worse things for parents to be than overinterested in their daughter's friends, than a little too excited about telling them things about themselves that they might not know already.

So I just smile and say, "Thanks," and my dad and Ava reappear from his study carrying two Clyde Jones biographies and a few books about Westerns in their arms.

"Should we set the table?" Dad asks.

"Actually," I say, "we're here to watch a video, so I'm think-ing we'll just coffee-table it in the den."

"You have a den?" Jamal asks.

I nod yes, and Mom, now back to us, clasps her hands and says, "A movie!"

Charlotte and I exchange glances.

"Guys," I say to my parents. "I don't want to be rude but—"

"Oh, it's fine," Dad says.

"Yes, right," Mom says. "We don't mean to intrude. Gary, we could watch our own movie. That sounds fun, doesn't it!"

If Ava Garden Wilder were the star of her own film, the scene during which she watches her dead mother in a minor movie role would look something like this:

```
Ava sits in a small, dim room alone. She
sits close to the screen, and when her
mother appears, she turns up the vol-
ume to better hear her voice. When the
scene is over, she rewinds the tape and
then her mother reappears. She touches
the screen and it's a poor substitute
for the woman she wishes she knew. She
hits rewind, then play. Rewind, then
play. Everything is cast blue by the TV
screen; her face is tear soaked.
```

But this is not a movie, this is life, and I hear Ava say, "Actually it's fine with me if you both want to watch with us."

"What movie is it?" Dad asks.

"It's called *The Restlessness*."

"Oh yeah," he says. "Scott Bennings. I haven't seen it since it came out in—what?—'92? '93?"

"Do you know *everything*?" Jamal asks.

"Don't encourage him," I say.

Charlotte asks, "Are you sure, Ava?"

I explain to my parents that Caroline Maddox, Ava's biological mother, has a small part in the movie.

"A waitress," Ava says. "In an important scene. I don't want to watch it alone. It's fine if it's emotional for me, right? It doesn't need to be a private thing."

"Oh, honey," Mom says. "Feel completely at home. You just let it out if it hurts. Gary and I are honored—*honored*—that you will include us in this moment."

Dad is nodding in concerned agreement, but I see something else flash behind his eyes.

"Let me guess what you're thinking, Dad. You're thinking: I'm about to see Clyde Jones's daughter in a movie, and not a single one of my colleagues or a single film critic knows that she's Clyde's daughter, or even that Clyde Jones had any children."

Dad furrows his brow.

"Of course not," he says. "I'm thinking about Ava and how important this must be to her."

"You can be thinking about both," Ava says, smiling. "It's okay."

I have an urge to send Charlotte a secret text from across the room about how wonderful Ava is, but I don't. My willpower has suddenly become stronger than I knew it ever could be.

"Okay," Dad admits. "It's both."

We all carry our plates down my wide family-photo-lined hallway and into the den, which is basically a shrine to my parents' eclectic interests. Where else can you find a framed flyer for a 1963 protest against the savage police beating of civil rights activist Fannie Lou Hamer hanging directly next to a framed poster of *Beverly Hills, 90210*, signed by the entire cast of the 1993 season?

One of the few areas where my parents' professional passions overlap, though, is music, most significantly the rise of West Coast gangsta rap. They can talk for hours about it, analyzing the evolution of music videos, from the low-budget Snoop Dogg/Dr. Dre collaboration of *Nuthin' But a "G" Thang*, which celebrates Long Beach and Compton over a backdrop of humble house parties, to the opulent candlelight, champagne-filled set of *2 of Amerikaz Most Wanted*, released only three years later.

I turn on the VCR, Ava hands me the video, and soon the screen (which hangs on the wall flanked by giant original photographs of N.W.A and Tupac on the left and my parents many framed diplomas on the right), is playing the opening credits of *The Restlessness*.

Blue light and snow over Chicago. A jazzy song.

The story is pretty simple to follow. It's all kind of a nod to the noir genre, with a mysterious loner protagonist trying to solve a murder mystery before the police do. The plot is fairly predictable but the tension in the den is high anyway, because we don't know when Caroline Maddox will appear. All we know is that she's a waitress in the pivotal scene, so we assume that she won't be on-screen until the movie is at the very least half over.

Even though the wait is inevitable, no one eats much past five minutes in, and Ava doesn't eat at all. No one moves or says anything, and as is the case with many of my ideas, I start to worry that coming over here was a bad one.

Ava and Jamal are sitting on a love seat, my parents and Charlotte on the couch. I'm alone in a chair where I can see them all through my peripheral vision, and everyone is stiff and nervous. So many things could go wrong. Maybe Caroline Maddox doesn't even speak. Maybe we only see her from the neck down, a hand and arm refilling a coffee cup in the foreground while our moody detective broods at the counter. Or, even worse, what if we do see her and she's a terrible actress? What if Ava is embarrassed and we all rush in to say Caroline wasn't that bad but she can tell that we're lying?

An hour and five minutes in, I begin to feel ill. I have to remind myself to breathe. I have no idea what's going on in this movie, only that, at some point, the scene will change to the inside of a restaurant and I will implode.

And then, here it is:

The camera pans to the outside of a steakhouse, and suddenly we are in it. The detective sits in a booth alone, awaiting a blond woman who may or may not be his daughter.

"Can I get you a drink?" a woman's voice asks, and the camera reveals Caroline Maddox.

We all gasp, because there is no doubt that it's her, even for my parents, who haven't seen the photo. She has the same red hair as Ava, the same perfect nose.

And I get this feeling. Like when you're a little kid and you make a fort out of chairs and blankets pulled off all the beds of the house, and when you're inside the light is different, and you're lying on pillows on the floor and you need a flashlight to read even though it's the middle of the day. It feels like the people in this room are the only people in the world. Like all the life outside must be holding still and quiet, giving us these moments.

The camera stays on Caroline's face as she waits for an answer. I was expecting her to be the jaded waitress who cocks her hip and chews gum and seems distracted or annoyed by her customers, but she isn't. When she asks if she can get the detective a drink, she means it.

"Scotch," he says, and we all gasp again, because the camera is now back on him and it would be too painful, too cruel, if that was all we saw of Caroline. Something is happening. He pats his pocket and pulls out a matchbook and narrows his eyes. Something has been solved, but I don't know what. He gestures, and—thank God—here Caroline is again.

"Are you ready to order?" she asks.

"Change in plan," he says. "I'm going to have to take a rain check on that drink."

"Oh." Her pleasant, professional courtesy is replaced with confusion, but it's more than that. It's concern. She smooths a strand of hair behind her ear. The camera stays on her for longer than it probably should, considering that this is an important moment that is in no way about her.

"Listen. If you see a blonde come in here, tell her something for me, will you?"

Caroline nods.

"Tell her that she duped me but I'm on to her. Tell her no daughter of mine would run around with Mack's boys."

"Okay, I'll tell her," Caroline says. "Sure you don't have time for that scotch?"

"Tell you what. If I live through the night, I'll be back to celebrate."

Suddenly, I want the detective to live.

"What's this guy's name again?" I ask.

Jamal says, "Max."

"I really want Max to live," I say, and everyone murmurs in agreement.

Unfortunately for all of us, Max dies five minutes later, and the blonde never does go into the steakhouse, and the movie ends.

"Can we watch her scene again?" Ava asks, and I rewind the tape and find the part and press play. My dad stands up first and walks over to the screen, and soon Ava follows and then Mom and Charlotte and Jamal all at once, until we're all standing just a couple feet away, staring into Caroline's face at eye level.

"She's beautiful," Dad says.

"Such a kind face," Mom says.

And I nod yes but as they all watch Caroline, I look at Ava, her hair fallen out of its ponytail, her hand raised to her mouth, her green eyes fixed to the screen, unblinking, taking in the sight of her mother.

Chapter Thirteen

At 4:40 a.m. on Sunday morning I pull up to the Echo Park house and text Rebecca that I'm here. When I look up from my phone I see Morgan's truck in their driveway, which I guess is something I should have considered as a possibility. There's no reason that seeing her should be any more awkward than it's been the last few weeks—it could actually be less so now that we know where we stand—but I'm disappointed at the sight of the truck anyway. I wanted to feel like the art department expert on this excursion and every time I'm with Morgan it's clear that she's the more experienced one.

Then Rebecca appears, shutting her door behind her, carrying two travel mugs and Morgan's keys.

"Good morning," she says through my rolled-down window. "I borrowed Morgan's truck."

The 110 has never been so empty as it is now, before 5:00 a.m. on a Sunday morning, but when we get to the Rose Bowl, people are already lined up to get in. I'm used to the bustling, friendly version of this flea market, the eleven o'clock version when everyone is there to make a day of it, meandering in and out of booths and breaking for burritos at the food trucks. At 5:00 a.m., though, no one is meandering. Everyone is eagle-eyed, targeting specific booths, inspecting the vintage furniture and clothing and decor and either placing them on giant metal carts or slapping SOLD signs on them and continuing to the next thing. These people are vintage-shop owners, ready to sell what they scavenge here for two or three times the price, or they're decorators, furnishing the houses of private clients, or they're from the art departments of movie studios. They, like me, are looking for what will make the set transcend an artificial invention, the addition that will make audiences believe that what they're seeing is real.

Rebecca takes the color swatches I've put together for her and goes off in search of rugs for Juniper's and George's houses. I target the stands that sell art, still unsure of what I should be looking for. Yesterday afternoon I lay down in the middle of Toby's living room and stared at the wall for an hour, thinking that maybe the answer would come if I wasn't searching through magazines and online shops for it. But all I got was blankness so I called Ava, feeling more nervous than ever waiting for her to answer. I know that Charlotte is right and I shouldn't even be hoping for anything more than friendship. But the things that I wish for are rarely within my control.

I asked her, "What do you think Juniper would hang on her walls?"

"I don't know. Maybe, like, floral images? Because of the botany?"

"Tried that."

"Let me think."

I could hear her breathing in the space between raspy sentences. I tried to picture her in her room at the shelter but I didn't know what it looked like, and honestly I couldn't imagine Ava Garden Wilder living in a place like that.

"Family photographs," she said. "The script doesn't talk about her family, but she seems like the kind of person who would miss them."

Something in that felt right to me, but unless I found models to pose as her family it would be pretty much impossible to pull off. And it isn't the aesthetic I'm going for. I want a set that feels romantic, emotional. A place where someone would dream about a different kind of life.

Now, sifting through hundreds of pieces of art, I find something: a painting of a woman with a long neck and a soft smile.

Portraits.

It's similar in feeling to what Ava was thinking, but has the potential to be more beautiful. Juniper will have drawings and paintings of strangers on her wall, old things found at flea markets and thrift stores. She surrounds herself with images of people so she'll feel less alone.

Rebecca texts me a photo of three rugs with a question mark. I text back, *Yes, No, Yes.* And I visit four art stands and find six portraits that I love.

Driving back at eight with a few rugs and a chest of drawers in the bed of the truck and my portraits stacked on my lap, Rebecca says, "We watched all the audition reels last night."

"Oh yeah?"

She nods. "Your friend is good."

"Yeah, she is."

I wait.

"How good?" I ask.

Rebecca smiles.

"We'll see," she says.

—

Ava meets me at the Hollywood Goodwill. There are thrift stores I like better, smaller spaces with carefully curated stock, but we need dirt-cheap artwork and I am willing to comb through the stacks to discover it.

"Portraits," I tell her when we get to the corner where the art is. "The apartment is mostly blues and greens, so if anything matches that color scheme let's be sure to grab it. But a couple pieces could pop, especially if they're good ones; if you find a couple red pieces don't hold back."

"A variety of sizes?" she asks.

I nod. "They'll all be hung together on one wall. I'm looking for mismatched styles and sizes. I already have six but could use at least ten more."

We get to work, sifting through everything from framed band posters to amateur oil paintings. Ava starts a pile and I add to it, and I find that I like working with her. The way that she isn't asking me what I think of what she's finding, how she's just moving fast and efficiently, knowing that we'll look through them all together when we've finished.

"Half of these portraits are of Jesus," she says. "I'm assuming it's okay to skip over them."

"That would cast Juniper in a different light."

"*It is morning. Juniper stands before a wall full of approximately sixteen Jesuses in various sizes and styles.*"

I laugh and Ava smiles down into the stacks, working again, and I have to force myself not to look at her.

Theo is supposed to make his final callbacks today, and with every hour that passes without hearing, I am struck with both hope and dread. Hope because I know that Ava has a good chance, even though she's an unknown, even though he doesn't know about Clyde. She was that good. And why would Rebecca bring it up if the news was going to be bad? But I know Theo had a lot of actresses to choose from this time around, and I really want this for Ava. We don't need another setback now when things have been going so well.

I flip through a few landscapes, an abstract in muddy browns, an old circus poster. Then I find a pen-and-ink portrait of an old man and I add it to the pile.

"Emi," says a voice I recognize, and I turn to find Laura Presley.

"Oh, hey," I say.

And then I remember what I wrote in her yearbook and feel a little embarrassed, because when I wrote it, I never expected to see her again.

She's looking at Ava so I introduce them.

"That's quite the stack you guys have," Laura says, her eyes darting from Ava to me. She's holding a suede jacket with fringe and a pair of pink sunglasses.

"It's for a film I'm working on," I say.

"Cool," she says. I can tell she wants to see, but I don't have time to show her everything and explain it all, so I just say yeah and smile and wait for her to walk away.

"Great finds," Ava tells her. "I love the fringe."

Laura looks down at the jacket as though she'd forgotten about it.

"Thanks," she says to Ava. Then, to me, "I didn't see you at graduation."

"Yeah, Charlotte and I left right after the ceremony."

"You aren't very sentimental, are you?"

"Only about some things." I wait for her to respond but she doesn't, so I say, "Well, it was nice to see you."

She laughs like she gets the point.

"Okay, Emi," she says. She looks at Ava one more time, and then she says good-bye and walks away.

I turn back to the artwork and shake my head at Ava.

"Was she looking at me strangely?" Ava asks.

"She probably thinks we're dating," I say. "Laura and I went out for a while junior year."

"Oh," she says, and she blushes a deeper red than usual.

"What is it?" I ask.

"I just didn't know you liked girls. Well, I thought you might, but I wasn't sure."

"You weren't?" I ask, but I guess I shouldn't be so surprised. People talk about coming out as though it's this big one-time event. But really, most people have to come out over and over to basically every new person they meet. I'm only eighteen and already it exhausts me.

"Sorry," I say. "I just figured you knew."

She shakes her head no.

"I'll put it this way," she says. "When you grow up in the desert and the only people you're allowed to hang out with are the people who go to your mom's church, and the girl you think is in love with you turns out to not be in love with you at all, there's a tendency to feel a little bit alone in the world."

"But I mentioned Morgan."

"Morgan isn't always a girl's name," she says.

She locks eyes with me, her blush fading. There's a confidence in the way she's looking at me that makes it difficult to know what to do or say next. Especially when all the things I *want* to do and say are not the things I should.

"Yeah, well, this Morgan is a girl," I finally say, remembering the strands of this conversation, pretending that what we're actually talking about is Morgan and not what Morgan represents about me. "We had this on-and-off relationship for the past year, and she didn't want to let me go, but at the same time she wanted to date other people and it was just really confusing."

"Oh." Ava nods in understanding and then shakes her head in sympathy, her gaze broken, her blush returning, all traces of confidence escaping.

And I realize that what I've said makes it seem like I want to get back together with Morgan, when I don't. Especially not now, with Ava standing here next to me in Goodwill, a pile of portraits at her feet, her hair pulled to the side in a ponytail, a wisp of it fallen on her graceful neck, her eyes wide and vulnerable, clearly embarrassed by presuming that I'd find her attractive just because I like girls.

In the conversation we're not having, the one that actually isn't about Morgan at all and is instead about Ava and me, I would be saying, *When you look at me this way I want nothing more than to kiss you.* I would be saying, *Maybe I did know you figured I was straight. Maybe it felt safer that way.* I would be saying, *Could this be a good idea—you and me?*

Instead I say, "But I finally got over her."

Ava, looking at the bin of small pieces of art instead of at me, asks, "Do you see her a lot?"

"Yeah. She's working on the film. She kind of got me the job."

"How can you do that? I don't know what I'd do if I had to see Lisa again."

I shrug. "You're probably still in love with Lisa," I say. And then, "I'm ready for something new. Someone new, I mean."

She reaches into the bin, moves a few framed pictures aside. I can see a smile tug at the corners of her mouth but she still doesn't look at me. She lifts out a small portrait of a woman in a thin green frame.

"I'm not in love with Lisa," she says.

A buzz comes from inside her purse. She sets the portrait on top of the pile and pulls out her phone.

"Hello?" she says, and then she turns to me, her hand flying to her mouth. "Yes," she says. "Hi, Theo."

I stare at her with my eyes wide, not breathing until she says, "Yes, of course I'm still interested. Yes, I can come right now."

She hangs up.

"They want me to come in and read for the part. I can't believe this."

"You're perfect for it."

She laughs, incredulous.

"I have to go. But wait! Let's take a picture first. Who would have ever imagined that my life might change while digging through art bins at Goodwill?"

She reaches into her purse, saying again how she can't believe this is happening. But I can. This is what was supposed to happen, what needs to happen. It's one of the steps that leads to the happy ending I imagined for her at the Chateau Marmont, the character doing what she didn't know she was capable of, an early hint that the film you're watching is of the life-affirming kind.

And I'm wrapped up thinking of the scenes that will follow: Ava on set, embodying Juniper. The press conferences and business lunches. The red carpet and first screenings. Some minor setbacks to temper the triumphs, moments of stillness and of action. She's the perfect person to be cast into this life: so beautiful and kind, so sad beneath all of that charm. Ava's holding her phone out in front of us, not just celebrating a moment but making it into a scene the way a perfect character would.

But.

A character in a movie doesn't startle you with a tight grip on your waist when you imagined she'd have a lighter one; she doesn't smell like the morning, or press her soft face against yours, so close that you feel her eyelashes against your cheekbone as you pose for a photograph together, tilting the phone up for the best light, pulling it farther back to get the setting, working on the composition so the clutter of the shop frames the photograph but together, in the center, are both of you.

Chapter Fourteen

"Do we need real dinner?" Ava asks when she appears in my doorway a few hours later. "I feel like baking a cake."

A grocery bag is propped on her hip. I peer inside: flour, olive oil, eggs, baking soda, strawberries.

"A celebratory cake," she adds, grinning.

"It's official?"

"I was the only one they called back."

"I knew it!"

I take a step back and let her in, saying, "Cake is clearly the perfect choice for a celebratory dinner."

"I'm so glad you agree."

"So tell me about it," I say as we head into the kitchen.

"I don't even know what to say. All we really did was fill out some paperwork but it was still one of the most exciting afternoons of my life. Just think about it. Less than two weeks ago I was knocking on your door with no idea why I was here. Now I'm acting in a film with famous people. I'm SAG eligible." She shakes her head. She scans Toby's apartment. "I have friends," she says. And then, more quietly, "I feel like I belong here."

"That's because you do," I say. "Acting is in your blood."

"It still feels unreal."

She steps over to the sink and turns on the hot water. She washes her hands slowly, her eyes the kind of far away that makes it easy to stare at her without fearing getting caught. Her hair is still in its side ponytail, but this time every strand is perfectly in place. I wonder what Theo thought when she walked in his door, whether she looked as luminous to him then as she does to me now.

"Before I left Leona Valley, when I pictured my ideal life, this sort of thing never even entered into it."

"What did you picture?" I ask her, leaning against the kitchen counter while she rinses strawberries.

"Well, I was trying to be smart about it. I thought I could get a job in LA and commute for a few months until I earned enough to be able to rent a room somewhere."

"Commute from Leona Valley?"

"Yeah. It would have been really long but it would only have lasted a few months. Then I would have moved out the right way, with money in my bank account and a place to show up and work five days a week. Maybe a couple of friends here already."

"So what happened?"

"Well, I thought I would find a job at a bakery, because baking is something I'm good at. And the hours would be crazy— the shifts start so early in the morning—so I thought I would save time on the commute and it would also be a good escape because I would be out of the house before Tracey got up."

She's put all the ingredients in a neat cluster on one side of Toby's counter and is now finding measuring cups and spoons.

"Let me know if you need any help," I say.

"Cake pan of any kind?"

I nod and find one we thrifted from the Rose Bowl a couple years ago. We bought it because it was this great coppery color, not because we had any intention of using it. I hope it works because it's all Toby has.

"Great! I've got it from here."

I hop up onto the counter, out of the way of her prep area.

She's quiet for a moment, taking stock of everything she has, and it dawns on me that she's making this cake without a recipe, which is not something I even knew was possible.

She cracks the first egg into a glass bowl in one quick motion.

"So anyway, I researched all of these bakeries and I thought of a way I could prove myself considering that I was a teenager with no formal experience. I chose seven bakeries and made seven full-size German chocolate cakes from scratch. I drove out here and delivered them all, and one by one, the people who worked there looked at me like I was crazy."

"Why?" I ask. "That sounds like a great thing to do to impress people."

She shrugs. "I thought so, but it didn't help that most of the places I went didn't have traditional cakes. They were all very gourmet. Like with bourbon and sea salt, or classic cakes with a spin, like vegan Red Velvet made from beets. Lots of olive oil cakes, which I had never even heard of, but that now I love. Anyway, only one baker at one bakery ate a slice of my cake in front of me. It was the La Cienega Bakery and it was the owner who was there working, and when she tasted it she told me it was delicious but that they weren't hiring. I still held out hope that someone would quit and she'd have an opening. That's who I thought you guys might be when Jonah said a woman had called me. I thought it would be a perfect birthday present to be offered a job."

"Instead you got us."

She smiles. "When I pictured having friends here, I saw us crammed into a tiny apartment. I imagined waitresses taking community college classes or aspiring chefs working as line cooks. I thought we'd probably live in a sketchy neighborhood and pool our money to make stir-fry for dinner."

"Are you disappointed?"

"No. I mean, don't get me wrong; that kind of life sounded incredible. But," she says, looking up at me, "what could be better than this?"

—

Forty minutes later, the cake is in the oven. I'm laying the portraits we bought out on the floor to determine how they should hang, and Ava is reading her own copy of the script, pen in hand.

Charlotte lets herself in.

"Thank you, Ava. Whatever that is, it smells amazing and I am starving," she says, dropping her computer bag onto the couch.

"Why not 'Thank you, Emi'?" I ask.

"Because all you know how to cook is pasta and scrambled eggs."

"And toast."

"Yeah, but you usually burn it."

"Not true," I say. "It's a matter of preference. I happen to like my toast crisp."

"Still," she says. "There's no way that amazing smell is thanks to you."

"She did find me a cake pan," Ava says, laughing.

She's clearly amused but I'm not because I don't want her to think I'm some loser who can't toast bread. I want her to think that I'm that fun kind of girl who will bake cookies on a Tuesday night, or make french onion soup on Bastille Day.

"Don't be mad," Charlotte says. "You have to leave *some* talents for the rest of us."

She smiles at me and I can't help but smile back because it's a pretty nice thing to say.

"Fine." I shrug. I turn to Ava. "Secret's out: I can't cook."

"I can't decorate," she says.

"That doesn't bother me," I say, and it comes out flirtatious, and I want to keep going, so I say, "I'm terrible at math."

"I'm a bad speller."

"I don't even know my multiplication tables."

"I can't do a real push-up."

"I wanted to learn Spanish but I can't roll my *r*'s."

"Wow," Charlotte says. "This is interesting," which is a cue to stop but I could keep going forever, listing all my flaws in order from the most innocuous to the least. I am afraid of spiders . . . I fall in love too easily . . . I have fierce spells of self-doubt. Because in the conversation beneath this one, what we're really saying is *I am an imperfect person. Here are my failures. Do you want me anyway?*

"I want to hear all about everything," Charlotte says to Ava.

"She's SAG eligible," I say.

"I know. I was there when they signed the paperwork. Rebecca and I are redoing the budget for the third time. What did you think of Benjamin?"

"Oh, he was there?" I ask, surprised that Ava didn't mention him right away.

She nods.

"He was . . . nice," she says.

Charlotte and I laugh.

"You don't have to like him just because he's famous," I say. "Or because he's your costar."

"It's not that I don't *like* him. Like I said, he seems nice. It's just that in movies he's so sexy. I don't find many guys that attractive, but even *I* understand the appeal. Like his role in *Call Me Yesterday*? When he's all brooding and misunderstood? But today he was just kind of . . ."

"Oh, we totally understand," Charlotte says.

"It's the collapse of the fantasy," I add.

Ava cocks her head.

"It applies to almost anything. You know that scene in *Call Me Yesterday* that takes place in the back room of the school?"

"Yeah?"

"You know how it's super-dark and claustrophobic?"

She nods.

"That room actually had no ceiling and only two walls. It's in a giant warehouse. Nothing claustrophobic about it. And you know that fight scene where Benjamin's all shirtless and sweaty? I bet between takes he put on a robe and drank Perrier. You'll see how it all happens. We work so hard to create an illusion and to make it seem real. But for us, the more you know about what happens behind the scenes, the more difficult it is to maintain the fantasy."

"Does it spoil things a little?" she asks.

"You just have to make an effort to forget."

"Which doesn't work a lot of the time," Charlotte says. "Watching a movie with Emi is like getting a tutorial on how films are made. *Look at that shot! They must be using natural light. That backdrop is so fake.*"

"I'm not *that* bad."

"You're pretty bad."

"But when a movie is really good, it's easy to forget."

Charlotte nods. "That's true."

Ava closes her script and looks at the cover.

"I think our movie is going to be really good. Don't you guys?"

I nod yes and this moment almost feels like a premonition. Here we are, in the room where we will shoot the first scenes, with the girl who will play Juniper working on her lines and the beginnings of the set in place. These portraits are everything I wanted them to be; I can already picture how they will look on Toby's wall. And even though we still don't have George's house or the grocery store, even though I've been starting awake most nights worried about all I need to do, there is a calm in this room that assures me that we are exactly where we are meant to be.

Chapter Fifteen

Theo and I have appointments at five potential locations for George's house.

The first one is infested with rats. The second has a terrible, unidentifiable smell and I end up coughing so hard that Theo says, "Let's get out of here. Run for your life!" The third one has such cramped rooms that it would be impossible to fit everyone inside with our lights and the cameras. The fourth is too modern with high ceilings and stainless steel everywhere.

We are desperate by the time we pull up to the fifth.

We park and walk up to it. Paint is peeling off the walls of the house in thick strips, but we try to stay optimistic.

"I don't think we could use it for the street-view shot," I say.

"Nope," Theo says. "No way."

"But we could choose a different house for that."

"Right. No big deal."

A middle-aged woman pulls up in a dirty car and sits there for a moment, digging through a giant purse.

"You figure that's her?" Theo asks.

"Probably," I say, but she doesn't look over at us or appear to be in any kind of hurry.

Eventually, though, she gets out of the car and crosses the street toward us.

"Patricia?" Theo asks. "Hello."

"You have an accent. Are you legal to live here?" Patricia asks, scrutinizing his face.

"Yes, in fact, I am. But as I said on the phone, we're only looking for a one-week rental for a film."

She looks at me and then back to him.

"How old is she? I can't rent to minors."

I laugh but Theo tries his best to keep his composure even though this woman obviously suspects him of some statutory rape–immigration scandal.

"This is Emi. She is eighteen years old. But it wouldn't matter anyway because she is not interested in renting the space. I would be renting it and only for a week to shoot a film."

"You got insurance?"

"Yes. I have insurance."

"Is it pornography? I can't have pornography shot here."

Theo seems on the verge of exploding, but he runs his hand through his hair and smiles down at her.

"It is not pornography," he says in a voice that is part polite, part menacing.

Patricia sighs and unlocks the iron gate and then the front door.

"Go on in," she says. "I have some calls to make."

We make a quick lap of the house—splotchy carpets, dingy walls with water stains from what must have been a leaky pipe, dreary lighting in most of the rooms. How difficult is it to find just a humble, decent house?

I expect Theo to say we should move on, but instead he says, "Well, Emi, what do you think?"

"It would be a pretty bleak interpretation," I say. "Is that what you're going for?"

"It isn't what I had in mind exactly, but I'm feeling desperate. It's a good day rate."

"That's true."

I know how important the good price is, and also that it's my job to take whatever we can get and then transform it into something we want. So I do another lap and I look for opportunities this time.

When I get back to Theo, I say, "Let's go for it."

Already, I know of a few things I could do to make the space nicer. If a cluster of framed artwork hung over the water damage on the main living room wall, for example, the house wouldn't appear to be on the verge of collapse. Morgan could affix coral-colored wallpaper to plywood that we could prop against the kitchen walls. I could beg for more curtains. I could make this work.

I tell him some of my ideas and he says yes, over and over, so fervently.

"Emi," he says. "You're a miracle."

I savor that sentence, allow myself to bask in it. Hope it might revive some of my lost confidence. And then I follow him out to the front steps where Patricia is waiting, a fresh coat of hot pink lipstick smeared on her lips.

"So, one hundred dollars a day, you said?" Theo says.

"That'll buy you until three."

"On what day?"

"Every day. I'm going to need it after that for viewings."

"Three is quite early."

"And if someone rents it before then, the deal's off."

"What do you mean?"

"You know, if someone signs a lease."

"This isn't what you said on the phone," Theo says.

"Put yourself in my position. I need to find a renter. What if I find someone to sign a year lease but they need the place right away. Am I supposed to say no because you need it for a week?"

Theo's hands fly to his head. Towering above her, he says, "Please. If you will. Put yourself in *my* position. How can I accept an agreement that could mean that even if I were half-way through the week of filming, I could have my location pulled out from under me. Then I would have half the scenes that are meant to take place in this house completed, but the other half undone. What would I do then?"

Patricia is fazed neither by his impressive stature nor his argument.

"I have to make a living. A hundred a day is a real bargain. I can give it to you day-by-day but that's all I can do."

"So you're saying that I have to decide whether it's worth this so-called *bargain* you're offering me for a piece-of-shit house with water damage and stained carpets to risk losing *days* of shooting to a hypothetical renter?"

He's yelling now, and Patricia's hot pink mouth is hanging open and I try to lighten things up by saying, "Well, looks like we'll be moving on, right, Theo?" in a kind of happy-go-lucky lilting way.

And then when no one responds I walk to his car and wait by the passenger-side door.

—

After venting for half an hour as we inch along the 405, Theo finally falls silent. I let him have a few minutes and then I say, "So is it safe to change the subject?" and he says, "Please do."

So I ask him about scene 42, the scene Ava read to audition for the part, because I've been thinking of what they told me the day I accepted this job, that they had envisioned the entire scene playing out as Juniper tells the story: the flower stand and the florist, the city street.

"Right," he says. "We ran out of money. It was one of the easier things to cut. But even with a spectacular Juniper, it's a long time to hold an audience's attention."

"I've been thinking of ways to create the illusion of a set."

I'm taking a risk by bringing this up because really what I'm suggesting is a directorial decision and I don't want to overstep. And it's also a departure from the style I showed him and I don't want him to doubt me. But he tells me to go on, so I take the chance.

"Well, there's the possibility of really tight shots, close-ups of hands, flowers, the tissue paper, Juniper's face, and the florist's face. We could shoot it basically anywhere outdoors because we wouldn't see much of the background."

"Interesting," Theo says.

And even though I know *interesting* can be a euphemism for "terrible idea that I will disregard immediately," something in the way he says it makes me think that he doesn't mean it that way, that the concept really does interest him, so I keep going.

"I think it could work because it's kind of the way memories are. They're private, and shooting them so close would convey intimacy."

Theo runs his hand through his wavy brown hair. His phone rings and I see it's Charlie, the DP, calling, but Theo hesitates before answering and instead ignores it.

"Go on," he tells me.

"What the scene is about, at least to me, is Juniper finally trying to connect with someone. Instead of spending all this time obsessing over a stranger, she realizes that making a real connection with a real person—not just an illusion of who someone might be—is worth taking a risk. So she tells a story that has the potential to humiliate her. She shares a memory. It's a huge moment in the film so it would work for it to be stylistically different. It wouldn't even be as good to show a wide shot of Juniper at the florist because it would look like everything else. This scene should look and feel like a memory, and we could pull that off—*you* could pull that off—by cutting between her sitting in the break room telling George the story, and the close-ups of images that help us *feel* the story."

"I'm liking this," Theo says, and then his phone rings and it's Charlie again and he tells me he has to take it. "Let's work on this concept," he says as he answers. "Come up with some things to show me."

As he talks Charlie down from some kind of lens crisis, I think about what I could include in the scene to convey memory and sadness, and soon I am thinking about the set I would create if this were a movie about me. If I were trying to show people how it once felt to be with Morgan I would show the shimmering blue water of the pool at her apartment, and the line she rigged on her back deck because her unit has a washing machine but no room for a dryer. All those tank tops and pairs of bright underwear in the sun. It would be a soft nostalgia, a faded romance.

But the *Yes & Yes* scene isn't only about sadness; it's about yearning, too.

Yearning is a red-haired girl sitting on the hood of her silver sedan, reading about Marilyn Monroe. A cherry orchard at night, houselights at a distance. It's the painstaking neatness of a paint-by-number sunset, a yellowed letter held between graceful fingers, a cautious step into the sun-filled lobby of a famous hotel.

It's the way I feel every time I think about Ava.

Soon I'm feeling the same ache that descended after Ava's audition, and then a similar urge to savor it. Out the window, downtown Los Angeles comes into view, that sprawl of tall buildings in the smoggy haze, the people too far away to see. In a year or so some of those people might enter a theater to watch our film. The lights will go down, allowing them to drop into themselves for as long as the movie lasts. And if I choose flowers that are the perfect shade of red, tissue paper with words subtle enough for them to overlook at first and then, later, clear enough to make them cringe, they may find themselves feeling the same way I am now. We'll all be feeling for Juniper but actually feeling for ourselves, for how it is to be heartbroken, how it is to be alone, and maybe, if we're lucky, how it is to be ready to open ourselves up to the fragile hope of something new.

—

Charlotte laughs forever when I tell her about Theo and Patricia.

"He said all that? No way."

"Yeah," I say. "He had a minor breakdown. I thought he was going to start kicking things."

"Poor guy. We should find him somewhere perfect."

"I actually have an idea," I tell her. "I thought of it when we got back, but Theo was pissed off again and didn't feel like talking. You know when you try to cheer someone up but it's clear they aren't in the mood? They want to wallow for a while? That's what he was doing. Anyway. What if we ask Frank and Edie?"

"That's a great idea."

"I know. I don't know why I didn't think about it before. I guess I just got swept up in the film and forgot about them for a little while, but their little cottage is sort of perfect."

"Yeah," Char says. "It's totally an old-person house but it's nice. Is it coral?"

"I can make it coral. That's no problem. I just don't know if Edie would be up for it. She seemed pretty set in her ways."

"We could buy her cookies and drop by."

"Brilliant. *Plain* cookies."

—

An hour later we are armed with a dozen sugar cookies in a pink box, on our way to Long Beach.

"I wonder if Frank and Edie know who Lenny is," Charlotte says.

"We should ask them. Maybe we should call Ava and see if there's anything else she wants us to try to find out."

Charlotte smirks at me.

"*What?*" I ask. "It's *her* family we're trying to find out about."

"You're right. Do you want me to do it?"

"Sure."

Ava picks up when Charlotte calls, and I listen to Charlotte explain why we're headed to Frank and Edie's.

"We thought we'd ask them about Lenny," she says. "Just in case they remember him. Is there anything you want to know? Yeah, Long Beach. Ruby Avenue. Um . . . yeah, I guess that would be okay. All right, I will. See you soon."

"She's coming?" I ask.

Charlotte grimaces. "Not the most professional move on our part."

"Yeah, not really," I say, exiting the freeway and turning right onto Ruby Avenue. "But it's okay. We met Frank and Edie under strange circumstances. We don't need to get super-professional with them all of a sudden. And at least she's part of the film now."

When we get to the house, the station wagon is in the driveway; the front door is open.

"Hello, Frank and Edie," I call inside. "It's Emi and Charlotte."

"Is someone there?" Frank calls. I can see him working his way out of his chair and walking over to us.

"Girls, hello!" he says from halfway through the room. Soon, he is standing in the doorway, welcoming us inside.

"We brought you guys cookies," I say.

"Plain ones," Charlotte says.

"Edie will be thrilled," Frank says. "The perfect afternoon snack. She's getting her hair done right now. Gretchen, our daughter-in-law, takes her every Tuesday. Such a sweet girl."

We follow him into their living room and it's even more right for the film than I'd remembered. The plastic-covered maroon couch, the careful piles of magazines. Frank has the wood-paneled television tuned in to a Dodgers game, a vintage TV tray with brass legs set up in front of a mint green easy chair. Everything is old but in such good condition. I take a closer look at the TV tray—the top of it is a fruit basket design in a muted color palette of gold and—*yes*—coral.

"Frank," I say. "I'm here with a request."

"Oh?"

"Last time we were here I believe that we told you what our jobs were."

"Yes, you did. Every time Edie reads something about *The Agency* she talks about you. Very exciting. And you're both so young."

"We started working on a new movie. It's very small but we hope it will get picked up by a big studio after it's been made."

"It's called *Yes & Yes*," Charlotte says. "The script is really beautiful."

"I'm the production designer," I say, and I get such a thrill from saying it that actually gives me goose bumps. Frank is watching us deliver this information so patiently, looking at us with these wise old-man eyes, turning his ear just the tiniest bit toward us when we speak so that his hearing aids will work.

"I was wondering whether we might be able to use your home in the film," I say. His white, wiry eyebrows shoot up in surprise.

He turns his head to survey the room as though he's expecting to find himself suddenly elsewhere.

"Here?" he asks.

"Yes," I say. "Unfortunately, we have a limited budget and could only offer you a hundred dollars per day, but we have a very respectful crew and we'd only need five days. And maybe it would be exciting to see your house in a movie?"

"Why our house?" he asks, so I explain the part to him and I can tell that he likes the idea of it because he keeps looking around in awe and saying, "Who would have guessed?" and smiling.

"I'll talk to Edie," he says. "It's fine with me, but you know who's in charge around here."

He winks, and just as I'm winking back, Ava calls, "Hello?" from the doorway.

"I can't remember the last time I had so much unexpected company," Frank says.

Charlotte says, "This is Ava."

"Come in," Frank says, and when Ava steps inside I get goose bumps again but for an altogether different reason. Her hair is swept off her shoulders with bobby pins. She's wearing a camisole as a tank top, a light green satin that makes her eyes even brighter, makes me want to be nearer to her.

"Hi," she says to all of us, and the rasp in her voice is enough to make me swoon.

But then I remember what she's here for and that I didn't have time to give Frank any warning.

"Frank, remember how we were looking for Caroline Maddox last time we were here and you told us that she had a baby?"

He nods yes.

"We found her. This is Ava."

Instead of turning to Ava he looks harder at me. At first I thought he might not have heard me, but then I realize that he's just taking a moment to process this news, and I feel a trace of what I felt when I opened the door to Ava that first night. Like I'm trespassing again.

"I hope it's okay that I came," Ava says.

He finally turns to her.

"Sure, sweetheart. Sure. Come into the living room. Let's have some of these cookies."

He turns off the TV, and I feel even worse because clearly all he wants is to watch the Dodgers in peace and here we are ruining it.

Charlotte places the pink box on the coffee table next to all the magazines and opens the top. The cookies glisten up at us. Frank reaches for one.

"I suppose you want to hear the whole story."

"If it's okay," Ava says. "The woman who adopted me never told me what happened."

"That's a shame."

Frank takes off his glasses. He rubs his eyes.

"I don't like to think about this sort of thing," he says. "When I was a young man I fancied myself a philosopher. I enjoyed thinking about the tragedies of life. I thought all the feeling out of everything. But not anymore."

"I'm so sorry, Frank," I say. "We didn't mean to upset you. We should have called before we came. I just got the idea about using your house for the movie and—"

"It's all right," he says. "So I'm upset. So what? It's your life." He glances at Ava and nods. "If you have a right to anything in this life, it's to know your own history."

He takes a bite of the cookie. Takes his time chewing and swallowing. We sit in silence and wait.

"So this is what happened," he says. "When Caroline first moved in she would tease me about the state of the garden. *Pitiful*, she told me. *You think you can do better?* I asked her, and, well, she showed me. In a matter of weeks she cleaned it up, got it blooming. We would have long talks sometimes when we were out there working. She was a dreamer. Always imagining an extravagant future. A penthouse overlooking the ocean. That's what she wanted someday. But for the time being, we had an arrangement about the flowers. She was to keep them pruned and watered, and we would help her out with the rent. She did it for a little while. But then she took a turn. It was clear just to look at her. Soon the garden was overgrown and the flowers were starting to wither. We hadn't seen Caroline around for a couple of days. I started getting upset. Edie wanted me to take the responsibility away from her, but I knew she couldn't afford the full rent, especially with the baby. With you, I mean.

"I had been calling her, you see? Calling and calling and she wouldn't answer. But I knew she was around. Her car was in the lot and at night she'd have parties. Some of the neighbors would complain and once in a while Edie would go up there but I never wanted to get into it. You see, I really liked her. I thought she was the sweetest girl. She only showed me her sweet side. Maybe that's why I looked the other way when she was a few days late on the rent and when she didn't do the gardening she was supposed to. I was getting to the point where I was going to have to give into my wife, you see, and raise Caroline's rent.

"I called that morning but, no surprise, there was no answer. And then later on, in the early afternoon, we heard sirens. They aren't too unusual for this area, but they got louder and louder and then stopped right outside, and I went out there and asked the paramedics what was going on. Told them we owned the building. They said they got a call about someone in apartment F and I said, 'I'll get the key.' I ran up after them—I wasn't such an old man then, you know—and I opened the door and they let me follow them in. The baby was crying. *You* were crying. I could tell something was very wrong. And then there she was, your mother, Caroline, and there was no mistaking that she was dead already."

We're quiet for a minute. Ava looks pale. I want to reach out and hold her hand but something keeps me from it.

"Did you find out who made the call?" Charlotte asks.

"No," Frank says. "We never did. But it was made from the apartment."

"So someone was in there, alive, when Caroline had already died?" Charlotte asks.

"That was my understanding."

"Maybe it was Tracey," Charlotte says.

"Or Lenny," I say.

"Lenny? The name doesn't sound familiar." Frank shakes his head. "It could have been anyone, though. I wasn't acquainted with her friends. Actually, there's one thing I could check."

He leans forward. Charlotte walks to his chair and offers him her arm.

"Thank you," he says, and she helps him stand.

"We have these files over here. All of our old tenants. Everyone has to provide the name of a person to contact in case of emergency. We've never been good about clearing it out."

He opens the drawer of a black metal cabinet and in spite of myself I make a mental note that we'll have to take it out of the room when we shoot. It's a cool piece, but too office-like and altogether the wrong color.

"Here we go," he says, and we all lean forward to hear him. This could lead us to Lenny, whoever he is, or it could lead us to someone else entirely, someone who knew them all and could answer all our questions.

He adjusts his glasses. He squints.

"Tracey Wilder," he says. "Should I write down her phone number and address?"

We all sigh.

"That's okay," Ava says. "I already know her."

Frank shuffles back to his chair. This time it's me who helps him sit down.

"I could get used to this kind of treatment," he says to us with a wink.

"Anytime," I say. "But we should go, let you watch your game."

"Don't you want to wait for Edie? You can ask her about your movie."

"Okay," I say. "But we can watch while we wait."

"As long as you don't mind . . ." He picks up the remote and clicks the game back on.

"Can I ask you something else?" Ava says when a commercial comes on.

Frank nods.

"Where was she when you found her? What did she look like?"

"What did she look like?" Frank asks. "Well, sweetheart, I'm sorry to say, but she looked dead. I don't know how else to describe her."

"Was she in the living room?"

I brace myself for the answer, remembering what she told us at the Marmont, that she imagined carpet.

"No," he says. His eyes are watery. "She was on the bathroom floor with a needle in her arm. There was nothing pretty about it. I'm sorry."

A moment later the door opens and Edie steps inside dressed in a red suit and flat black shoes, her hair curly and stiff and much closer to brown than to purple.

"What?" she says, squinting to see us all. "We have company? Oh, it's Emi and Charlotte. You came back to see us! And who did you bring with you this time?"

"Sweetheart," Frank says. "This is the baby. Caroline's baby."

Edie blinks. "Oh my," she says. "Oh, dear, really? Come. Let me see you."

Ava crosses the room to stand with Edie in a patch of sun.

Edie touches her hand to her heart, and then reaches out and takes Ava's hand between her own.

"You poor thing," she says.

Ava tries to smile but it doesn't last.

"Frank was telling us about the day you found her," Charlotte says.

"It was a terrible day," Edie nods. "But look at you now. So pretty."

"A terrible day," Frank echoes.

"Yes," Edie says, her gaze never leaving Ava's face. "But look. You grew up anyway."

Chapter Sixteen

My phone rings at 2:23 a.m., a Los Angeles number I don't recognize. I pick up, heart in my throat, unprepared for the terrible news that might come.

"Hey, it's Jamal."

My mind was swarming with police officers telling me something happened to my parents, hospital receptionists saying, *Come immediately.*

He says, "Sorry to call so late. It's just Ava—is she with you?"

"No," I say. "She isn't at the shelter?"

He hesitates.

"She got kicked out tonight," he says.

"Why?"

"She was upset and . . . I don't know, I don't think I should get into it."

"Should we try to find her?"

Charlotte's up now, standing in the doorway.

"What's going on?" she asks. I tell her what Jamal told me, and then I offer to pick him up.

"Oh, man," he says. "Things around here are tense right now."

Charlotte cocks her head at me, waiting for an answer.

I shrug, but then Jamal says, "Whatever, fuck it, come get me." He gives me the address. "*Don't* come to the door," he adds. "Just pull up and I'll run down to you."

Five minutes later Charlotte and I have traded our pajama shorts for jeans, grabbed my car keys and our purses and are pulling out of Toby's driveway headed for downtown Los Angeles. The streets are deserted in Venice and the freeway traffic is nonexistent. Once we've exited, the skyscrapers tower around us, a lit window here and there, glowing like a partially inhabited ghost town.

We follow the directions on my phone and soon we're on a part-commercial, part-residential block and something runs into the road and I slam on my breaks to discover that something is Jamal, now jogging around to the back and letting himself in.

"Really?" I ask. "You thought it would be a good idea to run in front of my car as I was driving?"

"You were going a little faster than I expected. I thought you saw me."

We sit in silence for a minute as I try to get my heart rate back to normal. Eventually, Jamal says, "If you could pull away soon that'd be great. I'm not supposed to be doing this right now."

I drive around the corner.

"So where should we look?" I ask.

"Honestly?" Jamal says. "I have no idea. All I could think of was your place."

Charlotte says, "It might help if you tell us what happened."

"I don't know. I feel weird about this. She really likes you guys and I don't want to change the way you think about her. She's a great girl."

"We know she's great," I say.

Charlotte smirks at me. "We've actually had a similar discussion," she says, "about her greatness."

"All right." He takes a breath. "So, it's like this. I don't know what you guys did today, but when she came home she was a mess."

"A mess how?" I ask.

"Throwing shit around her room, saying things I didn't understand. What happened?"

"We had to go to the apartment where Caroline used to live," I tell him. "It was for the movie, but Ava wanted to come and ask questions so we let her."

Charlotte says, "She wanted to know about her mom's death."

"And they told her?"

"Yeah," I say.

"And then what?"

"She left and we stayed to talk about the film. The land-lords are letting us use their house for a set but Edie—she's the wife—she had five million questions for us."

"Let me get this straight," Jamal says. "You're telling me that Ava sat there and found out how her mom died, and then you just let her drive away?"

Neither of us says anything.

"Like it was no big thing?" Jamal asks.

"Shit," I say.

"I should have gone out there with her," Char says.

"She seemed okay, though," I say, but the truth is I wasn't paying close enough attention. Edie was there and she wanted to know about the film and there's so much that I need to do that I just let the conversation move in that direction. I just said, "Okay, talk to you soon," when Ava said she had to go.

"Where should we start?" Charlotte asks. "Maybe back to Frank and Edie's?"

"Yeah, that makes sense. She might want to go back to the apartment by herself."

"All right," Jamal says. "Let's go."

Back on the 405, I ask, "Why did they kick her out?"

"She was acting pretty wild. The counselors tried to talk to her but she slammed the door in their faces. I told them she just needed some time, but they're used to some pretty serious shit, you know? They kept saying she could be a danger to herself. I was like, 'Nah, you don't know Ava. She's not like that.' I knew she just needed a little time, but they forced their way back in. She had a bottle of vodka on the table."

I say, "They kicked her out for that?"

"There's a zero-tolerance policy."

We exit Ruby Avenue for the second time today.

"It seems irresponsible to kick someone out when she's in distress like that," Charlotte says. "I mean, I feel bad enough that we let her go this afternoon, but we didn't know that she was upset."

"They were going to let her spend the night," Jamal says. "But she didn't want to stay. She has issues around that stuff, you know."

When we get to Frank and Edie's place, her car is nowhere in sight. We park and walk down their long driveway, but the only car there is the beige station wagon. We circle the block. No silver car.

"Where now?" I ask.

Jamal says, "I have no fucking clue, man."

There's worry in his voice and I can understand why. The streets are deserted. When we do catch sight of someone, he isn't the kind of person we'd feel good running into in the middle of the night alone.

"Was she drinking before she left?" Charlotte asks.

Jamal's quiet.

"It's possible," he says. "I don't know."

"I feel like shit," I say. "Why didn't we at least call her when we left?"

"Let's just find her," Charlotte says. "What about Clyde's house?"

"Clyde's?" Jamal says.

"If she's thinking about her family, why wouldn't she go there?"

"That makes perfect sense," I say. "I don't think she's been there before, but it's an easy address to find."

I head back to the freeway in the direction of the Hollywood Hills, feeling the kind of hopeful that verges on certain. I can picture her there, sitting on his front steps looking out over the glittering lights of the city. We'll get there and she'll be grateful for our company. We'll sneak around the property, look through all his windows, lie in the bottom of his empty pool like the kids in *Rebel Without a Cause*, but unlike James Dean and Sal Mineo and Natalie Wood, we'll end the night feeling better.

I step on the gas and my car heaves itself up the winding hill, turns into the driveway.

The circular drive in front of his house is empty. She isn't here.

I stop the car in front of his house.

"What now?" I ask, trying not to sound as defeated as I feel.

Jamal opens the door and looks around.

"Could she be parked somewhere else?" he asks.

"I don't think so," I say.

"I'll take a quick lap. Just to be sure."

Charlotte and I get out, too. We lean against the car and look at the house where all of this started until he comes back to us.

"Nothing," he says.

We all climb in again.

"You've called her, right?"

"A million times. Straight to voice mail."

"Maybe her phone's battery's dead," Charlotte says.

"I feel terrible," Jamal says.

"Me, too," I say.

"We bought that bottle of vodka together. Weeks ago. We drank most of it together, too. I didn't even get a chance to tell them it was part my fault she had it. She was just gone."

"What about her house?" I ask. "What if she went back to see Tracey?"

"Yeah," Charlotte says. "She had more questions. Maybe she thought Tracey would tell her."

"I don't know," Jamal says. "She says she never wants to go back."

We're all quiet for a while, and I wonder if we're about to give up for the night.

Then Jamal says, "But in a moment of weakness, who knows, right? Let's go check it out."

We barely talk on the ride to Leona Valley. I exit where I did before, but then take a wrong turn and have to backtrack a few blocks.

I turn on to her street, not expecting to see her car there, but there's a silver sedan parked midway up the block, right across from her mother's house.

"Is that it?" I ask.

"Yeah," Jamal says. "Yeah, that's it."

I park behind her car and open my door. I can't imagine her here. It was more of a wish than an actual guess, so I walk up to make sure it's really hers.

She's inside, stretched across the backseat, bobby pins falling out of her hair, hoodie bundled up as a pillow. I know I should look away, but I can't bring myself to do it. There is something kind of moving about seeing someone sleep—I've always felt that. But *this*. It feels bigger than that. Like I could understand so much of Ava if only I could be suspended here for a little while. Like I could look into her heart.

A few seconds later Jamal and Charlotte appear next to me.

"Should we wake her up?" I whisper.

"Nah," Jamal says.

"Are you sure?" I ask. "She looks so lonely."

"She knows where to find us when she wants to," he says. "I just needed to know she was okay."

I look at Charlotte and she nods, so I force myself to turn away from Ava and back toward my car. The sun begins to rise as we get on the freeway, and by the time we're dropping Jamal off it almost looks like daylight.

"Call me if you hear from her?" I ask him.

"Yeah," he says. "You, too, okay?"

"Yeah."

"Thanks," he says. "Sorry if I was hard on you earlier."

"We understand," Charlotte says.

He nods, looks up at the shelter.

"Hey," he says. "If it's okay, let's keep this little adventure to ourselves. It's no big thing. She'd just be embarrassed if you knew what happened tonight. She's really into you guys."

"Us?" I say. "*She's* Ava Garden Wilder."

Jamal raises an eyebrow.

"Yeah, that's her name," he says.

I want to tell him that it's more than just a name. It's where she comes from, who she is, but before I can he says, "Later, y'all," and jogs up the steps.

We drive most of the way back home in silence.

"What did he mean, 'That's her name'?"

"You know what he meant," Charlotte says.

"No, actually. I don't."

"He's saying she's Ava Garden Wilder. Raised in Leona Valley, did drama in high school, ran away from home, works at Home Depot. He's saying that she's just a girl."

"This is Hollywood," I say. "You get to be anyone you want to be. Norma Jeane Mortenson became Marilyn Monroe, Archibald Leach became Cary Grant. Spike Lee's first name is actually Shelton. Ava has been Ava Garden Wilder forever. She just has to embrace it."

When we get home it's almost six already, so we collapse onto the bed and sleep for an hour and then we make coffee like zombies and get to work.

Part 3

THE APARTMENT

Chapter Seventeen

Juniper's apartment is introduced like this:

```
INT. JUNIPER's STUDIO APARTMENT—DAY.
A small bright space filled with PLANTS
and BOOKS.
```

So I've used the plants and books as the starting point and chosen everything else based on them.

This morning Charlotte and I dug through piles of old art books at thrift stores up and down Sunset Boulevard. Stripped of their jackets, they are faded tan and pink and green cloth. I'm going to stack them in corners of the room, using them as makeshift side tables. We're stripping the film history books and DVDs from Toby's bookshelf, but I'll keep his novels on the shelves as they are. Juniper would definitely read novels.

My dream is to create the impression of potted plants hanging from a beam in the ceiling, but Toby is not an indoor plants kind of guy, and I doubt his landlord would appreciate huge holes in the walls. I have no idea how this will work, but I'm browsing a West Hollywood nursery anyway, choosing the plants I want while Charlotte negotiates a loan from the owner. I'm relying on Morgan to create one of her perfect illusions.

"Okay, here's the deal," Charlotte says, walking toward me from the office. "He'll let us rent up to thirty plants for $15 a day, but we have to keep them really healthy, or else he'll make us buy them. How does that sound?"

"Good."

"Choose what you want and put them on this cart, and then I'll do all the paperwork with him and get directions for when to water them all while you go across the street to get pots."

"This is why I need you," I say.

"We still have three other tasks on our list for the day."

I nod and select my thirty plants of various sizes and textures and shades of green. I choose one with yellow flowers to put in a prominent place, and then I let Charlotte deal with the business side while I start looking for pots. But I only find a few that are right, because Juniper would not have matching sets—she would have whatever she could find at the time.

I talk the woman at the register into giving me a deal and then I head back as Charlotte is loading the plants into the back of my car.

My phone rings. Ava.

"Hey," she says. "Guess what? Everything went through. I have access to the bank account."

"So cool," I say, setting the pots in the backseat. "Are you rich?"

"Yeah. I think I am. I just bought myself a forty-dollar lunch." She laughs. "And I got a manicure."

"That's awesome," I say.

"So I need to find a place to live."

I wait, but she doesn't mention getting kicked out so I just say, "We have a couple more errands right now but you could come over after and we could start looking."

"I have a better idea. I'm going to get a room at the Marmont. Meet me there when you're done?"

"Looks like Ava came into a lot of money," I tell Charlotte as she shuts the trunk. "She's checking into the Marmont this afternoon."

She widens her eyes.

"Long term?"

"I don't think so. Just until she finds a place."

"Still," she says. "That's expensive."

"Seriously."

"Did she say anything about last night?"

"No. I guess she doesn't know we went to look for her."

I call Jamal to let him know I heard from her.

"Yeah," he says. "She left me a message when I was at work. Said she was getting a room at some fancy hotel. You gonna go check it out?"

"Yeah, a little later."

"Cool. And remember to keep last night between us if that's all right."

"Sure, that's fine."

"I don't want her feeling weird about it."

"Makes sense," I say. "It was no big deal."

"All right, cool. See you later then."

—

When I get to the Marmont, I find Ava leaning against the outside wall of a poolside bungalow, wearing gold-rimmed sunglasses shaped like John Lennon's, her hair cascading down her shoulders in loose waves. She is still in the green camisole and cutoffs from yesterday but she is barefoot. I've never seen her feet before. All slender and graceful, like they aren't even used for walking.

She leads me inside, where her boots are kicked off across the floor and her purse is hung over a chair. She doesn't have any bags and even though I don't ask her why, she says, "Jamal's coming later to drop off my stuff."

She stands at the center of a red rug. Orange light beats through the window; the edges of her glow.

"Is this what you pictured?" she asks me.

I don't know what she means. But, no, I could have never pictured anything quite as glamorous as this. She is almost too bright to look at.

"When you had me come here the first time. You thought I might come back. Right?"

"Oh," I say. "Yeah. I guess I did."

"When I was booking the room I asked the man where Clyde used to stay. He said this one so that's what I chose. Come here," she says, sitting on the edge of the bed. "Clyde slept here. All those years ago. Can you believe it?"

I kick off my sandals and join her on the bed, unsure of where this is headed.

"I wonder how many women he brought to this room," she says.

Our bodies are so close. I watch as she moves her hand even nearer, until her fingers with their short, perfectly smooth nails are almost touching the soft underside of my knee.

And if she's trying to seduce me right now, I will admit that it's working. My heart beats fast and hard. I can't look at her mouth without imagining it on mine.

This is the moment where I'm supposed to lean in. This is when everything starts. But I can't do it. All at once, Ava feels like a stranger. And it's my fault. I thought that inviting her here a couple weeks ago was such a perfect idea, that creating a glamorous future for her was a nice thing to do. I even thought it was generous, for me, to take the time to show her this place, to tell her about Clyde. But I think I always pictured myself here, with her. If I'm being completely honest, this chance is probably what I hoped for: To have a fling with the granddaughter of a legend in a Chateau Marmont bungalow. To get to be with her when she was still a secret, before the world got ahold of her.

What a stupid thing to wish for. A handful of thrilling days. A good story to tell later. Like what Clyde wrote in his letter to Caroline when he was talking about her mother: *a few minutes in the spotlight on the arm of someone famous.*

Ava is doing exactly what I once hoped she would do, but now, when I picture us together, we're lying in a cherry orchard or I'm watching her bake a cake or we're hunting for treasures in thrift shops. The memory of her curled up on the backseat of her beat-up car in the desert, entirely unaware of me, is enough to make my chest ache. But I don't recognize the Ava I've gotten to know in the girl next to me now. I search her face, but her sunglasses are still on and I can't find her.

There is only one chance to get a first kiss right. I can't shake the feeling that if I kiss her now, it won't be the right version of her I'll be kissing.

So I say, "I brought my laptop. What neighborhoods are you thinking? West Hollywood? Beverly Hills?"

She straightens up, moves a tiny bit away from me, but barely misses a beat.

"Actually," she says. "I was thinking Venice. Somewhere with a view of the ocean."

I rise from the bed, wondering if I'm making a mistake to let this moment go. My laptop is cold and heavy when I sit back down. I open to the browser and hand it to her.

"Oh," Ava says, looking at the screen. "The Internet is locked or something."

"You just need a password. The front desk will give it to us."

Ava stands up and grabs the key.

"You can call them."

I cross to the desk, pick up the phone, and dial zero.

"Hey," I say. "What's the Internet password?"

I read it out to Ava and she enters it. She smiles.

"Success," I tell the man on the other end. "Thanks."

She does a search for Venice apartments and barely ten minutes into looking, she says, "Found it."

"That fast?"

"It has an ocean view. I think it's exactly what Caroline would have chosen. Want to see?"

I'm sitting at the desk now, and I don't know if I trust myself to get back onto that bed with her.

I shake my head.

"I'd rather wait to see it," I say. "Surprise me."

She slips her phone out of her pocket and calls the broker, sets up an appointment for just a couple hours from now.

"I have to look the part, right?" she says when she hangs up. "Where should we shop?"

"I have to go over to Rebecca and Theo's for a meeting," I say. "But *you* should go to the Beverly Center."

"The Beverly Center. Okay."

"It's just a couple miles from here. Take Sunset to La Cienega, and then stay on La Cienega until you hit Beverly."

She nods. "I can do that," she says.

"Venice apartments are hard to come by. It'll be competitive. If the clothes don't work on their own, you could always play the Clyde card."

She's up now, grabbing her keys, slinging her purse over her shoulder.

She grins at me.

"I'll see what I can do."

—

Charlotte and I get to Brooks Avenue at a little after nine, park near the beach, and stroll by the skaters and punks and tourists who look a little afraid of what they've gotten themselves into. I pull out my phone and double-check the address she gave us.

This is a nice building. I mean, *really* nice: white-painted brick with art-deco-style ornamentation. The door to the building is locked so we press a button, and soon Ava's voice comes through the small gold speaker.

"Is it you?"

"Yeah, it's us."

"Take the elevator! Penthouse! Three-twenty-three!"

"Penthouse?" Charlotte says.

I widen my eyes like *I know.*

Then there's a buzzing, which lets us into the lobby. In the elevator, we select *P* for you-know-what, and a screen asks us to enter a code, so we press 3-2-3 and the doors shut and we glide upward. When the elevator opens, we find ourselves on the roof, facing the ocean right in front of us, the Santa Monica pier to our right, its Ferris wheel lit up, silhouettes of palm trees against the dark sky.

We turn around to an apartment made of glass.

Ava stands in the doorway, dressed in high-waisted white jeans and a blue-and-white polka-dotted blouse. She has on bright red lipstick and a pair of shiny, bright red heels, a long string of pearls around her neck.

"Are those real?" I ask her.

"Of course they are. I had to look like a girl who belongs in a penthouse."

Charlotte and I laugh, and Ava takes a seat on an outdoor sofa that must have come with the place. She rests her feet on an ottoman, crosses her ankles. I would hardly have recognized her.

"I went to Bloomingdale's and told the woman to make me look rich."

"It worked," I tell her.

A moment later, Jamal appears next to her, in sagging khaki shorts and a gray ribbed tank top that shows off his muscular body. They couldn't look more incongruous: She's dressed for a lunch meeting at an upscale restaurant and he's dressed for a day at the beach.

"Finally," he says, holding a bottle of champagne by its neck. "We can pop this open."

"We felt like celebrating," Ava says.

"I can see why," I say.

"We don't have any cups, though," Jamal says. "I had to go to five different liquor stores till I found one that didn't card me, and all that time I didn't think about cups."

Charlotte and I both have water bottles, so after Jamal accidentally sends the cork ricocheting off the roof, he fills our tins and then he and Ava pass the rest back and forth between them.

"How did you get this place?" Charlotte asks. "Didn't you need rental histories and references?"

Ava takes a swig out of the bottle.

"Clyde was right," she says.

"How so?" Charlotte asks.

But I know what she means: "Money can open doors," I say.

She nods.

"I told the manager I could write him a check for the full year right now, and then he went to the bank and deposited it and called me back and said the place was mine. It was good timing. Terrence and I just finished the bank paperwork this morning."

"Bank account in the morning, Chateau Marmont in the afternoon, penthouse in the evening," I say.

"Yeah, if Terrence is watching my money, he'll be impressed," she says. "But I didn't have much of a choice."

I don't trust myself to say *Why not?* in a way that's even remotely convincing.

Instead I say, "Show us the inside."

She takes us on a tour of the penthouse. One by one, she flicks on the lights. I can imagine what it must look like from above: a glass house, lit up and glowing in the night. Inside, it looks like it's sprung from the pages of *Dwell* or *Architectural Digest*. Pure white walls, high ceilings, thick-planked wood floors. A bedroom with a closet the size of Toby's old dorm room. A bathroom with a Jacuzzi tub and a shower that takes up half the room and has no door. A modern, airy kitchen opens onto the living room.

"Isn't this the best kitchen you've ever seen?"

I nod, but I actually like my kitchen at home better, and even Toby's tiny kitchen. I understand that this is full of nicer, more expensive appliances, but without pots and pans, cutting boards and mismatched mugs, bowls of fruit, and magnets on the refrigerator it feels too sterile.

"If you need any more locations for filming," Ava says, "you're welcome to use any rooms you want." She's standing in the middle of the cavernous living room under light wood beams and the yellow glow of recessed lighting.

"That's so nice of you," I say, but the truth is that the place has no soul. I haven't seen a single scratched floorboard.

"Don't you think it's great?" Ava asks me a little defensively, and I don't want her to be defensive, because doesn't she deserve this? After everything she's been through, shouldn't she end up with a dream house on the rooftop of one of the most exclusive buildings in Venice?

"It's beyond great," I tell her. "We just need to get it furnished. Let's go look at the view again."

Back outside, everything feels less sad. The skaters are doing tricks on the street below us; the Ferris wheel on the Santa Monica pier spins and spins; from somewhere in the distance comes laughter.

"Can you believe it?" Ava asks. "Last night I was living in a shelter. A few months ago I was living in my car, sleeping under overpasses, hoping no one would find me."

"You were untethered," Jamal says.

"Yeah," she says. "I guess. I never thought of using that word before."

"Marcy used it on me," he says. "I hadn't thought of it either."

"Who's Marcy?" Charlotte asks.

"One of the counselors at the shelter."

"The only nice one," Ava says.

"Not the only nice one. The least strict one. The youngest one."

"It doesn't matter," Ava says. "We never have to go back."

"So you're going to live here, too?" I ask Jamal.

"Nah," he says. "She wants me to, but it's not in the master plan."

He smiles when he says it, looks out over the ocean. I don't question him until later on, after Ava has fallen asleep on one of the outdoor sofas and Charlotte has taken a chair on the other end of the roof to e-mail one of her future professors about something. Jamal and I are sitting together a few feet away from Ava, still looking over the water.

"So explain this to me," I say. "You could live in a shelter or you could live here, and you're choosing the shelter?"

"This place is crazy nice," he says, "but it wouldn't be real for me."

"But you could live here for free, right? Quit your job? What would you want to do if you could do anything?"

He smirks. Shakes his head.

"What?"

"Not everyone's like you," he says.

"What's that supposed to mean?"

"Don't get upset."

"I'm not upset."

"We're friends now, right? So I can tell it to you straight."

"Yeah, okay," I say, trying not to feel hurt already.

"We don't all have it figured out. We don't all have internships and college all lined up and our parents' credit cards."

"I don't have my parents' credit card. I make my own money."

"For some things, yeah," he says. "But we don't all have *dens* with pictures from the ghetto in *frames* on our walls."

"It's not like that," I say. "That makes it sound terrible. My parents care about that stuff, they spend all their time teaching people about it. My grandfather—"

Jamal holds his hand out. I stop.

"I like your family," he says. "Your mom told me about a lot of stuff I didn't know."

"And she called you handsome and graceful."

"She did," he says. "And I'll always love her for it. But my point is that we don't all have brothers getting us fancy jobs in movie studios."

"I get it," I say. And I do. But I still don't want to hear it, don't want to think about the conversations he and Ava must have about me when I'm not around to defend myself.

"What I'm saying is this: The shelter got me my job. And I finally got promoted so now I even get to work decent hours, on the floor, not doing stock. The deal is I work there until I have enough money saved up to get a place, and then the shelter hooks me up with an apartment. I keep the job, I pay part of the rent, and the shelter pays the other part. It's not something I'm trying to get out of. It's not just for the money, even though the money is something I need. I've seen the building where I'll live. It's cool. Near downtown on a quiet street. I need to start my own life and it can't be here. I mean, look. This might work out for Ava, but I'm still a kid who's only been to the beach one other time in my life."

"You mean Venice Beach?"

"No," he says. "I mean the ocean. I mean *this*." He extends his arms toward the coastline. "This."

"But you grew up here," I say. "How did you only come once?"

"If you'd ever been to where I grew up, you wouldn't call it 'here.'"

"What's it like?"

"Pawn shops. Check-cashing stores. Liquor stores."

"Sure," I say, because these places are everywhere.

He holds up his hand as if to say, *Let me finish*, so I shut up and look out at the dark sky and listen.

"Empty buildings," he says. "Guys on the street all day. Fields covered in trash. Street signs full of bullet holes. Boarded-up windows. People who look decades older than they are. Grandmas who just take every tragedy like it's expected, just take another kid into their houses and act like it's not crowded already, like it isn't a burden to feed another one."

"All right," I say. A concession. He's speaking like he's in a trance, like he could go on for ages, but also like it hurts him.

"Guns," he says. "Guns everywhere. I got my first gun when I was twelve. A gift from my cousin. We went out onto the street and I shot it into the sky. Everything went silent."

"So what happened?" I ask. "Why did you leave?"

"My grandma died. I was in the foster system once, before she got custody, and I sure as hell wasn't going back again. There were plenty of ways for me to make a living in the neighborhood, but I didn't want her looking down from above, shaking her head in disgust."

"What about the rest of your family? Do they know where you are?"

"Pops is locked up. My mom's dead."

"So is mine," Ava says.

I don't know when she woke up, but she's sitting now, pulling a hoodie over her legs, and Charlotte's walking back toward us, sitting down next to her.

Jamal turns to Ava, eyebrows raised in skepticism, but she doesn't elaborate.

"All right," Jamal finally says. "It can be that way. But it's the other way, too."

"What do you mean?" Ava asks.

"I mean Caroline is dead, but Tracey is alive. That's rough, but you still have one mother."

"But she doesn't want me."

"I don't know about that," he says. "We'll give it some time. Check back soon, you know?"

"When you really want to find someone, it isn't that hard. I should have known all along that she wasn't looking. I feel so stupid."

"There's nothing stupid about wanting to be loved," he says. "Believe me."

We sit together for a little longer, and then Charlotte and I get up to go home.

"You'll help me decorate, right?" Ava asks me. "Figure out what to buy? After the filming is over, I mean. I went to this place to try to buy a mattress today but I didn't know what I wanted, and it would have taken a few days to get delivered anyway, so after a while it just seemed pointless. I left without choosing anything."

"Sure," I say. "I'd love to do that."

"We have the read-through tomorrow," Charlotte reminds me.

"Right," I say. "Ava, are you ready for that?"

She nods.

"We'll see you then," I say.

Before Charlotte and I step into the elevator, I turn around to get a last glimpse of them for the night: two formerly homeless kids, sitting in front of a bare rooftop penthouse with an empty bottle of champagne.

Chapter Eighteen

I wake up nervous.

Today is the day all the actors assemble in Theo and Rebecca's apartment and read through the script from the first scene through the last. This usually happens earlier in the preproduction schedule, but because Ava signed on so late, it's happening now, just two weeks before the shooting begins.

I should have told Ava what to expect from the day. Should have told her how important it is. I start to worry that I've gone overboard with all the Clyde stuff. What if she takes her rags-to-riches glory too far? What she wore yesterday was the perfect costume to score a penthouse, but today shouldn't be an act. As an unknown in a lead role, she has a lot to prove.

"She's going to be fine," Charlotte says as we climb into her car.

"But what if she shows up like all hung over or something?"

"She wasn't even drunk last night. How would that be possible?"

"I don't know how it would be possible. All I know is that my stomach hurts for her."

"Just relax and focus on your own job. Let Ava's stomach hurt for itself. Or, even better, trust that she'll do well. We have no reason to doubt her."

And when we get there, I see that Charlotte, as usual, is right.

Ava is making the rounds with Rebecca as her guide. She is holding her hand out to shake, confident but modest, professional but warm.

The actors are gathering around the table while members of the crew find spots to sit on the periphery. Charlotte and I scavenge two chairs just as Rebecca and Ava reach us.

"No introductions necessary in your case," she says.

Even though we were together yesterday and last night, seeing Ava in this context makes my heart race. She smiles at us and widens her eyes, almost imperceptibly, but enough to let us in on the secret that she's a little bit nervous. I watch as they move on to meet Grant and Vicki, who apologize for the bad timing but whip out their measuring tape anyway.

"We still have *all* your costumes to figure out," Grant says as Vicki measures Ava's waist. "Nice tank, by the way," he adds.

Her outfit is deceptively simple: tight jeans and a silk navy top that makes her shoulders look amazing. A couple of bangles hang off one wrist and delicate gold earrings appear every time she brushes her hair from her face. When she steps away I notice her signature boots and think of them kicked off on the Marmont floor, when we were sitting so close to each other.

I wonder, again, if I made a mistake.

Charlotte and I get out our scripts and pens. This is only the second time I've been included at a read-through, and the first time I was surprised by how much I picked up on that I hadn't when I read it to myself, even though I had studied every scene. So I'm ready to be inspired, to be reminded, to find new opportunities to bring the sets to life.

Then, behind me, I hear Ava say, "Hi, Morgan. So nice to meet you."

I can't help it: I turn to see them.

Rebecca is the one talking but Morgan is looking at Ava, and I can only imagine the things she is thinking. When she told me about the vastness, I'm sure that the Avas of the world were what she was imagining: talented and gorgeous, utterly free and a little bit wild. But as Morgan looks at Ava, Ava turns to look at me, and I suspect that the Morgans of the world are not who Ava would want in return.

At least I hope they aren't. I allow myself to believe that flirtatious and fickle isn't what Ava wants. That, more than invitations to Hollywood parties and Silver Lake brunches, Ava wants someone who will love her back.

"All right, everyone." Theo's voice carries through the room, a happy, festive thunder. "Please take your seats."

Soon, the chatter dies down; the people all settle.

"Look at you all," Theo says.

We have filled the apartment, everyone smiling.

All the actors for all the speaking parts, from Juniper and George to the nameless customer with only one line, sit around the dining room table, Ava, Benjamin, and Lindsey next to one another at one of the heads. Those of us in the crew have taken over the adjoining living room. Charlie and his volunteer camera operators and key grip got here early enough to snag the sofa. Michael and his brother sit on the floor. They got here the latest because Kim, the USC student who is assistant directing, forgot to tell them about the meeting until a couple hours ago.

"Everyone always forgets the sound guy," Michael grumbled as he came in, but even he looks happy now.

As the weeks have gone by, word about the project has been spreading. Instead of our bare-bones crew we now have a script supervisor and an onset photographer, who stand, holding hands, in the doorway, peering into the dining room. We have gaffers and a best boy and three grips who will set up the lights and keep track of equipment; they sit next to the buffet eating cookies and sneaking glances at Ava and Benjamin. There are others, too: a girl with pale blond hair who looks about my age, a guy with an ironic mustache. I don't know what they'll be doing yet but they have notebooks out and look ready to work.

"Can you feel the energy in this place?" Theo asks. "My God, it's beautiful. Most of you are doing this for free. Those of you who are getting paid are getting nothing close to what you're worth. I know that and I thank you. Sincerely. I thank you. I couldn't imagine a better group of people. If I had ten million dollars to make this movie, I would still choose you. I mean that."

He takes a breath, extends his arms to the people at the table.

"These actors," he says, "are about to stun us with their talent. Let's begin."

He and Rebecca share a love seat, each of them with their own copies of the script.

Rebecca begins to read:

"Scene one. Interior. A small Los Angeles grocery store. Bright summer light

shines through the windows. Juniper, 19,
stocks jars of baby food in an aisle.
George, mid-40s, stands behind the register staring out the window. Enter
Miranda, in a blue dress. She picks up
a red plastic basket, a grapefruit, a
box of oatmeal, a bar of chocolate. She
falls. Juniper drops a jar of baby food.
End scene.
"Scene two. Interior. Grocery store.
Juniper stands behind the cash register.
George places lemons in a basket near
the window."

Ava has the first line. I can feel everyone in the apartment holding their breath.

"The jar cut her ear," Ava says. She has her script open on the table but she isn't reading it.

Benjamin James, however, has his eyes fixed to the page when he responds, "It did? I didn't notice."

Ava touches the top of her right ear.

"Right here," she says.

And with these few words she's already proven herself. She's understated, wistful, everything she's meant to be. Theo and Rebecca exchanged pleased looks, and I turn to my script, my stomach not hurting at all, and read along as the scene continues.

GEORGE

Her skirt was blue, like this.
                    (points to a magazine)

JUNIPER

Lighter, I think.

GEORGE

Maybe, but not much.

Silence.

GEORGE

You know, in ancient times, when someone
had a seizure people thought it meant
they were inhabited by demons.

JUNIPER

That's ridiculous. How do you know that?

George shrugs.

JUNIPER

What do you mean 'in ancient times'?

GEORGE

Ancient. You know, people in Babylonia
or something.

JUNIPER

Babylonia? Did you read this somewhere?

GEORGE

I don't remember. It's just something I
know.

JUNIPER

How do we know she even had a seizure?

GEORGE

What else could it have been?

JUNIPER

It could have been just some weird reaction to something, or an anxiety attack,
or something. We don't know.

GEORGE

Okay! Whatever. It was what it was.
Someone comes into the market. They look
up; it's not her.

GEORGE

I was not implying that she was inhabited by demons. Obviously.

JUNIPER

You weren't implying anything. I know.

—

I have a canvas bag full of home-decorating magazines and catalogues, four tacos from my favorite truck, and a large *aguas frescas* to share. Thankfully, a man is leaving Ava's apartment as I arrive, and he holds the door open for me. I press the call button to the elevator with my elbow, then *P*, then 3-2-3. The doors shut and send me on my way to Ava's.

I am arriving unannounced.

I want to surprise her.

We haven't spoken since the read-through and I didn't even get a chance to tell her how amazing she was because Morgan caught me right after it was finished to talk about the next steps for the sets. And now two days have passed, bringing me closer to the looming deadline for Juniper's apartment.

But I can't stop thinking about Ava.

So, here I am, setting down the bright pink juice to knock on her door, armed with everything I need to help her brainstorm decorating ideas.

She opens the door in plaid pajama bottoms and a thin T-shirt and I try not to look at the gorgeous way it clings to her.

"Surprise! I come bearing lunch and decorating ideas," I say.

"And I am still in my pajamas at noon," she says.

But she smiles and lets me in anyway.

She glances down at herself, blushes, says, "Let me just, um . . . I'll be right back."

"Sure," I say, and she pats off down the hall.

So I find myself alone, for the moment, in Ava's place. Though it's only been a couple days since she moved in and it's still mostly empty, she has filled one corner, under a sky-light, with the things that she owns. And I realize that I have never seen how Ava lives. I never went inside the shelter. She didn't let me into her old room. She didn't have any of her own things in the Marmont, and the only other time I came to the penthouse it was bare.

I cross the room to the kitchen and set the tacos and juice on the counter. I see that she has bought herself a few things:

Two heavy red skillets, one large and one small.

Three cookbooks: on baking bread, on making jam, on French desserts.

A deep copper pot that looks almost too beautiful to cook with.

A small yellow bowl full of peaches.

I notice the faint sound of music and voices. It's coming from the other side of the living space, so I cross to the corner under the skylight, where Ava has laid out a colorful blanket. Sitting on the blanket is an old TV/VCR, playing *The Restlessness* with the volume down low. Next to that is the paperwork for her lease. I hadn't seen her signature before. It's simple, assured: a strong *A, G,* and *W* with flowing lines after each. The screenplay to *Yes & Yes* rests there, too, opened to the audition scene. Next to the line, "I threw them away," Ava has written, "Remember: long pause."

And then there is the photograph of Caroline out on the sunny street in her ripped jeans and flannel, neatly placed next to Clyde's letter. I take it out of its envelope. Reading it again, now, the phrases feel different.

some kind of beginning . . .

the possibility of a change of heart . . .

*I don't know how a father is supposed to say heartfelt things,
or express regret, or give a compliment . . .*

It's possible that you feel alone in the world . . .

It's like they suddenly mean more, and I can't even finish
reading because I'm afraid I might cry.

A perfectly sharpened pencil and a pink highlighter sit
next to a to-do list. *Practice lines. Buy plates, cups, silverware.
Decide about boxes. Find a good coffee shop. Finish letter to
Jonah. Humane society?*

Footsteps come from behind me. I turn around to find
Ava dressed for the day, her hair pulled back in a ponytail, her
mouth pinker than usual, as though she put on lipstick and
then changed her mind.

She says, "I always wish there was one last shot of Caroline's face. Like, the camera would just linger on her looking
out the window, waiting to see if Max comes back."

Instead, the screen goes dark and the music for the credits
begins.

"I haven't gotten plates yet. I couldn't find any that felt
right. And since I'm starting from scratch, I want everything I
buy for myself to mean something. Maybe we can find something in one of those."

She gestures to my bag full of magazines as she heads to
the kitchen.

Even though I chose them all carefully and brought only
my favorites, I now realize that I don't want to use anything
in these magazines. Not *Anthology* with its full-page spreads
of the warm and bright houses of the creative and fortunate,

not *Apartamento* with its international flair and naturalistic feeling.

I don't want to open any of them. I don't want to look away from what Ava has already placed in her home.

My eyes tear up again and I don't know why. I'm not even thinking about Clyde's letter. I don't even understand what's happened.

Until Ava comes back with the bag of tacos and the *aguas frescas* and two gray-and-white-striped cloth napkins. She sits on the edge of her blanket, in front of the few things that she owns.

"We can pretend that it's totally normal to eat without plates or forks, right? Picnic under the skylight," she says.

And I understand what this is.

It's the opposite of the collapse of the fantasy.

It's what happens when the illusion pales in comparison to the truth. I'm seeing her for the first time. Not Ava Garden Wilder, the rags-to-riches granddaughter of Clyde Jones. Not a tragic, romantic heroine.

Just Ava.

And I am utterly in love.

—

"I always wait to see her name," she says, looking at the screen.

I lower myself next to her, grateful that she's looking at something other than me.

I can't eat. I can feel how close she is to me. There is a square of sunlight on her knee. A diamond of sunlight on her face.

I force myself to look at the names as they scroll by.

It always amazes me to think about how many people work on a film, especially big studio productions, so I try to distract myself with the credits. I don't even understand what all of the jobs are. The names roll on and on, and Caroline's name flashes by but I don't look away yet. The *Yes & Yes* credits will be so short, and my name will be there early, all by itself in the center of the screen, and I'm thinking about that as I watch the names of all these strangers and wonder what they're doing now, if they made it to the positions they wanted, or if not what became of them, and then I see a name that leaps out at me but it's gone in a moment and Ava says, "Okay, I'm sorry, you probably don't have much time," and I say, "No problem," and try to shrug off the feeling that I may have seen something important.

"These tacos are delicious," she says.

She takes a last bite and I have to look away. Even that is so beautiful it hurts.

"We should sit outside," she says. "Look through what you brought. Did you see the view when you came up? It's totally different in the daylight."

"That sounds great," I manage to say.

She stands up first and we get as far as the doorway before I blurt out, "I saw something in the credits that I didn't notice before."

She turns around to face me.

"A second assistant director credit for a guy named Leonard."

Her eyes widen.

"It's probably nothing," I say.

But she's already heading back to the corner. She kneels on the blanket and rewinds and then we watch the credits again.

"When is it?" she asks.

"Later on."

"But you said director?"

"The second AD gets people coffee. It's not exactly high profile."

Caroline's name passes.

"Soon," I say. "Here!"

Ava presses pause. The name vibrates at the top of the screen: Leonard Pine.

I pull out my phone and search his name.

"Something's here," I say, opening the first link that appears, and I don't tell her that it doesn't say Leonard—it says Lenny—because I can't stand the thought of disappointing her if he isn't the right person. "He's a producer now."

"Is there a number for him?"

"Yeah, for his office," I say. "I don't know if—"

"What is it?" Ava asks.

I tell her and she dials.

"We don't know it's him," I say. "It's such a long shot."

"May I speak to Leonard?" she says into the phone. She waits for a moment. "Ava Garden Wilder. Yes, okay."

She looks at me and shakes her head. "She's never going to connect me. We'll have to go there."

"Let's just see what happens. Maybe I can find someone who knows him."

"Yes," she says into the phone. "Yes, Ava Garden Wilder. Is this Leonard? Lenny?"

The knuckles of one hand are white from grasping the phone, and then she reaches out to me and squeezes my shoulder with the other as she says, "Yes, her name was Caroline. Yes, I can come now."

And I know that this is a major breakthrough. I know that all I should be thinking about is Lenny and what he's about to tell us. But, instead, what I think about is how her hand squeezing my shoulder feels like a kiss.

She lets go.

Touch me again, I want to tell her. But I don't.

Chapter Nineteen

"We found Lenny," I tell Charlotte when she answers.

Ava is pulling her beat-up car out of her fancy garage and I'm sitting next to her in the passenger's seat even though I'm due back at work in twenty minutes.

"Are you kidding?" she asks.

"No. And I know we're supposed to be putting up the artwork but I'm sort of headed downtown right now."

"We can do it tonight," she says. "It's fine. This is amazing. How did you do it?"

"I'll tell you everything as soon as we're done."

"You'd better," she says. "I can't believe I'm missing this."

"I know," I say.

"It's fine. I'll do as much on my own as I can. I'll tell Rebecca you got some great idea and ran off to make magic happen."

"I love you," I say.

"Yeah, I know," she says. "Call me as soon as it's over."

And soon we are parked in a twenty-dollar-an-hour parking garage, riding a silver elevator to the thirty-seventh floor of a sleek office building, stepping out into a lobby with a pristine white carpet.

"How often do you think they have to replace this?" I whisper, but Ava isn't looking down. She heads straight to the guy at the desk and tells him that Lenny's expecting us. Then a door opens and a tall man with thinning brown hair and a white linen shirt appears. He looks at both of us but soon his gaze shifts to Ava only. A faint smile flickers and vanishes across his

angular face, and then he ushers us in. We follow him down a hallway and into a corner office with a view of Los Angeles I've never seen before, so different from Ava's view from only three stories up. From up here, it would be easy to forget that life exists below you.

Lenny sits in his office chair and I leave the seat across from him for Ava while I take the sofa behind her, a little out of the way but still close enough to hear everything he says.

"This is my friend Emi," Ava says. "She drove me." Which isn't true, but I nod and say hi, because I understand that kind of lie the way I understood from the moment she said she'd go straight over that I would be with her. Some things are just impossible to do alone.

"Emi," he says. "Hello."

He gives me a weak wave and I lift my hand in response, aware that these are the first words exchanged among us.

Finally, Ava says, "I have some questions."

"Yes, of course you do," Lenny says.

This isn't the response I would have expected. The child of a dead woman he used to know suddenly appears in his office almost two decades later, and he knows that *she* has questions?

But he lifts his hands over his head in a motion of surrender, and sweat beads on his cleanly shaven face, and each time he looks at Ava he averts his eyes as though she were too much to behold.

And then he launches into the past as though he's known this moment would someday come and has preserved the story in some easily accessed recess of his brain. And here is his moment. And here we are. So he tells us everything.

It turns out that Lenny and Caroline went way back, grew up down the block from each other.

"What do you know about her parents?" he asks.

"I know that her mom is dead. I know Clyde Jones was her dad."

"How did you find out?"

"From Emi," she says.

"My friend and I found a letter hidden in a Patsy Cline record," I tell him. "We bought it at his estate sale."

"Wild. I really think that besides Caroline's mother and Caroline—well, and Clyde, of course—that I was the only person alive who knew that for a long time. Mrs. Maddox—Valerie—was a terribly bitter woman. I've never met such a bitter woman, and believe me, I've met a *lot* of women."

I laugh and say, "*Okay,*" but Ava doesn't appear amused by him. She's the way she was the first time in the Marmont, when she asked me if we knew how Caroline died: focused and intent, bracing herself for the answers she's been searching for almost her whole life. And here, finally, is someone who can talk about her whole life. The only person who can and is willing to, already mentioning Clyde and Caroline as though they were just people, not clues in a mystery, not elusive characters in a cinematic life.

"Valerie's house was always dark and she walked around in her robe all day, and poor Caroline, she only wanted to be happy. She ate dinner at my house most nights, but then Mrs. Maddox would get angry and keep her inside for a week. After a while Caroline could come back, but she always had to do her time at home in that horrible, dark, dusty house, with her mother pacing around smoking cigarettes and thinking about the man who betrayed her. For years she never even told Caroline that Clyde was her father. Caroline found out eventually when a letter came when her mom wasn't home. Apparently Clyde tried to send money and letters for years, and Valerie had them sent back. I found that out later, a couple months after Valerie died. Caroline and I were in our twenties and we met Clyde at a restaurant."

I don't think of myself as an entirely trusting person, but everything Lenny's saying fits what we already know, and there's something about the way he's telling us this that makes me believe him.

"Caroline was pregnant with you," he says.

"So that's how he knew my name," Ava says.

"No. She didn't tell him. She was upset about seeing him. It was just too much for her. It's hard to believe, but it was the first time they ever met. He explained it to us that day. He and Caroline's mom had a fling—it only lasted a week or two—and he didn't even know she was pregnant until a mutual friend told him. Until Caroline found that letter when she was about eleven, she didn't have any idea who her dad might have been; and then when she *did* find out, her mom polluted her mind with these accusations: He was fame-obsessed. He would never admit that Caroline was his. The money he sent was to pay them to keep their mouths shut. I guess it was her word against Clyde's, but the man I met that day didn't seem like any of the things Valerie made him out to be. He seemed sad and lost and a little bit desperate. But Caroline didn't know how to react to everything. She didn't tell him what she was planning to name you. She hardly said anything.

"He knew your name because he found *me* somehow. I got a call from him one night, just a couple weeks after you were born. He wanted to know about you, but mostly he wanted your name. I told him Ava Garden and he laughed. He said something like, 'Caroline is more like me than she would like to believe,' which I chose to interpret as a comment about family and rejection. That she would prefer to invent a last name than to carry one on. That all of them were root-less—Clyde and Valerie and Caroline and now Ava. Clyde was raised by relatives, you know. An aunt and uncle for a while, a grandmother, passed back and forth in this big family."

"I didn't know that," Ava says. "He mentioned that he was an orphan in the letter, but I didn't know the specifics."

I *did* know it, though, and I don't know why I hadn't thought to mention it before.

"Yeah," he says. "A lot of people theorize that that's why he was so private. I was always touched by that, though. That he would just want your name."

"It was for a bank account," Ava says.

Lenny looks surprised, but then he shakes his head.

"Maybe he wanted to know for the account, but he also wanted to know just to know. Believe me. I could hear it in his voice. I never told Caroline about that call. She thought that meeting him had been a mistake and she was spinning out of control. The guy who got her pregnant was just a one-night stand, so she was on her own and she was scared."

He looks stricken for a moment.

"I hope you weren't hoping to find your father," he says. "Caroline never knew his last name but she wouldn't have tried to find him anyway."

"Why not?" Ava asks.

"It just wasn't like that. Caroline chose him for a good time one night, not to be a father to her child. And then we were sort of together by the time we met Clyde. I was never into the kind of life she led. Drugs didn't sit that well with me. To be honest, they fucked me up, and not in the intended way. But I would have done anything for Caroline and it was beginning to seem like the only way I could be with her was to live her kind of life. So I did, for a little while. And then one day . . ."

He turns his chair away from us, toward his majestic view, but he's hunched forward the way people are when they're about to pass out and someone tells them to put their head between their knees. After a while he turns back around to face us.

"Look," he says. "Whoo! I just gotta say this. I've been carrying this thing around with me for years. For all your life. Holy shit. Okay."

First Ava, then Frank, then Edie, and now Lenny. I don't know when so many strangers will ever cry in front of me in such quick succession and with such feeling again. I try not to look away because it's clear: He's giving us this moment. I don't even know what he's about to say but I already know that remorse is part of it.

"And then one day she wasn't answering my calls. I had been over the night before. Over with a lot of other people. I left before the party was done and I wanted to call her before going back the next morning because I didn't want to find her with somebody else. I was faithful to her but only for my own sake, so I could pretend we really had something. Caroline was the most honest woman I've ever known. Once she told me that she could love me but she couldn't be true to me. I said, *Where's the commitment in that?* And she said, *That's the point: There is none.* And that was the last thing we ever said about it. But I never wanted to catch her with another man, so I liked to give her warning when I was headed her way. I had been calling and calling and she didn't answer, so finally I went. I tried the door but it was locked so I used the key she'd given me and I let myself in. She wasn't in the living room and I knew that something terrible had happened because the record player was spinning and spinning but no sound was coming because the record was over, and the baby was crying. *You* were crying. And not the strong kind of *Pick me up* or *Feed me* crying, but a weaker, desperate kind. I made my way down the hallway and I found her in the bathroom. I forced myself to touch her even though I knew right away that she was gone.

"Let me tell you: In that moment it was like my whole childhood was undone. All those dinners we had together that my mom made us. All the games we played. All the growing up we did. All the sex we had. All the conversations that felt important. They were obliterated. They were fucking *gone.* I was alone in the world and the world was an ugly, brutal place. I made it to the phone and I dialed nine-one-one and when the operator answered I told her that a baby and her mother needed help and I gave her the address and then I left the phone off the hook and I got the fuck out."

He stops talking and the room is painfully silent. That kind of loss he's describing? Just one look at Ava's face shows that she's felt it, too.

I want to confess. I thought that her story was comprised of scenes. I thought the tragedy could be glamorous and her grief could be undone by a sunnier future. I thought we could pinpoint dramatic events on a time line and call it a life.

But I was wrong. There are no scenes in life, there are only minutes. And none are skipped over and they all lead to the next. There was the minute that Caroline set Ava down and the minutes it took her to shoot up. There was the minute that Caroline died and all of the minutes before Lenny discovered them. The minute he left Ava there, still crying, and the minutes before the ambulance came. And all of the minutes that followed that, wherever she went next, whoever held her, so many gaps in memory that must have been filled by something important. I want to apologize for not realizing sooner that what I felt in Clyde's study was not the beginning of a mystery or a project. She was never something waiting to be solved. All she is—all she's ever been—is a person trying to live a life.

~

"Later on, I tried to keep in touch with you," Lenny says. "You probably won't believe me. I could have tried harder, I'm sure. I bought you a trampoline when you were a kid," he says. "Do you remember that?"

"That was you?"

His face brightens, a flash of happiness in the midst of his sweating, teary nervousness.

"But," Ava says, "the guy who bought me the trampoline was with Tracey."

"Tracey," he says. "Right. That was a strange time in my life."

"You had a relationship with her, too?"

He nods, a little sheepishly.

"Tracey always had a thing for me," he says. "I don't want to flatter myself, but she did. She was a kid with us, too. Caroline knew her even longer than she knew me. After I found Caroline, I dropped out of reality for a while. I left town. I didn't think I'd be a suspect or anything, but I was sure I'd be questioned. I had all these nightmares about lie detector tests. I was afraid of being humiliated. I was just . . . I was wrecked. And your mother," he says, leaning closer to Ava, "she was the love of my life. If you ever repeat that to my wife I'll deny it. But she was. God, was she a special woman. She could have been a great actress. She could have been a great mother if she weren't so incredibly fucked up."

He leans back in his chair and swivels toward the window. For a few moments, we all take in his breathtaking view of Los Angeles.

"She was crazy about you," he says. "There's no way she did it on purpose."

But he says it like he's trying to convince himself, and it becomes clear that this is yet another thing we won't ever know. If Caroline intentionally took more drugs than her body could endure. Why Clyde couldn't be a better father. What Ava's life would have been if Tracey had not become her mother.

"But back to Tracey," Lenny says. "I had a few wandering years. I traveled all over the world. I was getting clean, finding myself. I tried to be a Buddhist but couldn't make all the sacrifices. I could only go so far. Then I returned to LA ready to pick up where I left off in my career. Luckily I still had some friends in the business and they gave me work. I had been thinking about you a lot. Wondering how you were. I abandoned you. I knew the ambulance would come and they would take you away but that isn't absolution. I know that. Now that I have kids of my own, I can hardly believe the coward I was then. But as I was saying. I got back to town and I looked Tracey up. She wasn't easy to get ahold of, but eventually I found her, and she had me come over to this god-awful motel where you were living, and we spent a long time commiserating. She's the only one, besides you now, who knew what I'd done. I confessed it to her that night but she had already suspected it was me who called the police. We ended up sleeping together. You're old enough to know that. I woke up to you staring at me, standing at the foot of the bed. You'd been asleep already when I got there the night before. You look so much like Caroline. You did even then. I thought, I'm going to see how far this can go with Tracey. We had Caroline in common. We had you in common. You and I had fun for a while. Tracey and I, not so much. Eventually we both knew that we weren't right for each other. She was still living a pretty rough life, and I had changed. I asked her if I could still spend time with you and she said yes, but keeping up with her wasn't easy."

"We moved around a lot," Ava says.

"'A lot' doesn't even come close. Seems like Tracey had a new boyfriend every couple weeks. At one point, when I started getting really nervous, I asked her if she'd let you stay with me for a little while, just while she got back on her feet, but she said no."

"*Why?*" I ask. I can't help myself.

He looks at me, then back to Ava. "You made her feel safe," he says. "That's what she told me. She said that she would never go too far as long as you were with her. She told me that you saved her life in more ways than she could explain."

Ava shakes her head. I can see her fighting off tears.

"That isn't how she feels now."

"Well, no. That was before all of her transformations. I suppose AA or some self-help guru or Jesus saves her life now."

Ava looks surprised at the bitterness in his voice.

"Yeah," she says. "Exactly. Why did that happen?"

He leans forward, buries his head in his hands. Finally, he sits back again.

"I don't know all the details. We'd been out of touch for about a year, and she called me and asked if I could meet her for lunch. You were in school, I guess. She was wearing a lot of makeup because someone had beaten her up. It was pretty ugly, I remember, even with her attempts to hide it. She wanted money. She needed to pay to get her car fixed and then she was going to take you and go to stay with her parents for a while in Arcadia. I gave her the money, and she left for her parents' a few days later."

"I remember staying there. They had a yard and a lot of books."

"Right. You guys stayed there for a couple of months. She was in rehab and she thought it might work for her that time.

She was trying really hard and I felt better, knowing that you were with her folks. Then, she met a guy who said he could help her and she moved way the fuck out there. To Leona Valley."

"She's still there."

"Really," he says. "I guess I already knew that. I just didn't want it to be true. I got married seven years ago. Our first year of marriage, my wife got all excited. She wanted to send out holiday cards. We got our picture taken wearing Santa hats and posed with the dog. Amazing, isn't it?—the things we'll do for love. She asked me for a list of addresses, and I thought about you guys. I gave her your name and address and she sent it out. I didn't know if you'd remember me, but I'd hoped that you would. But then the letter came back in the mail. Someone had written 'return to sender' and I tried to tell myself that it wasn't Tracey's writing, that it was the writing of a stranger, but I think I knew. Secretly, it was what I expected."

He looks at his watch.

"Damn," he says. "I pushed back a meeting in order to see you, but I can't push it back any longer."

Ava stands up and I stand up, too.

"So, look," he says, walking us back down the hallway toward the lobby. "I know that to you I'm just some distant memory. Maybe less than that. But will you keep in touch with me? Just now and then. Give me your address, my wife will send you a holiday card."

"She's going to be in your business soon," I tell him.

"That right?"

"I have a part in a film," she says. "A small film."

"Not that small," I say.

"You take after your mother," Lenny says. "In the best ways."

"That's how we found you," I tell him. We're all in the lobby now, and Lenny gives the "one minute" gesture to a group of eager young men. He turns back to me.

"From *The Restlessness*," I say.

He cocks his head.

"I saw your name and we made a wild guess."

"Caroline was the best part of that movie," he says. "Don't you think?"

We say, "Yes," and he says, "Thank you," and then he beams at Ava, regret still clouding his face, before turning away from us and ushering the men in. He shuts his door and then we are back in the silver elevator, plummeting down to the street.

Chapter Twenty

I have to make up for lost time. I talk to Toby in the morning, tell him all about *Yes & Yes*. He's excited, but I can tell he's also skeptical. I don't tell him about the famous actors who'll be in it. I don't tell him that I'm using his apartment. But I do tell him about my design ideas, and about them he is not skeptical. He congratulates me. He wishes me luck. He shows me some photos of locations he's found in London and they look opulent and larger than life, just as they should. Then we say good-bye, I shut my computer, and I start packing up all of his stuff.

Charlotte works on the DVDs and books; I take artwork off the walls, framed photographs and souvenirs from his travels and mementos from movies off his shelves. Charlotte takes pictures so we'll know how to replace everything when we're finished shooting. I move the sofa and roll up the shag rug, ready to replace it with the ones Rebecca found at the Rose Bowl. The orange chair stays, but I'll be covering it with a Southwestern-style blanket to tone down the color.

Charlotte and I wrap up Toby's dishes, which are too modern for Juniper. Instead, we'll use Rebecca and Theo's plates and bowls and mugs, handmade, from San Francisco. They're way too expensive for Juniper, but this is the movies, after all, and the simple feeling of them is perfect.

"Hey," Charlotte says. "Did Ava call you?"

She's looking at her phone and I realize I don't know where mine is, which only happens when I lose myself in this kind of project. I find it under a pile of pillows on the couch.

"Yeah," I say. "Twice."

"Me, too," she says.

"Did she leave a message?"

"No."

"Not for me, either."

"We can call her later," Charlotte says, and I set my phone back down and keep working.

A few minutes later there's a knock at the door and Morgan walks in.

"You made it!" I say, and I can feel Charlotte's disapproval over my enthusiasm, but I can't help it. Morgan's here to rig the hanging plants contraption; she's here to affix wallpaper to removable panels. In other words: She's here to make my dreams come true.

But only some of them.

"Did you doubt me?" She laughs.

"No," I say.

"Though she had every reason to," Charlotte says.

"Hey, Charlotte," Morgan says, ignoring her comment.

Grudgingly, Charlotte says hey back.

I show Morgan my plans for the apartment and she's the perfect person to help me because she's done this sort of thing so many times. She knows, for example, how low the plants should hang in order for them to be in a lot of the shots.

"Once I worked on a set where I did all of this detail work on the wall near the ceiling," she tells me. "First I put up this molding and then I painted it gold and blue. Really intricate. And then, when the movie came out, it wasn't even in it. The camera never panned that high. One thing you need to do when a shot is being set up is stand with Charlie and look at the monitor. Be sure to tell him when you want something in the shot, when you think it's important."

"I'm allowed to do that?"

"Oh yeah," Morgan says. "They'll expect you to do it. And be prepared for him to ask you for changes, too. Like if he's trying to get a certain shot but he needs it to be simpler, or something's in the way."

"I'm so glad you're telling me this."

"There's more," she says. "But first let's talk about this hanging thing."

I show her the pots I've collected, explain that I'm going to be borrowing some others from my parents' house and from Theo and Rebecca's jungle-like yard. Many of them will sit on the low wooden table in place of Toby's TV, but I want a cluster of them to hang by a window to the right, not blocking the light, but catching it. I show her some red twine I found.

"I want this to be wrapped around the pots as if it's hanging from a hook in the ceiling."

"That'll contrast well with the green."

"And I want them to be at various heights, and a lot of them—a dozen at least. There's that scene where she's watering her plants and crying, remember? I want the plants to go on forever."

"But no holes in the ceiling," she says.

"Is that possible?"

"Anything is possible."

She takes some measurements, sketches something out, and then tells me she's going to pick up some supplies.

"We have a friend who might be able to get a discount," I say. "Let me see if he's working."

I find my phone again and see that I have a text from Ava: *Finding Caroline's death certificate. Meet me downtown?*

I text back: *Can't today. I'll call you tonight.*

Then I text Jamal to see if he's at work and he is. *Any chance you could share your discount?* I write.

Gotta keep this job, he responds. *But I am happy to provide you with unparalleled customer service.*

So I tell him to expect Morgan; tell Morgan to ask for Jamal.

"Okay," she says. "I'll pick up everything I need and come back. But first, come out to the truck. I have something you might want."

Charlotte shoots me a glance from where she's been wrapping dishes in old copies of the *LA Weekly*. She thinks this is a ruse to get me alone, but I ignore her and go outside anyway.

Morgan's saying, "I thought about it after you described your ideas for Juniper's apartment but didn't want to bring it up in case it didn't come through, but then this morning I got a call, and . . ."

And there is my sofa: green and gold and soft, sitting in the bed of Morgan's truck.

"So can you use it? It's no problem to take it back if you can't."

"Yes," I say. "I can definitely use it."

She lets down the gate and we carry the sofa into Toby's house together, and then we set it down in the living room and I thank her as though it doesn't mean much. Like it's just some nice thing that anyone would do.

My phone buzzes with a new text: *I have to wait two hours! Wish you were here with me.*

Oh no! Wish I could be there, I write.

Morgan says, "I'll be back in about an hour."

"All right," I say. "See you soon," but I'm distracted, realizing I don't know what Ava's really looking for out there in whatever bureaucratic office she's waiting in.

Tell me when you get it, I write back, even though I don't know why she needs Caroline's death certificate. Maybe she just wants more closure than Lenny was able to give her.

—

"Let's hang the pots," Morgan says hours later, after she's been to Home Depot and back, after I've finished a dozen small tasks and she's built the hanging contraption in the courtyard and installed it in the living room.

So we hang them, one after another, terra-cotta and porcelain and tin, orange and white and silver, full of all of these leafy green plants. She holds open the red string and I place the pots inside.

"Watching you work is incredible," she says. "I can't believe how good it's looking in here."

"I couldn't do it without you."

She shakes her head. "You're much better at this than I am."

"Not true," I say.

"Yes," she says, "I have the skills but you have the vision. If I had taken this job this would look like a normal apartment, but you're making it look like its own world. If anyone ends up seeing this movie, you're going to be celebrated for it."

And I don't say this flirtatiously; I say it straight. I look into her eyes and I thank her. Because no matter how flawed we were as a couple, as collaborators we're perfect together.

But as good as it feels to be with her now, when Ava comes over later it will feel even better. I want her to see what I've made. I want to hear about her day. I want to see what's between us now that the mystery is as over as it will ever be.

—

But when Ava walks through the doorway later, she doesn't even look around.

"So they wouldn't give me a copy of the death certificate but I got to see it," she tells me. "Under cause of death it says 'drug poisoning' and I asked them what that means *exactly* but they didn't know."

She drops her bag and all of these papers and books on the table where we're standing, and I try not to be disappointed that she doesn't notice it, because as of two days ago it was a boring table I got for fifteen dollars at a garage sale and since then I've laid these gorgeous green and blue tiles on its surface.

"So I went to the library and did all this research."

"The library," I say, smiling, thinking it will remind her of the night we met, when Charlotte and I told her that the library was where we got the clues that led us to her.

"Yeah, and I found a list of reasons for death, and all of these books about causes of death, but they're all medical books and law books so it's, like, impossible to understand what any of them mean."

"But doesn't 'drug poisoning' just mean overdose?" I ask her. "That's what Frank and Lenny both told us, right?"

"Yeah, but look, there are all these variations."

She picks up a book and flips through it, drops it back on the stack and finds another one, muttering things to herself about how she knows that it's somewhere in one of them I wonder whether this is what she was like at the shelter after she left Frank and Edie's, what I should do to try to calm her down.

"Here!" she says. "Okay, look. When a drug overdose is the cause of death, sometimes it says 'unintentional drug poisoning' and sometimes 'accidental drug poisoning,' but Caroline's doesn't have those words. It's ambiguous. It could have been accidental. But maybe it wasn't."

"Okay," I say.

"So what do you think it means?" she asks. "What should I do next? Should I call Lenny again? Maybe he could give me a list of the people who they used to hang out with, people who could have been there that night. Then I could try to find them and figure out who was there last."

"What would you want to ask them?"

"There's so much we don't know," she says. "I mean, maybe it was accidental, or maybe she meant to do it, but what if someone gave her too much on purpose? I should call Lenny, right?"

"I don't know," I say.

"You don't know if I should call him, or you don't know what I should do next?"

I take a moment. I could keep playing along, say, *Yeah, call Lenny*, pretend I want to know what secrets she'll uncover next. She's so eager her hands are shaking and I want to tell her what she wants to hear.

But I just can't.

"I don't know what you're trying to find," I finally say. "I don't know where you hope to be after you have all the answers."

Pain registers on her beautiful face.

I reach a hand out to touch her arm, right above her elbow.

"You think I'm acting crazy," she says.

"No," I say. "It's just that we've learned so much about her already."

Her eyes flick up to mine, and I feel something shift between us. Her face is so close all I'd have to do is put my hand on her hair and there would be no going back.

"Don't you want to kiss me?" she says.

Her eyes are boring into mine, inviting but also angry, and I let go of her arm and take a step back.

"I do," I say. "I do." But as she puts her hand on my waist to draw me closer, I say, "But not right now."

She flinches.

"Oh," she says, spinning around, gathering her stuff. "I'm sorry. Do I not fit neatly enough into your perfect life? How *stupid*," she says. "I was so stupid. When your dad took me into his office to show me all his Clyde Jones stuff it was probably just to amuse himself. And everything your mom said that night was out of pity. And you and Charlotte—you were just solving a mystery. You got your answers and now that's it. It's over."

"Ava," I say. "Stop."

She's trying to stuff everything into her bag but there's just too much of it. She's trembling and cursing and throwing a book that won't fit hard against the floor. And then she's giving up and sinking to her knees, and I want to step closer to her but I don't know if I should.

But I want to.

And it's in the precise moment I take a step toward her that Charlotte opens the door. She sees Ava crouched on the floor and freezes in the doorway.

"What's going on?"

Ava says, "I was just leaving."

Charlotte looks at me but I don't say anything because I can't speak.

Ava gathers into her arms what she hasn't been able to put away.

I cross the room to pick up the book she threw. It landed open and the pages are bent. When I hand it to her, she doesn't look at me.

I find my voice enough to say, "I don't think you should drive right now." It comes out small and meek. I barely recognize it.

"I'm okay," she says. The anger is gone but she sounds so tired.

"I can drive you," I say.

"No thanks."

"I want to."

She shakes her head and walks toward the door.

"*I'll* drive you," Charlotte says, still in the doorway with her purse over her shoulder. This is one of the reasons I love her. She doesn't ask any other questions, and even as she takes a few of Ava's books under one arm and puts her other arm around Ava's shoulders, I know she's doing this for me.

"We can take your car," she says to Ava. "Em, come get me in a little bit, okay?"

—

I pace the floor. I go into the bathroom and wash my face. I look at myself in the mirror for a minute. I force myself to just stay still and look.

And then I drive to Ava's place and park on the street. A moment later, Charlotte's climbing into the passenger seat.

"Is she okay?"

She shrugs.

"Is Jamal there?"

"I called him. He's on his way."

"Let's just wait here," I say. "Until we see him."

So we wait for a long time, without speaking, until a bus pulls up and he steps out, hurrying to her front door.

On the short drive back I tell her what happened.

"All I want is to go home and sleep but I have so much to do," I say.

I park in Toby's spot but I'm too wrecked to do anything else.

Charlotte reaches for the keys, turns the engine off. She gets out and walks around to my side, opens my door.

"Come on," she says. "I have to reply to some e-mails and then I'll help you work on something. You wanted to fill those jars for the kitchen, right? We can do that together."

I force myself out of the car and back into the apartment, where Charlotte tells me how great the table looks and the hanging contraption, too.

"Morgan's actually coming through for you," she says, which is the nicest thing she's said about her in over a year.

I nod.

Then she adds, "I wonder what she wants."

As Charlotte plugs in her laptop and heads to the bathroom, I pull flour and beans and dried cherries out of Toby's cupboards and find a flat of mason jars we bought. I'm taking the hinges and doors off the kitchen cabinets and lining the shelves with jars to provide color and light.

I know I should be rinsing out the jars but I just can't bring myself to do anything. I keep thinking of Ava saying *Don't you want to kiss me?* I've been wanting a moment like that, wishing for it, but I never imagined there would be anger behind it. Never thought she'd wield my life at me like some kind of weapon.

And I didn't think I'd say anything that would hurt her as much as I hurt her tonight.

Charlotte comes out of the bathroom, sees me standing here not doing the simple things I'm supposed to do. She leans against the counter next to me.

"I barely know her," I say. "But still."

"Come here," she says, and gives me a hug. I hang out for a second, rest my chin on her shoulder.

When I've had enough I say, "Okay, I'll wash the jars out," and she lets me go.

Chapter Twenty-one

Almost a week passes and I don't hear anything from Ava. As she spends her days in rehearsals, I immerse myself in the messy lives of the make-believe. Juniper and her plants and her longing. George and his coral-colored melancholy. I buy things and borrow things and mend them. I work with Charlotte and Morgan and then lose Morgan to *The Agency* and Charlotte to Rebecca, who needs her more and more for all the urgent, last-minute tasks.

Then, on Saturday night at our last official tech meeting before filming begins, Charlotte calls Ava to schedule a rehearsal. I cross the room away from her so that I don't have to listen to them talking, busy myself with sorting the day's receipts and checking tasks off my novel-length to-do list. Aside from a couple finishing touches, Juniper's apartment is complete, which is a good thing because we start filming the day after tomorrow. I've been working on our changes to George's set now, which is much more difficult than Juniper's because I could work at Toby's apartment whenever I wanted to, but I need to do most of the preparation for Frank and Edie's house without inhabiting it.

I'm checking off "frame photographs" when Charlotte taps me on the shoulder, hands me the phone, and walks away.

"Hello?" I ask.

"I want to apologize," Ava says.

Is it possible to get over a voice like this? Someday, I'd like to be able to hear her speak a sentence on the phone without it making me want to hang up, get in my car, and drive as many miles as it takes to kiss her.

"You don't have to," I manage.

"Please accept my apology," she says, impossibly raspy and sweet. "You were right to think I was acting crazy. And you did nothing to deserve any of the things I said that night."

"All right," I say. "It's accepted."

"I also want to tell you that I haven't been at my best."

I nod, but she can't see me.

"You met me during a difficult time," she says.

"I think I'm partially responsible for that."

"Maybe," she says. "But you're also responsible for making it better."

I don't ask her what she means by that, because I'm afraid she'll talk about the money, or that she knows a little more about her mother, or that she's only an announcement away from instant celebrity if she ever chooses to reveal that she's a descendant of an actor well known for having no descendants. In other words, I'm afraid that it would have everything to do with what I wanted for her, and nothing at all to do with me.

"I'll see you soon," she says. "I can't believe we shoot on Monday."

"Yeah" I say. "Everyone's really excited about you."

"I hope it's still okay with you. That I'm in it."

"Of course."

Here is what I want to say: *It doesn't matter that you're in the movie; I would be thinking about you all the time anyway.* I want to say, *It all leads to you. Not just the letter and the obituary, the articles and your birth date. But also this particular time in my life. The heartbreak and the art and all of the longing.* I want to say, *Every time I add a detail to the apartment I imagine you in it.*

Instead, I say, "You'll make a really great Juniper."

And she says, "So I'll see you Monday then?"

And I say, "Yes. I'll see you then."

And then I drag Charlotte out of house, saying, "We have so much to do, we have to go."

Once we're in her car she asks, "What was that about?"

I say, "You have to tell Toby."

"What?"

"You have to tell him how you feel about him. You have to tell him right now."

"But he's in England."

"I don't care."

Every breath I take feels jagged. Anything could make me cry.

"I reread Clyde's letter when I was at Ava's house. Remember how we thought he said nothing? It isn't true. I got that wrong, too. He says so much in that letter. It's all about the danger in leaving things unsaid. It's about failure. How could he have sat there with Caroline and not told her all the things that he wanted to? We all get so afraid. We need to be brave."

I knew that heartbreak was terrible, but never knew that I could feel this way over a girl I haven't even kissed.

"I don't know what I should have done," I say. "Maybe that day at her house, after I knew for sure how I felt about her, I should have just told her."

I lean forward and rest my head against the glove compartment. I don't mean to be dramatic, but I can't help it.

"What's the use in waiting until the right moment if that moment never comes?" I say. "What if the moment escapes you in the split second when your focus was elsewhere?"

I reach for her purse and find her phone nestled in a little pocket.

"God," I say, "you're so *organized.*"

She's wide-eyed and staring at me. I hand her the phone.

"Just call him," I say, and then I get out of the car and let her do it alone.

A minute later she knocks on the window and I go back inside.

"I left him a message."

"What did you say?"

"I said no pressure, but for the record I've had a crush on him since sixth grade. And that now I'm no longer in high school maybe we could hang out sometime."

I laugh and swat away the tears that have traitorously been dripping down my face.

"Emi," she says. "I'm sorry. I think I gave you bad advice."

I can't even respond. I've never known Charlotte to be wrong, but I do think she might have been wrong about this.

"It seemed too fast for you, after everything with Morgan. And it seemed like Ava really needed friends," Charlotte says. "But you can still be her friend, even if you're more than that. And you were right. She *is* great. She's fun and interesting and smart and nice. And beautiful. And talented. I was watching her rehearsal footage the other night. She's *really* talented."

"And she's a good baker," I say, these fucking tears still streaming down my face. "And I really think she liked me."

"So go after her," she says. "It doesn't have to be over yet."

"It's already so complicated now," I say. "And on the phone it was like she was trying to resolve everything so we could move on, work on the movie together. So things wouldn't be too awkward. There were all these things I wanted to say but didn't."

"So call her back and say them."

"No," I say. "It would be too much."

"Then just call her back and say something. Something that opens things up between you. You can move slowly, but you should move."

She opens her car door.

"Okay?"

I nod and she shuts it.

I dial Ava's number.

"Hey," she says, and she sounds surprised but glad to hear from me.

"Hey. There was something else that I wanted to say."

"Yeah?"

"I mean, there are a lot of things. So hopefully we'll have time, you know, to talk when the filming is over and we're all back to normal."

"I hope so," she says.

"But for now, I wanted to say this: I want to know who you are. I mean, apart from all of this we've been dealing with. Without the mystery and the Chateau Marmont. I thought that everyone would want that kind of huge, romantic story if it became available to them. But it wasn't a story, it was your life. And when I got to your apartment the day we found Lenny, and I saw you and how you lived, that's when I really understood that even without all the clues we'd pieced together and the new identity we'd made for you, you would have already been someone I'd want to know.

It's like the couch! The best things aren't perfectly constructed. They aren't illusions. They aren't larger than life. They *are* life. Part of me knew that all along, but I got it wrong anyway. What I'm trying to say is that I just want to know *you*. You don't have to be at your best. We can't all be at our best all the time. But," I say again, "I just want to know you."

I can hear her breathing on the other end, reminding me that she is there, that she's been listening. I hope that I've just rambled in a way that's romantic and not a way that sounds insane. It would break my heart if she didn't think I made sense, so I don't give her time to react.

"I have to go now," I tell her, and then I hang up.

I take a moment to breathe, and then I knock on the windshield but Charlotte doesn't turn around.

I knock again, harder, and she raises a hand to tell me one minute and I see that her other hand is pressing her phone to her ear. And when she turns around a minute later and hangs up, she's smiling.

"Was it him?" I ask her.

She nods.

"What did he say?"

"He said he'd been waiting all through high school for me to graduate."

"Are you kidding?"

"No," she says, and then she's leaning against the car door in a hysterical fit of laughter comparable only to that at Clyde Jones's estate sale.

"Wow," I say. "You and Toby. Fantastic."

"Don't be sarcastic," she says between breaths. "You're the one who made me do it."

Once she's regained her composure she asks, "How did it go with you?"

"I don't know," I say. "But I opened up something. At least I tried to."

"That's good," she says.

We sit next to each other, staring through the windshield.

"Charlotte," I say. "We both just did huge things. We need to celebrate, don't you think?"

"Champagne!" she says.

"Yes! But how?"

"We could just drive around to places until we find someone who'll sell it to us," she says, but it's clear from her tone that that prospect is not all that enticing. And it sounds pretty miserable to me, too.

"Oh, well, fuck it," I say. "Let's just get apple cider."

Charlotte double-parks outside of a store on Abbot Kinney while I run inside. I find the apple cider in a refrigerator, sadly positioned on the rack below the champagne, but I don't let it get me down. Instead I stride up to the counter as though I'm carrying Veuve Clicquot instead of Martinelli's, and the fatherly man behind the counter smiles approvingly at my choice.

He sets down a pen and a page of the *Times* and I glance at them expecting a crossword puzzle but instead finding the movie listings for the weekend.

He tells me what I owe him but I can't look away from the listings. He's circled several in red pen.

"Why are you circling movie times?" I ask him.

"I'm planning my weekend," he answers, in an accent I can't place.

"Are you going to see *all* of those?"

"Yes."

I hand him my cash.

"Is it, like, some sort of special movie weekend for you?"

"No, it's my routine. Where I'm from, we had to wait months, sometimes years for American films. Now, I see them on opening weekend."

I give him a slow smile, studying his face. It's lit up with the love of films. I turn slowly, taking in this store I've probably seen a dozen times but never actually noticed. When I started this project, I probably would have ruled it out. It's not at all romantic. There's nothing pretty about it. But it has good light. The produce is fresh and colorful, the aisles wide and well stocked. It's big enough for the crew but small enough to feel intimate, and I can easily see opportunities to play up its humble charms.

"My name is Emi," I say to him.

"Hakeem," he says to me.

"Let me tell you about a film I'm working on," I say, and ten minutes later I'm climbing back into Charlotte's car with yet another reason to celebrate.

—

On Sunday morning my phone rings and it's Ava.

"You know how you said I could call you when I needed a favor?"

"Yeah," I say.

"Does that still apply?"

"Is Jamal at work?" I joke, and I'm relieved when she laughs.

"No," she says. "But he's coming, too. So is this a yes? Can I pick you up at four?"

"Yes," I say.

"Is Charlotte with you?"

"No, we both slept at our houses last night. The apartment is off limits until we're done filming."

"Okay," she says. "I'll call her next."

I spend some time at the apartment in the middle of the day, watering the plants, rearranging some stacks of books, writing a grocery list for the refrigerator, some botany notes in notebooks that I scatter across the room. The best production designers are the ones who make the sets feel so real that if you didn't know better, you'd think the characters lived their lives there even after the filming stopped.

Then, at four o'clock, Ava and Jamal pull up to my house and I climb into the backseat. I direct her to Charlotte's house, and then it's the four of us, getting onto the freeway, and I recognize the direction in which we're heading.

"One request," I say. "No breaking the law on the day before filming starts."

"Granted," Ava says. "Speaking of filming, I saw some photos of the apartment. It looks beautiful."

"Thank you."

"If there's time before we start shooting, will you take me through it and explain everything? I want to know what I'm looking at. Like those photographs pinned on the corkboard by the hanging plants? Who are those people meant to be? Things like that."

"Sure," I say. "That would be great. I'll explain everything to you."

When we exit the 405 and pull onto the narrow highway that leads into the desert, Ava says, "This probably won't be very fun. But you don't need to do anything. Just be with me."

We all say okay, and my heart pounds so hard because I'm so worried for her.

Moments later we're parked in front of Tracey's house, and we get out of the car, four doors slamming shut. We don't get very far because Tracey is outside, watering the lawn.

She sees us all and her face goes serious. She looks younger than I expected, wearing jeans and a pink sleeveless shirt with a high collar, her brown hair pulled back in a ponytail and a gardening glove on one hand. Water sputters out of the hose onto the grass beside her. She crosses the lawn without saying anything and shuts off the water.

Jamal and Charlotte and I stay on the sidewalk next to the car while Ava rounds to the trunk of the car and takes out two boxes. I recognize them as Tracey's. They are sealed up, tied with strings of paper flowers.

She sets them on the grass and then takes a few steps toward Tracey, frozen on the path next to the little pink potted flowers. They've been spread out evenly now, a little farther apart than before to compensate for the one Ava smashed.

"Hi," Ava says.

Tracey looks past her, at us.

"Who are these people?" she asks.

"My friends," Ava says.

Tracey closes her eyes and shakes her head.

"*What?*" Ava says. I'm confused, too. We're all wearing normal clothes. We all look perfectly fine to me.

Tracey's head keeps shaking, shaking.

"Really, Mom?" Ava says. Tracey isn't looking at her, so Ava steps to the right, placing herself in Tracey's line of vision.

"You broke into the house," Tracey says.

"I tried to use my key."

"You went through my things. My personal things."

"I needed something."

"What?"

"My birth certificate."

"But you took so much."

"I wanted to know about Caroline."

Tracey shakes her head again and I wish I could close my eyes so I didn't have to see it. I thought that Tracey might feel some regret.

"I had so many questions," Ava says, making her voice slow and even, trying to sound like someone people listen to. "You never answered them, so I tried to tell myself that they weren't important. But, of course, it is important. Caroline loved me. *You* loved me. I read your journal. You said I was a gift."

Even from a distance, I can see Tracey's whole body tense.

"You had no right to go through my things."

"You said I saved your life."

"What are you talking about?"

"I found Lenny."

Tracey's hands fly to her face. When she drops them again, her eyes are wide and wild.

"You have no right," she hisses. "You need to let the past stay in the past."

"I do have a right. It's my *life*," Ava says. And I remember Frank's tired, sad eyes and how he was the first person to tell her the truth about what happened.

"I need to let go of the past," Tracey says softly.

"But I have a right to know where I come from," Ava says. "I've been learning all of these things I never knew. One thing I wanted to do was to thank you for taking me in. I know some of what you were going through. I know it was a really big deal."

"I don't want to talk about this. That was my old life."

"*Mom*," Ava says. "*Please*. We only have one life. *This* life."

Tracey turns away, like she's going to walk inside.

"Mom," Ava says. "I never had sex with Malcolm. We weren't even in the Sunday school room. We were outside. All we were doing was talking."

Tracey won't look at her, but Ava keeps talking anyway. And I remember what she told me when we were picking cherries, that she gave Tracey reasons to reject her.

"I never shoplifted from CVS. That makeup you found in my bathroom? Jessica gave it to me. And the night that you went looking for me in my room? I was just hanging out with friends at the movie theater. I wasn't doing any of the things I told you I was doing."

"Why did you torture me like that?" Tracey asks. "You were so cruel to me."

"I was giving you reasons," Ava says, "to not love me. I didn't know it then but I understand now."

I expect Tracey to give in at this, to assure Ava of her love, but she doesn't say anything. She just watches Ava standing there, crying and trying to explain.

The door opens and a boy appears in the doorway.

"Jonah!" Ava says, and steps toward him but Tracey turns around and shrieks, "Get back inside!"

Jonah stands, paralyzed, looking from his mother to his sister, and for a moment I think he might defy her, go show Ava that he's her family, but instead he retreats and the door closes slowly, but not all the way.

"I wasn't coming on to Lisa," Ava says. "What happened between us happened because of both of us."

Tracey shakes her head.

"Like that's going to make anything better," she says.

Ava says, "You aren't going to believe this but I found out that I had a grandfather, and he left me a lot of money. So I'm doing all right. You don't have to worry about me." She's struggling not to cry and it's so painful to watch her. "And I'm in this movie. I auditioned. A lot of other people wanted my part, but you know what? They wanted me."

Tracey is shaking her head. Shaking, shaking.

"I think you're afraid for me. Like, maybe you think I'm going to make the same mistakes you made. But I'm not. I'm doing really well. I just miss having a family."

The door swings open again and Jonah walks out, tears streaking his face, and he walks over to Ava, close but not touching her. For a moment, he stands between Tracey and

Ava as if he wants to be a bridge. Then he hugs Ava quickly but hard, and walks back into the house, shutting the door all the way this time.

"Mom," Ava says when she can speak again, "you had a tough time when you were young. That's okay. You did a lot of good, too. You took me in. You had Jonah. And look at us all. We're fine. Things are fine."

"You're wrong," Tracey tells her. "Things are not fine." She lets out a sob and covers her face. "Maybe I'm being punished."

"I try my best to be a good person," Ava says. "I wish that could be enough for you."

But Tracey turns and walks into her house, without even looking back, without saying good-bye.

Ava turns and steps numbly toward us. She walks past us all standing here and climbs into the front seat. When she starts the ignition, we get in, too. She drives down the block, turns the corner, and then Jamal breaks our silence.

"Look," he says. "I don't like talking shit about people's families, but I have to get this off my chest. Your mom is seriously fucked up. You know that? So you don't believe in God in the same way that she does. So what? So you're into girls. So fucking what. She needs to wake up and figure out that she doesn't get to decide every single thing about you. It's her fucking loss, man," he says. "I'm sorry but I just had to say that. It's her fucking loss."

Without warning, Ava pulls onto the side of the road. She pulls up the emergency brake and leans into Jamal, buries her face in his shoulder, her body quaking. She trembles and trembles and when she finally cries it doesn't even sound like crying. Nothing like that night in our living room with Clyde Jones on the screen looking out at her. Not like a few minutes ago, on Tracey's front lawn. Not even close to that. It's this gasping that makes Charlotte and me lock hands, makes me have to struggle against crying myself. It isn't *my* tragedy. It isn't me who knows for certain in this moment that I'm alone in the world. She has us, I know, but for all people talk about friends as being the same as family, I know that, really, they aren't. At least not when you're eighteen. Not when sometimes you need your mother.

I don't know what to do, but she brought us to be with her in this moment, so without overthinking the action, without wondering if it will be welcome, I reach through the seats and put my hand on her back as she cries. And then, right after me, Charlotte puts hers on her shoulder.

I know it's only a gesture, but I hope that it's something.

And after a little while, I say, "Let me drive us home. We can get delivery from Garlic Flower."

Ava sniffles. "I don't even have enough plates," she says. "And your apartment is a film set."

"We can go back to my parents' house," I say. "Let's go there."

She nods and opens her door and we switch places.

—

Charlotte calls the restaurant as I drive us out of the desert and back into the city, and we arrive at home just as Eric does.

"Perfect timing," he says. I hand him money and he hands me a bag full of warm food, egg flower soup and mu shu and noodles. It makes me hopeful.

My parents aren't home so I let us in and we carry everything to the den.

"Let's watch TV shows," Jamal says. "Some kind of series. Something cheesy."

So we eat our takeout and watch *Melrose Place*, lose ourselves in the early nineties hideous fashion, the day-to-day trials of the newly adult characters as they swim and work and spy on the neighbors. Ava isn't laughing, but she's eating. All things considered, she seems okay.

I watch the screen but all I can think about is us. We were on the verge of being together, and then on the verge of being strangers again. But what are we now?

I guess I was hoping for a cinematic love story. Like Clyde on his horse galloping toward the girl through dust clouds and brambles. "Well, hello you." His cocky smirk. The girl squinting into the sun after having waited for so long to be discovered.

But our film would have been more modern noir than Western: Two girls in Los Angeles solving a mystery. A late, enigmatic star. A beautiful woman, drugs, and sex. We'd be swimming in the Marmont pool, driving down Sunset Boulevard, our hair wild in the wind from passing cars. A secret love affair, kissing in Ava's trailer between shooting scenes, dodging paparazzi. All of it sounded amazing and so little of it was real.

But this is.

This is.

I thought I might get a cinematic love story, and I've gotten some of that.

But sitting here in my parents' house, with Ava a couple feet away from me, eating chow fun and watching *Melrose Place*, I realize that all of the sets and the props and the performances, the scripts that take years to write; the perfect camera angles and painstaking lighting, the directors that call take after take until it turns out right, the projections on the huge theater screens—so much larger and louder than life—it's all done in hopes of portraying what I'm feeling right now.

As much as I had wanted a love story out of a movie, I know now that movies can only hope to capture this kind of love.

—

Jamal leaves, heads back to the shelter to make curfew. Charlotte goes home to her mother.

"I know you're tired," I tell Ava. "And you can say no. But I have to go by the set one more time and I'd love it if you could come with me."

She follows me to Toby's place. We park next to each other and walk through the courtyard and up to his door together. I knew from the beginning that I wanted Juniper's apartment to seem lived in and I've tried to make it feel real. But even the stacks of books and the little basket by the door full of mail don't do enough.

Ava turns to me, her eyes pink rimmed, too tired for even her usual smile.

"This doesn't have to take long," I say. "We don't even have to talk. I was just thinking that maybe you could spend some time in here. Like, *live* here. Even a few minutes would help."

She nods. Lets her purse drop to the floor.

I take a seat in a corner chair that Morgan upholstered in

lime-green fabric and watch as Ava makes a slow lap through the space. In the kitchen, she takes a white enamel pitcher, borrowed from Theo and Rebecca's, and fills it at the sink. One by one, she waters the plants, and when the pitcher is empty, she sets it on the edge of a bookshelf next to a hanging fern.

She scans the novels and collections of poetry and pulls one out. *Twenty-one Love Poems* by Adrienne Rich, snatched along with most of the other books from the shelves in my mother's office. She kicks off her shoes, then sinks into the sofa and reads for twenty minutes. Then she places the book, spine open, on the coffee table. She makes a cup of tea, contemplating something as she stares into the ceramic mug. When she transfers the teabag into the sink, a couple drops land on the counter. She doesn't wipe them up. She crosses the room and, as she drinks, she studies the portraits. She looks for the longest time at one in particular. I found it by myself at the Rose Bowl when I was scavenging for George's house. It's a charcoal drawing of a young man, and something about his expression reminded me of Clyde when he was very young. When she runs her finger along the edge of the frame, it leaves the portrait just a tiny bit crooked.

She takes her last sip of tea and sets her mug in the sink. Her leather purse waits in the entry.

"Bye," she says to me, and walks barefoot out the door.

Chapter Twenty-two

We film today.

I wake up in my bed far before my alarm goes off. Everyone is meeting at Theo and Rebecca's for coffee and a final review of the scenes we want to shoot, but I got permission from Theo to skip the meeting and head straight to the apartment. I want to do a final walk-through, make sure everything is in order.

Out in the kitchen, my mother is cooking in her suit.

"You need to have a good breakfast, honey. This is such an important day for you!"

She's making her pancakes, the best pancakes in the world.

"I love you," I tell her.

"And I you, my strong and talented daughter."

When I was a kid, sometimes my mom had me do affirmations before school. She wanted me to grow up with a fierce belief in my own potential. So I stood and looked in the mirror and repeated the absurd things she said to me. But who knows? Maybe it did some good. I eat my breakfast and tell my parents a little about what happened with Ava and a lot about the movie.

"We've been missing you," Dad says. "I'm glad we have you home again."

"Yeah," I say. "It feels good."

They make me a little later than I had hoped to be, but I'm still the first one to arrive. I park and unlock the door and step inside, once again amazed by how different it looks from a week ago, and how, somehow, even with no budget and very little help or experience, I was able to make it look exactly as I hoped it would. Too soon, I hear another car pull up and stop. A door shut. Footsteps. All I wanted was a little time alone before everyone rushed in, but I guess everyone's excited and nervous and ready to begin.

There's a soft knock, followed by the door swinging open. It isn't everyone. It's Ava.

"Hey," she says. "I wanted to catch you before we started." She takes a breath. "Thanks again for coming with me yesterday."

"Thank you for wanting me to."

She nods, brushes a strand of hair off her face.

"How are you doing?" I ask her. "After everything?"

"Well, I didn't sleep very much," she says. "I was up all night thinking."

"About Tracey?"

"Yes," she says. "But also about you. That night when I came over, after I saw Caroline's death certificate, you asked me what I hoped to get from everything. And that hurt, because it was obvious, wasn't it?"

I shake my head.

"I don't know," I say. "I must be missing something because it isn't obvious to me."

"I was doing it for you," she says. She smooths her hair behind her ear. She takes a breath. "I have so much more than I've ever had," she says. "I know about where I come from. I have my own apartment and I have Jamal, who I know will be my friend forever. I have money. I have this movie, and all the possibilities that it could open up if I do well. But still. It's hard to let go of what I was to you for a little while. I've never been anyone's great mystery before. I doubt I ever will be again. It's not even what I want for myself, but it felt amazing, to be that special for a little while. For you to think I was that special."

"But you were more than that to me," I say. "The mystery was just how we started."

"I know that now. But I panicked. We saw Lenny and he explained all these things I'd always wondered about but all I could think was that I wasn't ready yet. I didn't want it to be over for you.

"Look," she says, and her words come faster, more urgently. "I don't know how you feel. But I just want to say this, and maybe it will sound incredibly egotistical or absurd but I'm going to say it anyway."

I can feel myself stop breathing.

She breathes deep. Says, "I can't stop thinking about you. I don't want to stop thinking about you. And you're this incredible person who does all of these amazing things. You have this job I didn't even know existed and everyone talks about you like you're a genius. You should have heard them this morning going on and on about this set, and it's all so deserved. I mean, all I have to be is decent today, because this room all by itself is enough to break hearts. And you have this beautiful life with your parents and your cool older brother and Charlotte and all your movies and records and insane knowledge of the city. When I said those things about myself compared to you, when I talked about your perfect life, what I was trying to say was that I wanted to feel worthy of you. The problem was that I didn't. But even though it's only been a week since then, I've figured a lot out. It might sound crazy, but even though you're this incredible, artistic genius of a girl, I do feel worthy of you."

I shake my head because I can't believe she's saying these things.

"Of course," I say. "Of course you are."

Everything feels fuzzy. Like there's humming all around me, and there is no way that she is saying these words to me but here she is, saying them, looking at me with those green eyes that I've been trying not to look too far into for all the weeks I've known her.

"But, wait," I say. "What about if you get famous?"

She shakes her head and laughs.

"I don't know what you're talking about."

"When everyone knows about Clyde and—"

"I'm not going to tell people about Clyde. I got some answers, and I got the inheritance and for those things I'll always be grateful. But I don't want anything else out of it. I don't want the world talking about him and my mother."

"Okay, but this movie is going to be big. I know it will be. And then where will that leave me? Even without Clyde, you'll be on the cover of *Vanity Fair,* and I'll still be behind the scenes while the whole world falls in love with you."

"So I'm in *Vanity Fair,*" she says. "Which I probably won't be, but for the sake of this conversation, we can pretend that I am. This is what, a year from now?"

I nod.

"Okay. A year from now. And the interviewer comes over and we're there together. And her piece begins with something like, Ava Garden Wilder and her girlfriend, production designer Emi Price, sit drinking lemonade on her rooftop deck."

I don't even know what to say to that.

"It sounds good, doesn't it?"

I nod. It sounds good.

"Last time I did this, I was in a terrible place, and I wasn't very kind and I wasn't ready to love anyone. You were right to say no and I'll understand if you say no again but I hope that you won't."

She takes a step closer to me.

"Don't you want to kiss me?" she asks.

She smiles just a little, a hopeful, sweet smile, but somewhere buried in it is that confidence that slays me.

I say yes and she says yes? and I nod and she touches my waist with one of her hands and I touch her face with mine, that spot where the sunlight landed on the day I really saw her.

We don't kiss right away. Instead, there's a moment when we just look at each other, the moment where, if this were a movie, the music would start. And surrounded by all of my careful details, everything still just a little more perfectly placed than it would be in life—the plants that cascade down the wall in their charming pots, the deep-sea curtains and the colorful jars, the fairy-tale sofa with its gold vines and plush cushions—and Ava's movie-star face, her Clyde Jones nose and her freckles and her beautiful green eyes, this could be the scene in the movie that everyone aches for. The moment where the thing that you wish for becomes the thing that you get.

When we tip our faces to the side, we do it in the perfect movie way—no awkward repositionings, no pressed noses. I swear: I can hear the music swelling.

But then.

Our lips touch. The imaginary music goes quiet. The room is only a room and we are the miracles. Her mouth is warm and human and soft, her hand presses hard and insistent against my back, her breasts press against mine. My hand grazes the delicate line of her jaw; there's the whisper of her hair against my fingers as we kiss harder.

We love films because they make us feel something. They speak to our desires, which are never small. They allow us to escape and to dream and to gaze into eyes that are impossibly beautiful and huge. They fill us with longing.

But also.

They tell us to remember; they remind us of life. Remember, they say, how much it hurts to have your heart broken. Remember about death and suffering and the complexities of living. Remember what it is like to love someone. Remember how it is to be loved. Remember what you feel in this moment. Remember this. Remember this.

Outside, cars are approaching, their engines cutting off, one after the next. And there is the shutting of doors and so many familiar voices, and everyone sounds excited and anxious but happy. Soon they're streaming in, and Ava and I are no longer alone, but the room is alive with beginning.

We step away from each other and Ava smiles, and her face is flushed and I feel this elated twist in my stomach when I realize that I will be able to kiss this face again when our day of work is over.

I will be able to hold her hand.

I will be able to talk to her whenever I want.

I will be able to want her without wondering if she wants me back.

Ava is swept away by Grant and Vicki, and I notice Charlotte watching me from across the room. She glances at Ava and then back to me and I nod yes. And living is beautiful. And she smiles because she knows.

The lights are already set up. Charlie's camera is on its tripod, pointed to our opening frame. In the bedroom, Grant is applying Ava's makeup while Vicki is standing back, assessing. I begin the last-minute steps to make the set perfect. I look into the monitor the way Morgan told me I should, and our first shot looks just as I had hoped. I prepare the first props: one of the ceramic plates with a piece of toast, a ceramic mug of peppermint tea. My toast comes out a little too brown, and when Ava sees it a few minutes later she smiles.

Her hair is straight, falling over her shoulders. Her eyes are lined with shimmery brown eyeliner and her lips are shining.

I will be able to make toast for her in the mornings.

I will do my best to get it right.

"Okay," Theo says. "Ava, remember, we can take as long as we need to get this scene. And you don't need to overthink it. It's just Juniper, existing in her apartment. We're getting to know her through her actions and her surroundings, so just, if you can, make yourself feel like you're home."

Ava nods. I watch her through the monitor. I wish I could tell Theo that the idea of home isn't always simple. It isn't the comforting direction he meant it to be. But, on the screen, I see Ava looking around at the set I've created for her. She moves from one place to another, lifting up the objects of an imaginary girl. And then she looks at me.

"Yeah," she says. "I can feel that."

"Okay, good."

Ava takes a seat at the tiled table. She has a book of poetry. She has her toast and her tea.

"All right," Theo says. "Are we ready?"

"Yes," Michael says, holding the sound equipment.

"Yup," Charlie says, from behind his camera.

"Okay," Theo says. "Roll camera."

"Camera rolling."

"Roll sound. Scene three. Take one. *Action.*"

The room holds its breath. Ava turns to a page and silently reads.

In a few weeks, Toby will come home, and he'll say, *So tell me what you did.* And I'll show him this footage, and it will look so professional, so beautiful. It might take him a few seconds to recognize that these are his walls holding up the framed portraits of strangers. His table, hidden under a bright yellow tablecloth. His windows with sea-blue curtains instead of their usual shutters.

He'll grin, say, *You made a movie, of course, how perfect.* And I'll say, *No, that's not it.* He'll cock his head, waiting for more. I'll take my time, keep him guessing.

Then I'll say, *I fell in love.*

Acknowledgments

Though I had been interested for a while in writing a novel about two girls in love, it wasn't until I went to Minnesota in the fall of 2011 that I decided for certain that I would. I was spending a few days in a suburb of Minneapolis, visiting a high school that had chosen my first novel, *Hold Still*, as a school-wide read. As part of my visit, I met with the school's Gay Straight Alliance. Seated in a large circle in the library, the students told me about their lives and asked to hear about mine. They taught me how important it is to share stories about love and hope, a lesson for which I thank the Champlin Park GSA; the students of Champlin Park High School; Terri Evans, Media Specialist extraordinaire; and all the RHRR committee members, past and present.

Katie Byron is not only my favorite production designer, she's also to thank for so much of this novel. A close friend of my dear friend Vanessa Micale, Katie was who I turned to when I realized what Emi's calling would be. In a series of passionate and illuminating e-mails, Katie described every position within a film's art department. She told me about the lengths she's gone to when working on films with small budgets, the challenges, the strategies, and "the love." I thought I was turning to Katie for technical advice on a small aspect of the story, but what she shared with me altered the trajectory of the entire novel. I'm sure I've gotten many technical things wrong, but I hope that I've captured the spirit of the work.

My cousin Danielle Diego generously facilitated a private tour of the Fox lot for me. Walking through the sets of televisions shows, and then past a facade of buildings that had been used in many different movies, I fully realized the extent to which filmmaking is a series of elaborate illusions. And then, stopping to admire the photographs of past stars that line the walls of Danielle's building, I was struck by the historical glamour of it all. These impressions turned into major themes in the novel, and I have Danielle to thank for them, as well as for a year's worth of answers to my follow-up questions.

Between drafts of this novel, Kristyn Stroble, Amanda Krampf, and I decided to turn *Hold Still* into a movie. We raised a micro-budget on Kickstarter. Many of our contributors were friends and family, and many were colleagues and readers. The experience of raising the funds and making the film left me humbled and grateful. I give immense thanks to our contributors, as well as to our actors and crew members, most of whom volunteered and all of whom approached the project with a level of dedication and artistry that left me touched and inspired. I am so proud of the work we did together, and thankful for the ways in which it influenced this story.

While Mia Nolting was at an artists' residency in South Africa, she offered me her beautiful apartment in Portland, Oregon, as the site of a private writing residency. I was desperately trying to produce a complete first draft, but I learned that long stretches of gray, rainy days combined with an abundance of solitude don't suit me. In between maddening writing sessions, I made myself tea in her small enamel pot, listened to her Patsy Cline record, and traded e-mails with her about the South African filmmaker she was quickly falling for and would end up marrying soon after. (Hi, Paddy!). Though I left with far fewer words written than I had hoped, the days away certainly enriched this novel.

Sharing drafts is always terrifying and exciting. Jessica Jacobs, with whom I've shared work for a decade, and Gayle Forman, who read a draft during our group book tour, provided me with early and invaluable feedback, as did my wife and my mother. Mandy Harris, Amanda Krampf, Peter Thompson, and Kathy Kallick all swooped in near the end with valuable insights. My long-time and ever-inspiring writing group (Lizzie Brock, Laura Davis, Teresa Miller, and Carly Anne West) gave me feedback through multiple revisions, and kept me motivated and productive throughout a time of great change.

Sara Crowe has been my dream agent and advocate for many years now. I remember well the rush I felt when she told me she'd like to represent me, and my gratitude and trust in her have only deepened since then. She helped get me through this novel's messy first stages and provided nurturance along the way. I'm so lucky to have her by my side. Thanks also to Rachel Ridout for her lightening-quick turnaround in a moment of doubt.

I am tremendously grateful to the talented and committed people at Penguin Books for Young Readers. From Theresa Evangelista, who gives my books beautiful covers, to Eileen Kreit, who gives them a second life in paperback, to Anna Jarzab, who gets the word out online. Thank you to Anne Heausler and Rosanne Lauer for their expertise, and Elyse Marshall and her team of publicists for working magic. Thank you to Melissa Faulner, who came to Dutton before this book's rush to publication and who has been a pleasure to work with. And, of course, thank you to my editor, Julie Strauss-Gabel, whose gift for discovering the heart of a story makes my novels so much stronger. If I were to apply the famous E.L. Doctorow quote to myself—the one where he likens writing a novel to driving through fog at night—Julie would be my headlights.

Originally, I hadn't intended for this novel to have much to do with family, but by the end family became an important part. Though my parents are not Emi's parents, they raised me in the same spirit, in a stimulating household full of art, music, films, and books, and with unwavering love, support, and belief in me. And though my brother is not Toby, we have found ourselves separated by an ocean for a couple years now, and I love the way his face looks on my computer screen. Thank you all for being mine. Thank you also to my beautiful extended family, near and far, especially my grandmother, whom I love dearly.

Finally, thank you to Kristyn Stroble, my lookout girl and getaway driver. Writing this book made me remember what being nineteen and in love with you felt like. Twelve years later, I feel the same.